C000258959

Storm of Arrows

On Campaign with the Black Prince

PAUL BANNISTER

© Paul Bannister 2019

Paul Bannister has asserted his rights under the Copyright, Design and Patents Act, 1988, to be identified as the author of this work.

First published in 2019 by Sharpe Books.

ISBN: 9781096491897

TABLE OF CONTENTS

HISTORICAL MAP

Historical characters

Thomas Holland Earl of Kent, Baron Holand 1314 – 1360. Knight and founding member of the Order of the Garter. Son of Robert de Holland of Lancashire. Mentor to the young Edward of Woodstock (the Black Prince) whose heroic principal commander he was during the Crecy campaign that began the 100 Years' War. Had a controversial marriage to Joan (the Fair Maid) of Kent.

Edward, Prince of Wales (Black Prince; Edward of Woodstock) 1330 – 1376. Raised by his father Edward III as a warrior, 16 years old Edward led the vanguard of the English army to a defining victory at Crecy after ravaging northern France. Edward assumed the insignia of three ostrich feathers and his 'Ich Dien' motto ('I serve') from the arms of the slain King John of Bohemia. He later stained his reputation by ordering civilian massacres. That, and his black armour, earned him his nickname. Edward pre-deceased his father, so never ascended to the English throne.

King Edward II (Edward of Caernarvon) 1284 – 1327. Noted for his 'heretical' and open love affairs with male courtiers, the calamitous king was tolerated by his queen but regarded with contempt by his barons After battlefield humiliation at Bannockburn, the estranged magnates rebelled and divided the nation in civil war. Edward did not learn the lesson and flaunted a romance with another courtier whose arrogance and presumption of royal powers snapped his queen's tolerance. Edward was forced to abdicate in favour of his son and died suspiciously soon afterwards.

Queen Isabella (the 'She-Wolf of France') 1295 – 1358. Daughter of Philip IV of France, she was married at age 12 to Edward II and largely ignored by her husband during his infatuation with Piers Gaveston, but she dealt pragmatically with the situation until after Gaveston's murder, when Edward began a relationship with Hugh Despenser. Isabella took her son the prince to France, raised an army, deposed her husband and put Edward of Windsor on the throne. In time, the young king seized control from his regents, executed his mother's lover and banished Isabella to remote Castle Rising, Norfolk.

King Edward III   (Edward of Windsor)   1312 – 1377.

Crowned king at age 14, Edward three years later led a coup against his controlling regents and regained his throne to begin a long and successful reign which saw the evolution of parliament and significant English military gains in France and Scotland. An excellent general who made his nation into a formidable military power, he was enamoured of Arthurian principles of chivalry which he did not always follow. Generally regarded as a popular and merciful monarch, he founded the Order of the Garter.

Queen Philippa   (Philippa of Hainault)   1315 – 1369.

Philippa was only 12 years old when she was betrothed to Edward of Windsor as a pawn to gain support for Queen Isabella's invasion of England, but the marriage was a success and Edward remained devoted to his wife until the end of her life.

Joan Plantagenet   (the Fair Maid of Kent)   1328 – 1385.

Joan, whose childhood guardian was Queen Philippa, claimed a prior, secret wedding at age 12 to Thomas Holland to gain a papal annulment of her marriage to William Montague, Earl of Salisbury. On Holland's death, she married her cousin the Black Prince and became the first Princess of Wales.

Piers Gaveston   Earl of Cornwall   1284 – 1312.

A courtier exiled for offensive behavior, he was returned to court on the accession of his lover Edward II and the new king lavished lands, gifts and affection on him, even appointing him regent in his own absence. Infuriated nobles eventually captured and executed the upstart.

Hugh Despenser the Younger   Lord Despenser   1286 - 1326.

The son of the Earl of Winchester, he was Edward II's lover and chamberlain. Unchecked by the king, he assumed regal powers and accumulated vast lands and wealth until Queen Isabella invaded England, deposed her unfaithful husband and had Despenser cruelly put to death.

Sir Roger Mortimer   1287 – 1330.

Self-appointed Earl of March, also Lord Lieutenant of Ireland. Imprisoned for armed rebellion against Edward II, he famously escaped the Tower by giving his guards drugged wine and descending a rope ladder to the Thames and a waiting boat. He fled to France, where he began an affair with Queen Isabella and aided the overthrow of her husband Edward II. His term as a tyrannous regent ended when the young king Edward III captured and executed him.

Robert de Holland: Baron Holand   1283 – 1328.

A follower of Thomas, Earl of Lancaster who was punished for his role in the death of the royal favourite Gaveston, Holland was pardoned, rebelled again and was imprisoned. He escaped and again was pardoned. Later outlawed for his rebellion and murders, he was captured and beheaded by Lancastrian rivals.

Thomas, Earl of Lancaster   1278 – 1322.

England's richest man and cousin of King Edward II, he captured and executed the king's lover Piers Gaveston 'for the stability of the kingdom.' Edward took another lover who ransacked the royal treasury and insulted the magnates. Civil war broke out and the rebel Lancaster was on the losing side. He was beheaded in his own feasting hall at Pontefract.

Henry, Earl of Lancaster and Leicester   1281 – 1345.

Thomas of Lancaster's younger brother and heir, Henry joined Queen Isabella's invasion force which overcame Edward II and the Despensers. Henry himself captured the king at Neath, was his custodian at Kenilworth and helped the young Edward III end Mortimer's regency.

Henry of Grosmont Duke of Lancaster. 1310 – 1361.

Garter knight. Son of Henry of Lancaster and cousin of King Edward III. He represented his father in Parliament when he went blind, became England's most powerful peer, saved Edward's sons in battle and was the king's most trusted captain.

Fictional characters

Hugh Mobberley.   Bastard son of Thomas Holland
Sir John Westwood tutor, mentor to Thomas Holland
Broggers   falconer
Andrew of Leatham master archer
Andrew Rosthorn   farrier
Joan the Palmer   Benedictine   canoness,
physician
Gaia DeJoie   Benedictine nun, French mystic

Chapter 1 - Mikelgate

Only a fingernail moon showed between the scudding clouds as our tired horses plodded towards the ancient bridge that led to York's city walls.

Before we could reach the span and cross the dark ribbon that was the River Ouse sliding between yew-lined banks, we must pass the outer walls and bar of the twin-turreted Mikelgate where an arched entry of squared Roman stone was imperfectly lit by a pair of burning hay bales.

An unusually-large contingent of guards stirred as we clopped closer and my father grunted. "Welcome to York, Thomas my boy," he said. "The king seems to have readied greetings for you. Or maybe it's the Scots who'll be greetin', by God's beard."

Easing my aching buttocks in the saddle, I made a questioning noise. "It means 'weeping' in the clans' language," he explained. "No, Father, I meant York – what is this castle?" "This is just an entry gate, but it is also the royal entrance to the city," he said. "Roman overlords, raiding Viking sea kings, the Conqueror himself and now the Plantagenets have all come this way, just as you do. You're entering like a royal, my son. Edward's probably eagerly expecting you."

I guessed he was joking and looked to see if he was smiling, but Father had half-twisted in the saddle to give a curt order to the serjeant, a Flemish mercenary crossbowman, who rode behind us. In turn, the soldier pulled his mount aside and spoke sharply to the men at arms who rode in our train.

Resisting the urge to turn and gawp, for father had warned my curious 13 years old self to be dignified, I could hear the clatter and jingle as our soldiers readied for the critically-inspecting eyes of other fighting men. We were all summoned by the king for a military campaign and we had come to join on this Tuesday after the feast of St Hilary, in the Year of Our Lord 1327.

We were riding between prosperous-looking stone-and-timber buildings with tile roofs, something I'd not seen before, approaching the bar when Father leaned closer: "There are four gates into this place, all of them small fortresses, and this, on the London road, is the most important way in through the city walls. In the morning, in daylight, you'll see the heads and limbs of malefactors rotting on spikes above these tall turrets." At once, I looked upwards, but the tops of the towers, four storeys above me, were shrouded in dark. Father chuckled.

He waved at the houses around us "These were the homes of the Jews. The first King Edward, Longshanks, expelled them all. Their old synagogue is on Coney St, just over the river. I don't know what it is now, probably a church – there are about two dozen of them here. That over there is Holy Trinity priory, it belongs to the Benedictines; there's another Holy Trinity church near the Minster, and in its grounds someone built some cottages, called Our Lady's Row. The rents pay for prayers for their owner, but as they're only one room wide I don't suppose they get much for them, so that fellow will not soon buy his way out of Purgatory."

Now, we were at the formidable Mikelgate Bar, which itself had a defensive barbican built onto its massive front. The gate guards were waiting, and Father pulled his horse Biter up short. He addressed the guard captain, who was politely deferential to this important-looking stranger knight and his several dozen men at arms.

"I'm Sir Robert de Holland, baron Holand, and this is my son Thomas. We are in the service of the Earl of Lancaster," Father declared, pushing aside his riding cloak to show the rampant white lion on its blue shield that comprises our family coat of arms. "That's Lord Henry, Earl of Lancaster and Leicester. He's my son's godfather."

The guard captain, impressed by the connection, saluted. "We have orders to show you to quarters, my lord," he said. "It's with the Dominicans, so it's good, although the city is full and men have had to be billeted in hamlets all around." Father nodded. "The more soldiers we have the quicker we'll put the Scots to bed." He gestured. "Lead on. My men will cope. John, you accompany us." "I'll tell your serjeant some likely places to bed down," promised the captain as we shook our mounts' reins and moved on.

We clattered under the portcullis, across the ancient stone bridge with its stinking public privies that emptied into the river below and through another gated fortification into the city proper, all the while following a guide on a stringy nag. He halted outside a large part-timbered building with a thatched roof. It looked like a homely house, but a sign above the low door displayed the quartered cross symbol of the Black Friars, the *domini canes*, the 'hounds of the Lord' which told me it was a hospice run by the Church.

"Some of the followers of John of Hainault are lodged here already, lord," the guide said, "but the abbot has held a room for you." Father thanked the man and gave him a piece of silver before we were shown by the porter to a horn-windowed stone chamber. It boasted a small table with a crucifix above it, a row of pegs to hang clothes and a single, largish bed comprised of a wool-stuffed pallet on a leather-strung frame. Father nodded: "Big enough. You sleep on that side, I'll take this, and John" – he gestured to the squire who accompanied us, "you take the door."

John, a competent young noble of excellent but impoverished family who wore his hair close-cropped and shaved high in the old Norman style, nodded, threw down his military cloak and prepared to sleep outside the door, stretched across the threshold. I noticed that he removed his long-bladed knife from the sheath at his hip and stowed it under the leather bag he had put down as a pillow. His short sword was close to hand, too, and he had looped around his wrist a leather thong fastened to its hilt. Nobody would pass him or disarm him while he slept.

While Father busied himself with saddlebags and sword, I rolled myself in my cloak and was asleep in moments, my prayers unsaid. Father wouldn't care about the omission and Mother wasn't there to see it. And in the morning, I would explore York.

Chapter 2 - York

The rumble of iron-tyred wooden wheels on stone setts woke me and then came a series of loud squeals from an indignant pig followed by a burst of laughter and someone calling out in a foreign language. Next, I was aware of the stench that came through the open window and it made me sit up. Father was already awake, moving quietly around the chamber. "What's that stink, Father?" I asked. "That's the smell of a city," he grimaced. "It's sewage and offal, smoke, animal dung and garbage. We're also near the fish merchants and their potent smells. Just be grateful we're not near the tanners – that's a powerful place that will really lay siege to your nose."

I swung my legs off the pallet, eager to dress and see the city. Where we live, in the shire of Lancaster, our nearest town is Ormskirk, and it isn't very big, a rural market town is all. I'd been there several times. As the son of Baron Holand who would one day inherit the title, it was important to my education to know about things like that, but this city of York was something different.

Father had been called upon by our overlord, the Earl Thomas of Lancaster, to provide fighting men and to join the king's expedition against marauding Scots. We were to rendezvous at York, and had travelled across the gritstone spine of England, across the windswept Pennine moorlands on an ancient Roman road that arrowed to their former colonial capital. Then, it was *Eboracum* which I knew from the Latin my tutor had taught me, but it had been Jorvik in the time of the Danes and now it was our solid English York, a place my tutor told me that was the site of the greatest cathedral north of Rome itself.

Mother did not want me to go, but Father said: "The boy will be thirteen, come Michaelmas. He's old enough to be married, Maud. He needs to know more about soldiering than just archery, swordplay and tiltyard quintain Saracens. It's time to expand his horizons past the schoolroom."

Mother had hurried to embrace me. "You ARE getting tall,"

9

she said, brushing a lock of untidy red hair from my forehead. It was an inheritance, she said, of my Angevin ancestors, of whom she had certain doubts. At this moment, she sounded regretful. I suppose she wanted to keep me as a small child but I resisted the urge to pull away from her. "We should trim those eyebrows, you're becoming quite the man." Then I did pull myself away, afraid she'd lick her fingers to smooth down my brows. "I'm fine, Mother," I said, irritated that my Father had seen Mother's smothering hug, and I made an unseen grimace as he grinned at me over her shoulder. I didn't care for open affection, and even as a child I knew my brain was cold, but my temper was sometimes terrifyingly hot.

My father had the same temperament and I had seen him hammer a pig to death after it lunged to bite him over the gate of its sty. "We have the old Berserker blood," he'd once told me. "They were wild men from the North and feared nothing and nobody. They say all the Angevins – King John was one – had black, hot tempers, and John certainly did. He'd bite his own fingers, or even the wall hangings in his rage, but an angry Norseman would butcher you, regardless of consequence. The legend is that an old duke of Anjou married a demon bride and the family has had a streak of the devil in it ever since."

***

I came back to the present, where Father was speaking. "Ready yourself old son, we'll be away for a fortnight at least, likely more if the king chooses to chase the rebels up there." At that, Mother abruptly released me and rushed off to sort out my cloak and small clothes. I thought I heard her stifle a sob, and wondered why, but it was time to pack the worn leather saddlebags and roll my cloak and fasten it behind the cantle of my saddle. I remembered to push my knee into my horse's ribs to make him exhale so I could tighten the girth and check that the bags were secure.

Finally, all was done, and I went back into the house and took a moment to touch for luck my grandfather's war harness that hung in the great hall alongside his two-handed longsword. Once again, I ran my fingers over the familiar, neat hole in the cuisse where some *balastier's* needle-point crossbow bolt had pierced grandfather's thigh and given him his lifelong limp. "Be with me, grandpa," I whispered, and wished I could just once more feel his hard hug and the rough bristle of his beard against my face. I could almost hear his gruff 'Crown of Christ!' that would make Mother flinch.

Then I hastened out into the yard where the troopers were cheerfully joshing each other, tightening gear and girths on their horses and making last-minute farewells of the womenfolk who crowded around to see their men leave. I swung up onto my palfrey Pilgrim and rode out proudly alongside Father at the head of the column and down the hill called Upholland Bank. We had long views from our small hill, far across a marshy plain dotted with meres and rich in wildfowl, and several times we traversed the reedy bogs on long, narrow causeways.

I felt purposeful and grown up, my enamel-hilted dagger at my belt, trotting along on smooth-gaited Pilgrim next to Father ahead of a jingling troop of men at arms and archers. Secretly I flexed my biceps. All the weapons training was giving me hard muscles. I was secretly proud, and I shivered a little with sheer pleasure.

As we rode, Father told me some things that would be useful to know now we would be entering the royal court. "I once was part of a plan to capture the previous king's corrupt male friend, his very close friend," he said meaningfully, though I wasn't quite sure why. "We took him and he was executed for treason," he said. I already had heard something of it: other, older boys told me of a man called Gaveston who had led the king, Edward of Caernarvon, into sinful ways. They sniggered when they spoke of it but they spoke with respect of our Earl Thomas, who with my father in his retinue was one of the nobles who had taken and executed Gaveston. Father said with a secret smile that the loss of his favourite infuriated the king so much that in his rage he bit himself severely on his drooping lower lip. He added unsmiling that those who acted in the plan were later punished. "Edward truly was a calamitous king," he said thoughtfully.

Father was among those who suffered, losing our lands before

I was born, but in time, he was pardoned for his role, got our demesnes back and even served in Parliament. He stayed loyal to our own Earl of Lancaster and in another, later political episode again acted for the earl and against the king, Edward of Caernarvon. As Father told it, Edward had a new corrupt friend, a man called Hugh Despenser the Younger who was wrongfully seizing power and wealth. It did not go well.

Father and our earl were on the losing side in a battle. "Lost all our lands again," Father said dryly. "But I did better than did Earl Thomas. He was accused of treason and lost his head to the axeman. They humiliated him and then tried and condemned him in his own hall. They called us Contrariants and we were tried without being allowed to speak in our own defence. Many were executed, but I was lucky. They locked me up in Warwick Castle, and then last year put me into Northampton Castle but I escaped down a rope and was away."

Some of his explanations puzzled me, but later I understood that Edward of Caernarvon, the father of the boy king Edward of Windsor was a Plantagenet from stock like ours. The word came from *planta genista,* the yellow broom plant that was the Plantagenet symbol, and we were going to see Queen Isabella whom men called the She-Wolf of France. After years of marriage that had somehow survived the storm over Piers Gaveston, the king had conceived another unhealthy affection. This time it was for Hugh Despenser, who took full advantage of his influence, to make great profit from the Crown, living and ruling in high style.

The queen could not bear to be around the arrogant popinjay, so took their son Edward of Windsor to France on pretext of visiting her father, then refused to return until Despenser was dismissed from the English court. The king's angry response was to put his and Isabella's other children into the custody of Despenser's wife, to strip away Isabella's lands and fortune and to arrest her household staff.

"By Saint Joseph's teeth, she was bitter about that," said Father. "Her husband the king had cast her aside for Despenser, so she slipped away to France with the heir and joined forces with her husband's foe, the magnate Sir Roger Mortimer. He had opposed Despenser over his wrongful seizure of power and was imprisoned in the White Tower for his troubles. A black-visaged villain he might be, but Sir Roger's a soldier and he escaped after drugging his guards. He fled to France, where he and the She-Wolf raised an army, invaded England and deposed Edward."

The rebellion against her husband worked, the king fled and our own Earl Henry of Lancaster, who was the king's cousin captured his kinsman at Neath and jailed him in Kenilworth Castle.

Despite his mincing ways, said Father, Edward acted with courage. "When he knew he would soon be captured, he sent away his companions, lest they be slain by the Queen's men, and faced his enemies alone."

Father drew a deep breath and continued: "Earl Henry and a brace of bishops went to see Edward in his cell and told him that if he abdicated he could hand the throne to his son, young Edward of Windsor. If he did not give up the throne, it might well go to another candidate. Henry said the king wept, but agreed, and the boy was crowned at Westminster at age 14. That was last February, on the eve of the Feast of the Presentation."

Father paused to consider and spoke carefully: "The king is too young to rule, so his mother and her friend Sir Roger act as his regents, making decisions for him until he is older. It is really they whom we are going to see, although the call has supposedly come from young Edward. He has pardoned most of those who plotted against his father, although the Despensers were executed for treason, and the old king is now held at Berkeley Castle."

I did not wish to ask exactly what the rebels had done, but thought it must have been a big plot, because the young king's regents forgave 350 people for their parts in it. I also knew that Father had been Earl Thomas' secretary for a long time and had acted for him to hunt down dissidents after an uprising.

Father was not just a secretary, he was a fighting man. He fought alongside his Earl in a losing battle at Boroughbridge, and despite imprisonment and losing our lands, he still acted loyally for our Earl. He had put down a rebellion in Lancashire, having his local rival Sir Thomas Banastre beheaded on Duxbury green. It was an act that would later cost him his own head.

"I still have enemies, Thomas," he told me, "and every day, I must guard my life. It is well that you are being trained in arms, for you are at the Earl's beck and may have to fight for him." I nodded and thought with pleasure of the time I spent at the butts, firing arrow after arrow into the targets, getting stronger and more accurate by the month. I enjoyed working with sword, horse and lance, but if I was to fight for the earl, I resolved to use the deadly English bow, the warbow. It seemed more clinical, more perfect, less personal. If Father had an enemy, my arrows could stop him before he could do hurt. In the meantime, I would practice hard at all aspects of weaponry – but I still wanted to be a longbowman.

Later, I better understood what Father was saying, for he would be unjustly accused and outlawed, captured in Henley woods and, like the earl he had faithfully served, was beheaded. But that was in the future. On this July day in the year of Our Lord 1327 I was bubbling with excitement at the prospect of going to York, filled as it was with men at arms, archers, knights and great nobles all gathered at the young king's command. I was going to war, but only after I'd seen the great cathedral, the markets and the crowds that must surely throng the streets.

"John knows this place and will take you on your rambles around York," Father said. "It's best for a boy to be protected, there are cutpurses and all kinds of rogues abroad these days." "What about you, Father?" I asked. "I'm going to find the Earl and maybe even see the king. I'll get a few of our men to escort me, too."

I liked John, who was an archer and whose other name was Westwood, and after we ate a snatched breakfast of bread, cheese and an apple in a room crowded with soldiers from Hainault, a place which John thought was near France, we stepped into the street outside. It was a narrow, muddy lane crammed with houses whose upper storeys leaned so far across the street that neighbours could almost shake hands from their windows.

A shallow trench ran down the middle of the lane as a drain, but the fishmongers who occupied several shops had choked it with the stinking offal they'd thrown there. I saw one merchant surreptitiously bathing a large fish with blood, and asked John about it. "The fish is likely stale, so he's making it redder to look fresh," he whispered. "Merchants have a lot of tricks, soaking cheese in broth to make it look richer, watering the milk or the wine. You have to inspect what you're buying, there's a lot of cheating that goes on." He paused, thinking. "The Persians say that only four fingers lie between truth and lies." I must have looked puzzled, then he demonstrated. He put four fingers up between his eye and his ear. My reaction, as I comprehended it: "Uh."

So, we rounded into the Shambles, where the butchers ply their trade, killing sheep and cattle on the spot, right there in the street. Sometimes they captured the dying beast's blood to mix into sausages, sometimes they just allowed it to flow into the fetid swamp that was supposed to be a cess trench that ran down the street's centre. It was worse even than the fishmongers' midden, with pigs, rats, dogs and the occasional feral cat rooting through to seize some rotting tidbit that was swarmed with flies. A voice called from above and I looked up just in time to step back as a servant emptied a chamber pot of night soil from an upstairs window, spattering our legs with foul liquid. "That's against the law in London," said John indignantly. "There, you have to empty it into the river, or carry it out of town. These folk in York are just backward!"

John and I took new care as we exited the lane to find ourselves in a warren of small streets thronged with archers and men at arms. The influx of strangers had sparked an impromptu fair, with stallholders selling peppers, wax and scarlet dyes, ale and bread; pedlars hawking everything from fruit pies to wine, milk, cheese and onions, soothsayers claiming to tell fortunes and poulterers offering the geese they had tied to their stalls while chickens and ducks, legs trussed, flopped about on the ground alongside. Probably I was gaping open-mouthed, for the poulterer shouted cheerfully to me: "Can you eat a goose, boy?

If you can't, at least you can make whistles from its leg bones."

The very thought of roast goose made me salivate with hunger and I sniffed the aromas and looked longingly at the vendors who hawked cooked sausage or chicken from baskets slung around their necks.

Some food vendors worked from more permanent premises, using houses with a pair of horizontal shutters that opened directly onto the street. One shutter swung upwards and was propped open to make an awning, the other turned down and rested on two short legs to form a counter. On them, the goods looked more promising: a spicer displayed his wares: salt, honey, olive oil and vinegar, while two bakers in friendly competition offered floury bran loaves still hot from baking. I watched as an apprentice not much older than me used a long-handled wooden spade to take from the oven some thin loaves of oatmeal clapbread, slapped out and flattened for baking, and some cocket, which was baked as a disc and carried the imprint of a medallion.

Under guild laws, the bakers were not allowed to accost a potential customer who was paused before a rival's stall, but the bakers themselves exchanged badinage while she studied the offerings. I heard one of the flour-daubed bakers loudly tell his rival neighbor that he need not worry, the customer wouldn't notice how he was trying to cheat her by shortchanging her on the weight of his loaves. "If he has, he's for the pillory," muttered John. "They'll hang his loaves around his neck and he'll be pelted with filth, and fined."

Trade guilds formed mutual-aid societies for their members, restricted competition, and strove to guard standards, yet tradesmen often cheated their customers, he said. Bakers would add stones to increase the weight of their loaves; chandlers would adulterate wax tapers with lard and skimp on the prescribed 4 lbs of tallow per quarter-pound of wick. Beadmakers must discard any beads which were not perfectly round, makers of knife handles were forbidden to trim them with silver, hiding the telltales which helped to pass bone off as ivory. Even the menders of old clothes were forbidden to press or fold garments so they resembled new ones.

Here was a barber, shaving a customer seated on a stool right out in the street. The man had a small apple tucked into his cheek, to stretch the skin for a smoother shave. "At the end of the day," said John, "someone gets to eat the apple." I shuddered. Further along was a dyer's place, where the tradesman had arrayed jars of soapwort, nut gall, tartar salt and madder, with a small jar of precious saffron kept in view but well out of reach of any thief. These unprepossessing ingredients would be turned into bright colours for the linens and occasional silks worn by fashionable ladies. It was all absorbing, each street a living tableau of traders and the services they offered.

Next, we saw a laundry, where laundresses were soaking bed linens in a wooden trough filled with caustic soda and wood ash. "They'll soak, then pound them, rinse everything and spread them on bushes to dry." I looked around the muddy street. "Bushes?" Yes, John told me. Behind those high walls were a good number of gardens, even small orchards that were out of public view.

"Goodwives grow things there: beets, lettuce, shallots, herbs for medicine as well as for flavouring food. Lamb with mint sauce – ummm," he closed his eyes at the memory. "Some here in York even have wells of sweet, wholesome water, because there are layers of gravel in the ground that filter even the foulest fluids. Canny people build their houses on those gravel beds so they'll always have clean water to drink, and a way to water their crops, too." "What else?" I asked, eager to hear more. "Well, you've had marigold and lavender on your stew at home, and violets chopped with lettuce and onions as a salad, haven't you?" I nodded. I could recall Mother supervising the kitchen maids at home. "The gardens are also good for growing fruit: raspberry canes, currants, apples, pears and plums. In France, they even grow grapes, but the weather is warmer there than here."

We were still paused outside the laundry and an apprentice walked out from the rear of the store with a bundle of furs. "I've beaten these well," he told a stout, red-faced woman. She nodded and took up a flagon of liquid. John politely asked her what it contained. "Bless you, sir," she said, "just some wine, lye and fuller's earth mixed with apple juice. It cleans the garment be it fur or wool. I rub it in, and spot-treat any stains with warm wine. If it's fur that has become stiff because of damp, I sprinkle it with flour and a bit of wine, let it dry, then rub it back to softness again."

Someone jostled me, for the narrow street was almost filled with people, almost all of them soldiers called to the king's service. A shepherd moving a dozen sheep struggled to keep his flock under control and a few raucous men at arms pretended to help him, only to deliberately scatter the animals as the herdsman shouted protests at them. John took my arm, "This way, lad," he said quietly, moving us towards an alleyway. "They're foreign troops and there could be trouble."

We slipped down the alley and then along another, wider one and emerged to the spectacular sight of the towering Minster right before us. Its forecourt was thronged with people watching a slack-line walker who was juggling three hens' eggs as he swayed just above their heads.

A crowd had gathered around a pageant wagon, something Father had told me about but which I had never seen. I knew that at Christmas and the Feast of Corpus Christi, the trade guilds would put on a pageant to illustrate events from the Bible, and the wagon was a horse-drawn travelling stage. This wagon towered above the crowd, its lowest deck higher than a tall man, and with an upper storey above that. Topping the whole wagon were two pinnacles or towers and at one end I saw there was a drum winch and grooved pillars to allow the stage to be lifted or lowered. The whole thing was painted and gilt and the sides and one end were opened so the crowd could see.

"The guilds knew that the city would be crowded, so they've pulled this out to put on a show although it isn't a feast day," said John. "In big cities like this, the guilds have their own pageant wagons and they'll go from place to place in a parade, stopping at designated stations to tell different Bible stories. The mercers here do an annual Doomsday pageant they say that terrifies people." He sucked his teeth and said thoughtfully that the crowds liked the entertainments, the church found them useful and even the town burgesses favoured the acts. "They can assess how large and wealthy each guild is by the quality of their pageants, and that way have a better idea how much to tax them."

Nothing was presently happening around the wagon, so we moved on and found ourselves watching a pair of jongleurs who fiddled while several stout goodwives danced with each other and screamed with laughter. A fellow in a dusty black robe with sewn-on cloth stars sidled through the crowd offering a 'magic potion' to restore virility but my eye was taken by a huckster with a board, a two pairs of six-sided bone dice and a leather cup, standing over a makeshift table. "Come find your luck at Hazard," he was enticing two peasants, calling to them from a gloomy corner under a cathedral buttress. "Win a gold piece." He held up a shiny coin, enticingly. "All you have to do is roll a higher sum than I do. It's easy." "Aye," muttered John. "The victim's pair of those dice are up against that fellow's weighted and shaved ones, so his big numbers always come up, and I expect that's not a real gold piece, either. No wonder he's operating in such poor light."

We moved towards the minster portal, gaping upwards where a great bell chimed to call to the missionary monks for prayers. On the five shallow steps that led to the vast arched doors, pedlars and clerks proffered holy relics, wheedling us to buy and save ourselves centuries in Purgatory. John snorted in derision. "Your father says the king and the old king were avid collectors of pieces of the saints," he muttered. "Personally, I can't think that having a feather from the wing of the Angel Gabriel or bit of fingernail from a scruffy hermit will influence anyone into letting you into heaven on Judgement Day." He paused and looked around before muttering cautiously: "But then, who's to know?"

However skeptical he was about the relics, I noticed that John glanced about to make sure nobody heard the heresy. I resolved to ask Father about it when I had the chance, while taking a look at the offerings of a man in monk's habit who displayed a piece of rock from Christ's tombstone and an actual wheat seed that had been sown by Isaac in the Bible, when he reaped a hundredfold.

Another monk called out to John, offering him an indulgence to forgive any ten of his sins, even ones he had not yet committed, his choice for only a silver penny, but my companion smiled grimly and gently pushed me into the minster. A pair of burly wardens stood watchful, to ensure that the merchants outside stayed out. They assessed us as genuine pilgrims however and nodded us through.

Inside was a great nave between pointed arches that soared to the sky and featured a lofty central tower whose wooden roof had been painted to resemble stone. Light poured in through beautiful stained glass that seemed to emphasize holiness and closeness to God, yet the whole vast building was a tumult of activity. Masons, carpenters, sculptors, ironworkers, painters and plasterers were creating a new cathedral on the Norman foundations of the old and the huge walls echoed to hammer blows, voices, the sound of saws and the squeal of sheaves as materials were hauled up high inside the great cavern.

We wandered through, blessing ourselves from the fonts of holy water until we came to the magnificent, octagonal Chapter House with its stunning display of stained, coloured glass windows and elaborate ornamentation. We peered in, then moved aside into a shadowed corner to watch as a pattering swarm of sandalled monks arrived to flock like starlings into the great meeting space.

There was a bustle as they fussily found their places, lined along the walls and propped against misericords in some exact order I could not understand. "Sorted by age," John muttered in my ear, "except for the ones who hold office." A tall, dignified man with three attendants in train strode in past us and the brothers rose respectfully as he took his place on a splendid throne raised up on a dais. "Archbishop William, he's from Melton," whispered John, who had lived in York and seemed to know everything about the place.

The churchman glanced around, spotted the open door and waved imperiously for someone to close it on our spying gaze. "He's probably going to talk to them about their sins," said John, making me snort with laughter. "He doesn't want us knowing about it." I wished to go back to see what the relic-sellers had to offer, so we dropped a coin in an offertory box and stepped back into the hurly-burly of the cathedral forecourt.

A slender, blonde woman the sombre black habit of a Benedictine nun was sitting on the minster steps in an eddy of the human tide sloshing around the cathedral forecourt. Before her, on a small leather box, were displayed some intriguing objects and I stopped to view them. "What are they, sister?" I asked politely.

"This, my young lord, is a thorn from the cruel crown which Jesus wore. It is imbued with holiness." "That one?" "That is the very basin with which Christ washed the disciples' feet, a truly sacred relic." The mendicant went on to display a scrap of the garment of Saint Paul and a dark mark on a piece of linen that she said was taken from the towel that wiped Christ's face on His way to Golgotha. "It might not actually be the blessed blood of Christ himself, we cannot be absolutely sure," she said, implying however that actually she was quite sure of its provenance.

I looked back at John, my eyes probably wide with awe, but he gently shook his head. "Remember what the Persians say," he cautioned me in a low tone. "Four fingers only lie between truth and lies." I knew what he was saying: four fingers' span is the distance between eye and ear. "We must be along, holy sister," he said, nodding to the nun in farewell. I must have looked pleadingly at her, for she impulsively picked up the sacred thorn, folded it into a scrap of wool and gave it to me. "It will keep you safe," she said. "Be blessed." I stammered my thanks and asked her name. "I am Gaia Dejoie," she said gently, "but my religious name is Sister Josse, a Breton word that means 'lord,' because I am dedicated to Our Lord's service."

Some mysterious thing happened and in all my life since that moment I am unable to say what it was. There was a crackling sense of power in the air, an ozone-like smell like a strike of lightning and Sister Josse's face seemed somehow illumined. My ears were buzzing but I clearly heard her voice speaking although her lips were not moving, and John later said he had heard nothing. The calm voice said: "One day you will be a great lord, Thomas Holland. You will be a knight of a most chivalric order and your actions will shape England's future for a century."

I know I was gaping, slack-jawed at her, when she got up, turned on her heel and glided away, leaving her small leather box abandoned. "How did she know my name?" I asked John, who looked blankly at me. "And this thorn, how do I pay her?" "Forget the thorn, she'll soon pick a few more," said John callously, but I didn't understand. I started to question him more, but he was preoccupied, saying: "I have a friend who's a goldsmith. Let's go and see him and perhaps we'll also look in on the smiths' street where they make weapons and armour." I nodded, too confused to speak, conscious that I was clutching the scrap of wool with its relic. For safekeeping, I carefully put it into my pouch, but although the wool was still there that night, the thorn had vanished.

Chapter 3 - Edward

My eagerly-anticipated visit to watch smiths making armour, swords and arrowheads was not to happen that day. One of Father's men at arms spotted us on Fish Street and rushed up to say: "We've been looking for you: the baron wants you back at the lodgings, and quickly!" so we set off in haste and arrived to find Father already dressed in his best. "We are to meet the young king and," he paused ominously, "more to the point, to meet the regents who rule in his place. Go and put on your good clothes, we are required to be there soon."

I hurried to our chamber and sorted through my wardrobe: high boots with folded-down tops of soft leather, close-fitting stockings and breeches, a long-sleeved tunic and a belted, sleeveless surcoat of red-dyed wool. That, and a cloak with gold chain to close it showed my status as a minor noble and should be presentable enough even at a royal court.

"Come on, boy," said Father, looking me over critically. He was ablaze in cloth of gold and baronial insignia and looked magnificent. "The king is lodged at the Treasurer's House with his mother the queen and Sir Roger Mortimer of Wigmore. They're the royal regents until he's older." I asked how old was the king now? "Just about your age," Father said curtly, impatient to be gone, and so we were out of the door, mounted and clattering across York.

Armed guards treated us with open suspicion when we arrived at the gates of the Treasurer's House, an old building covered in ivy, but Father took charge and we were soon being ushered into a reception room where Queen Isabella was sitting at a small table by the window, playing chess with a boy of about my own age: Edward of Windsor, the king of England. A steward announced us and Father and I bowed simultaneously, doffing our caps and making a leg as we did. The Queen spoke and I was surprised to hear her speak in a soft French accent.

"Sir Robert!" she exclaimed, rising from the chess board. She pronounced his name *Rho-berr*. "It is good to see you again!

How long is it since you served in Parliament?" "Six years, Madame, so it especially gracious of you to remember me." "We know and love our supporters, my lord," she said, "and you pleased us mightily with your actions against those creatures who corrupted the crown." I eyed her discreetly, I hoped. She was a handsome, not a pretty woman, not tall, with glossy dark hair that fell in waves to her shoulder. She had a longish nose and a heart-shaped face. I snapped out of a reverie as I realized she was speaking.

"Now, you must meet my son, the king." She turned and gestured imperiously to the boy, who was still seated, and who seemed to shrink from her voice. "Edward, I present Sir Robert de Holland, our good and faithful friend." The boy rose from his stool at the chess board and extended his hand, my father leaned over and touched his lips to the royal ring, a great ruby. Then I was ushered forward and imitated what I had seen. Next, to my consternation, the Queen said: "Sir Rho-berr come with me, we have much to discuss. Edward, continue your game. Master Thomas here will play my white pieces."

And so, unexpectedly, I was thrown into the royal court, a pawn facing a king. "Your Grace," I bowed, as Father had instructed me. I straightened in time to see the shadow of a grimace cross his face, but Edward made the first move. His eye had caught the coloured enamel of my dagger hilt. "May I see your knife?" he asked, politely. I looked at him, a tall, pale-faced boy, slim and almost diffident. He was dressed richly, as becomes a king, and was well bejeweled. He wore his hair in the Norman style of William the Bastard, shaved savagely high up the back of his head. By contrast, mine was in the old Anglo-Saxon style, long, to the shoulder and although I felt my dress was appropriate for the court, he far outshone me.

Secretly amused by his boyish request about my knife, but not daring to show it, I handed over the dirk I kept at my belt and he admired it then put it down on his side of the board, where he toyed with it. My mind was buzzing, half excited, half scared. Involuntarily, I blurted: "I'm going to visit the smiths and armourers, to see how they make things. My servant is taking me." His face lit up. "I'd like that," he said. "Can I come?"

And so it started, a friendship and an allegiance that lasted all my life. The self-effacing boy across the chess board became a brave and clement king who fashioned his nation into a power of Europe and whose lawmaking and administrative skills made him beloved of his subjects, over whom he would reign as one of England's longest-serving monarchs. He was imperfect, as all men are, sometimes intemperate but normally good-tempered and energetic. He was a lover of luxury, and was greatly inclined to military ways, but that was normal for a king in that age. All that was the future, unknown to me. For now, I let him win our first game of chess, as he was a poor player.

He was astute enough to realise I'd cheated, for I did it clumsily, moving my queen into danger hastily and without obvious consideration. "You did that on purpose, didn't you?" he questioned me. "Well, you have my knife," I said. "I didn't want to annoy you." He laughed and sealed our friendship. "You'll have to show me how to play better. There are some people I'd like to confound."

One of those, I later learned, was his mother's lover, Sir Roger Mortimer, the man who had imprisoned Edward's father and had effectively taken the throne. Edward of Windsor would be well advised to watch Mortimer in more ways than across a chessboard. "Confound, how?" I murmured, conscious that I'd had a couple of sharp looks from the dark-visaged, bearded man who lolled carelessly on a window bench across the chamber.

Father had left the chamber with the queen and I felt suddenly under threat. "Oh, just, you know, show someone that after all, I am the king," he said in a low voice, shooting a sidelong glance at the bearded man who had, or so I had heard in gossip was a man of terrifying temper. I felt I was swimming, and out of my depth. "But you are the king, your grace," I hissed. "We can't talk here," he said low-voiced and urgent then, louder: "Let's go and look at the stables." As we rose from the playing pieces, the bearded man spoke: "Are you leaving, Edward?" "Yes, I'm going to show my friend the horses, Sir Roger," and we slid from the room with a sense of escape.

In the courtyard, John Westwood was waiting and I saw his

eyebrow lift when he spotted me with Edward. "Your grace, my lord of Windsor," he said, doffing his cap and bowing. "My father's man, John of Westwood," I told Edward hurriedly. "He is the one who's going to take me to the armourers' workshops." Edward brightened. "That would be good. Can we go now?" He glanced up at the window above, where Sir Roger stood, looking down at us. "But I'd have to ask him," he said bitterly. "Let's just go to the stables."

So we went to admire the royal horses and boasted as boys do about what we would be and do when we were older. Edward was determined to be a warrior king in the chivalric mode of King Arthur, the king his adored grandfather Edward, the first king of that name had so admired, and that day he planted the seed that would inspire me to devote more time and effort to my military training.

Edward was very proud of his horses and pointed out one handsome chestnut destrier called Stamper that was just being led in after exercise. The horse was lathered, streaked white, jaws foaming. His sides were heaving and his head drooped but Edward was busy talking and did not notice at first. "He's fully trained for war. He leaps and kicks out backwards if anyone comes near to try and hamstring him…" his voice broke off as he realized how poorly the horse seemed.

"Andrew, what ails Stamper?" he called to a man who had just emerged from the stables, wiping his hands on a bundle of straw. The man ignored Edward and moved swiftly to the horse, seizing the bridle to look at the beast's eyes. "What have you done to him, you…" He began to berate the groom who had been exercising the horse, then shouted urgently into the stable for someone.

Edward spoke again: "Andrew Rosthorn, what has he done to my horse?" The farrier threw down the straws and spat. "Bloody well knackered him, your grace," he said grimly. "Will he survive?" Edward was obviously distressed; his anger would come later. "Aye, he'll live. Ah'll fettle him up," said Rosthorn. "Give him a good blood-letting. Give his blood some room in there and let out the ill-humours. Ah, here comes the lad with my fleam."

The stableboy ran across the yard to his master, bringing a wooden mallet with a head shaped like a round of cheese. In his other hand was a smaller iron object – the fleam - which would be inserted into a vein to bleed the horse. Later, I would have the opportunity to examine the knife-like instrument, one end of which was sharpened and shaped like a narrow, shallow spoon. The other end was blunt, rounded and the handle had a channel along it to allow blood to flow while the wound was held open. "Hold his head, lad," the farrier told the boy, but as the child caught the bridle, Stamper curvetted and began passaging about, rolling his eyes, putting his ears back and snorting.

"Soothe him, your grace," Rosthorn urged the king. "He knows you best." Edward took the bridle and caressed the animal's muzzle, then breathed into his nostrils. "He likes that," he said quietly. Certainly, Stamper calmed and Rosthorn moved up to caress the beast's neck and seek the big vein, isolating it with his fingers. "Give me that blood stick," he told the stableboy, who handed over the mallet. His fingers had found the vein, and with his left hand he placed the sharp curve of the blade over it. "Not across it, see?" he said. "You'd sever the vein, bleed him to death. You want to enter the vein along its length." Edward, eyes wide, was still holding onto Stamper's harness, "Hang on hard, horsehide is tough," Rosthorn warned. Edward nodded, and I saw his knuckles were white where he gripped hard.

"Just a sting, nowt much, lad," Rosthorn told the horse. He gave the fleam a solid, sharp knock on the back of the blade with the blood stick, slicing through the hide and piercing the vein at the first attempt, and the horse flinched. Edward kept the animal's head fairly still but there was still some sudden movement. The farrier had anticipated the reaction and followed Stamper's movement, keeping the fleam neatly in place.

A wash of blood pumped out, spattering Edward's face and as Rosthorn twisted the fleam to let more blood flow, steam rose above the sheet of thick red gore which ran down the chestnut hide, and turned the farrier's arm red to the elbow.

"How much will you bleed?" Edward asked. "Just about the right amount, your grace" said Rosthorn dryly. "There's a lot of blood in a horse." The farrier allowed a considerable puddle to flow onto the cobbles around the horse's hooves before Stamper seemed suddenly to settle. The beast's head came up, he gave a shuddering sigh and shook his mane, causing the farrier gradually to withdraw the fleam, reducing pressure and slowing the blood flow. Finally, he removed it altogether, reversed the instrument and pushed the blunt end into the small wound to seal it before wetting his finger and wiping the small incision. "Get some honey on that, stop infection," he muttered.

The farrier slapped Stamper on the neck, stepped back and looked over his patient. The horse whickered, his ears came up and he seemed suddenly at ease and indifferent to the small crowd gathered around him. The stableboy, who had obviously seen all this before, produced a small apple and Stamper gratefully took it and crunched it down.

"Take him in, give him a good rubdown and put some honey on that cut. When you give him his feed, add some horseradish and mint, make sure he has plenty of water and an extra blanket," Rosthorn told a groom who had just come on the scene, "and you –" he looked at the groom who had reduced Stamper to distress, "Ah'll talk to you later. You could have killed a fine beast with your stupidity." Edward scowled at the fellow. "Remove him from my stables," he commanded. "He put my horse at risk, I'll not have him near any of our steeds."

He turned away, "I'm glad Master Rosthorn was there, he likely saved Stamper's life. I'll tell the chamberlain to reward him." He paused and said thoughtfully "I'd like to know more about caring for horses, every knight should have that knowledge." It was typical of Edward, he was curious, and always sought to understand matters, yet he could be modest and wise enough to admit ignorance.

Too soon my father came looking for me, saying it was time to go, so I bade my new friend goodbye, John promised that he would take us both to view the smiths and armourers at work, and we set out across York to prepare ourselves for the campaign.

"A great expedition is mounting," Father told John and I. "We are to trap the rebel Scots against the Tyne at Newcastle and put an end once and for all to their raids and incursions. Sir Roger is assembling a great force." The words were hardly out of his mouth when we heard shouting. We rounded a corner and ran into a riot. A mob of men were striking at each other with staves, knives and clubs, others with broken heads were staggering away and hurrying swarms of men at arms were pouring into the square before us.

"Hainaulters!" John exclaimed. "They're Flamands, look at their tunics!" Father nodded. "Edward is to be betrothed to their princess and they've sent mercenaries to cement the bargain." He unsheathed his sword; John tugged his own short stabbing sword from his belt and we turned our horses into a small street where they nervously eyed a dozen pigs that had fled from the uproar. "Not a place for the boy," he told Father. "We should return to the lodging." Father shook his head. "No, it's full of those Flamands. If there's a fight it will be them against any English, and they'll know us by our insignia. Let's get back to the minster."

We started to turn our horses away when a group of men wearing the lion jupons of Flanders materialised and blocked the way. Father never hesitated. He drove Biter straight at them, grabbing my horse's bridle with his left hand while he leaned forward and swept his blade like a scythe. The foot soldiers scattered, but one stepped forward. Almost casually, Father turned his wrist and struck the fellow with the flat of his sword right across the temple. The Flamand dropped, limp, into the miry slop of the street just as John and his horse brushed up alongside me, knee to knee.

He too had his sword in hand and levelled it at one ruffian who seemed inclined to try for my horse Pilgrim's bridle. "Back, or I'll have your eye," John warned, and the fellow stepped backwards, slipping in the mud. A swift kick in the ribs to urge them and our horses were through the group and into an open street. "Forget the minster," said Father. "That square will be crowded and there will be fighting. Make for Clifford's Tower. The royal mint is there, it will be protected."

Father was correct. The bailey wall and massive gatehouse of the old Norman castle stood quiet and peaceful. No mob was going to bother to take on that impregnable place. We urged our horses up the steep mound, father showed his tunic with its impressive insignia, the constable hurried to open the gate and we were inside, and safe.

We stayed in the refuge overnight, by which time the royal troops had restored order, and Queen Isabella commanded our Earl Henry, who was one of three nobles acting as military advisors to the young king, to begin at once to move troops north to Durham and counter a new Scots incursion. Father, who had consulted with the earl, was pessimistic. "Mortimer and the queen think we can trap the Scots against the Tyne and so bring them to battle, but I fear they are a lot swifter than our army. We'll have to outflank them." And we hastened out of York.

Our cavalry went first, John Westwood and I among them, and everything was done hurriedly. Because of my father's status as a companion in arms of Earl Henry, who himself was a cousin of the young king, we rode at the head of the column, in the king's own party, and Edward and I had more to talk about than chess problems.

We rode hard, through moorlands, hills and valleys where there were no proper roads, just rough ground and John told me quietly that matters were not going well. "We've left our impedimenta far behind. The pack horses and the wagons can't keep this pace and the outriders who lead the way seem constantly to be making false alarms. They're being spooked by deer or wild cattle."

The race for the Tyne continued without pause except to tighten saddle girths or snatch a break to water our steeds and we covered ten leagues between sunrise and sunset, arriving at the river in an exhausted state. The horses fared badly, for we had outrun our supply train and there was no forage, oats or hay for the animals. John had wisely packed a loin of roasted beef in his saddlebags, and we shared that with Father, who took some to the king, but most of the cavalry had only bread which they had fastened behind the cantles of their saddles, and the horse sweat had soaked it.

For myself, after chewing a little beef, I rolled into my military cloak and slept on the ground, sore and exhausted, but John stayed awake all night, with the reins of our horses tied to his belt because it was too dark to find a place to tether them.

When daylight came, it brought a steady, roaring downpour of rain, swelling the river and making it impossible to ford. Nor had our supply wagons caught up to us, meaning we spent the day with growling stomachs, while our desperate horses ate leaves from a few trees we'd found. Eventually, Earl Henry located people who brought food to sell, making themselves a nice profit from watery wine and soggy bread. And so it went for a whole week. The rain continued unabated, our clothes and war gear were soaked, our horses had running sores on their backs and we did not even have wood dry enough to burn.

Finally, we had news of the Scots, and set off upriver to do battle. "They're in a good position," said John. "They're across the river and on higher ground. We have more men, but that's a good place to defend."

Edward rode out in front of our army, calling on us to fight well and to maintain our ranks. Earl Henry wanted to take the offensive, but Mortimer forbade it and we spent more uncomfortable, wet nights sleeping in our armour. Once, the Scots mounted a night raid, killing some scores of our men, and for several days we chased and tried to trap the invaders, but they escaped through swampy ground and we awoke one morning to discover that they had gone. The campaign had fizzled out.

On our journey back to York, I spent a few hours riding alongside Edward and he was bitterly disconsolate. "This was my first passage of arms and it failed miserably," he lamented. "It will drain my exchequer, too, I have to pay the Hainault troops a fortune. I vow by the Virgin that I'll never, ever again lead a mismanaged campaign like this one. I blame Mortimer for ignoring what experienced men advised, and my mother the queen abetted him."

"She even made me watch when they mutilated and beheaded Despenser, who was my father's friend. She said: 'Your hedger and ditcher of a father was a man of unnatural lusts. This one, his paramour, usurped my role and I can never forgive that.' She has become a bitter, vengeful woman and I must be wary of her now. Some whisper that Mortimer spied for the Scots, and the Douglas came close enough to capturing me. Maybe Mortimer and my mother deliberately mismanaged the whole campaign in hopes of getting me killed."

"You know," he said, twisting in the saddle to look at me directly, "my advisors did not train me for this, they did not inform me, they never ceased to squabble among themselves over the actions to take. It was badly done, and I swear I will make the decisions myself, once I have better knowledge. I can't have the queen and her paramour overriding me or my advisors. And, when I have sons, I shall teach them how to go to war, not thrust them unprepared into a shameful disaster like this."

His words burned themselves into my brain. I, too, would learn more about waging war. I wanted to be a fighting man.

Chapter 4 - Archer

"Thomas, bend your whole body into the horns! You're only using your arms. Frenchmen draw the bow, Englishmen bend it!" It was a cloudy, cool day and I was receiving instruction in archery from one of the most famous of the Cheshire archers, an amiable ruffian called Andrew of Leatham. In the three years since I first met our boy king, Edward, I had been training to be a fighting man, and while I was busily recruiting bowmen from the northern shires, archery had called me. Now I was receiving instruction from one of England's best.

Much had happened since I had followed the young Edward on a failed mission to repel the Scots. A treaty of peace had been agreed, Edward's deposed father the old king was dead at Berkeley Castle, probably murdered on the orders of the regent Mortimer, and the royal resting place in Gloucester Cathedral had become a place of pilgrimage, as had the spot in London's Newgate where the old king's heart was held in a silver casket.

My father Robert de Holland had been murdered in an Oxfordshire wood, some said by Lancastrian enemies with long memories of his part in the execution of Sir Adam Banastre a decade or more ago, and I had become the new Baron Holand, friend of the young king Edward of Windsor.

Our own late earl Thomas of Lancaster had conspired against the previous king, Edward of Caernarvon, and the good earl was captured, humiliated and lost his lands and titles before his appointment with the headsman and decapitation. But when the old king died, or was murdered, his newly-crowned son Edward of Windsor saw fit not only to restore the Lancaster lands and titles to Thomas' brother Henry, but also to appoint our new earl as his chief advisor and captain-general of the royal forces in the Scottish Marches. He even added the Earldom of Leicester and its wool-rich lands to Henry's Lancaster holdings.

Edward of Windsor and I had become close friends and he had appointed a magister to tutor me, to teach me Latin and to speak the court language of French. And while I followed those studies, I was also gaining skills at arms, horsemanship and above all, archery, my growing passion.

At court, I remained cautious and discreet, for Sir Roger Mortimer, the regent who acted for the young king was protective of his position and kept a close eye on Edward's doings and friendships and would brook no rivals. The regent spent lavishly and lived in grand style, with a household of 500 or more knights, pages, squires, kitchen and stable staff, and Edward complained privately to me about it. "He's filled the court with thieves and whores, has a circle of courtiers who fawn over him and thinks of nothing but feasting, hawking and hunting. The common people resent him, he squanders the treasury, he's a cuckoo in the nest! He is rude to my wife Philippa, when he should be grateful: it was her Hainaulter soldiers who deposed my father."

When I spoke to my mentor John Westwood about it, he only whispered cautions and implied that Earl Henry had quietly spoken of plans to oust the cuckoo, and with that I must be content, but I was 15 years old and impatient. "It isn't right that this Mortimer pushes you aside," I told Edward. "You're the king, dismiss him." "You could shoot him for me," he said airily. "Pop him off from a mile away."

It was our joke: I'd been attracted to archery more than to the knightly pursuits of horsemanship and swordplay. Edward had another driving force: he wanted to restore the Age of Chivalry. "You're a romantic," I told him, "besotted with the idea of re-enacting the court of King Arthur, of knights and ladies, of minstrels and dancing, bold deeds and courtesies." He laughed and agreed that he wanted to promote Christianity and militarism, to do good and live purely. Of course, some of it was lip service. I could agree to practising goodness and Christianity, I could be gentle with ladies and I'd learned my share of knightly courtesies and skills in the tiltyard, but my vocation was at the butts, where I could place an arrow of birch or beech into a handspan at 200 paces. When it came to dealing with my enemies, I'd rather simply kill them, and for all his chivalrous talk, Edward was no better.

He did not begrudge me my skills, for I'd worked hard at

becoming an archer: it takes years of physical work to attain the robust upper body needed to bend the great yew bows. Archery was encouraged as a sport and was of practical use as a means of procuring food: rabbits, small game, a goose or a duck could feed a family. And the king's verderers patrolled the royal chases with caution: it was not unknown for the poacher of a royal hind to spit the king's man with an arrow from hiding rather than be caught.

But to become skilled was a long and difficult road. Bowmen did not use the mere strength of their arms to bend their six-foot yew bows. Instead, the longbowman kept the right hand at rest on the nocked arrow and pushed the whole weight of his body into the 'horns' or nocked deer horn tips of the bow.

The draw weight to pull that hempen bowstring to the archer's ear was about the same as lifting a grown man with one hand, and that power could send an arrow more than 300 paces with deadly effect. At shorter range, an arrow with a needle-like bodkin head would pierce a knight's plate armour. Against most troops, we used curved broadhead arrows, vicious, edged-iron blades that will not pierce plate, but easily slice through the heavy leather Jack Coats favoured by infantry. They can pierce rivetted armour or even the links of Damascus mail and they inflict terrible wounds. Some of these arrowheads are not glued onto the shafts but instead are attached with warm beeswax. Once the wax sets, they can be handled normally, but if they hit a target and the shaft is pulled to remove the missile, it comes away from the head, leaving it buried in the body.

Even if the missile did not strike something vital, the buried arrowhead invariably causes a fatal infection.

For the past two years I'd been training with Master Leatham the archery instructor, doing considerable physical work and eating the king's good food. I'd grown taller, broader and stronger than most grown men despite my youth – I was still only fifteen summers old - and enjoying as I did the king's favour, was treated with respect for that as well as for my intimidating size. It was helpful that my training at the pel – a wooden post made to resemble a Saracen and used for sword practice under the hawk's eye and brazen voice of a weapons instructor – was better than average. Those who might think they could take on an archer at sword fighting were more cautious when they saw me hacking splinters from the pel set in the courtyard.

"Archers were not always regarded highly," said Master Leatham, "although we have always been well paid. It used to be that an armoured knight was judged the equal of ten men at arms and with his heavy horse to help protect him could even take on more than that. But then came the war bow, a longer weapon than usual that some call the English bow, or long bow. Now, an archer can kill a knight and we have new status and are feared by the French so much that they kill any archer they can capture. There's no ransom for us bowmen, so you fight to the death, and don't get captured, but you must train to be effective and to stay alive."

And train we did. Every village in England had a practice ground for archers, called the Butts. They were ranges where archers could hone their skills and usually consisted of circular, flat-topped turfed mounds about nine feet high on which were mounted straw-stuffed round targets marked with coloured rings.

We practised to the master's commands: "Ready your bows! Nock! Mark! Draw' Loose!" at various distances, with a minimum standard of shooting from a furlong away, which was 220 paces, but our war bows could send arrows for nearly twice that distance and a trained bowman would loose ten arrows a minute, all on target. A company of bowmen working together produced a sleet storm of lethal iron-tipped missiles that darkened the sky and rained death. "It's more important to have an unending supply of arrows than it is to have accurate archers," said Master Leatham. "That's because the army that runs out of missiles will lose, unless their infantry is superb."

"And, an archer must be strong," he cautioned. "Every arrow sent from your bow means pulling back the hempen bowstring, drawing it to the ear. It takes the strength needed to lift a man single-handed." I nodded. The longbow called for huge effort that exhausted my back and shoulders as well as my arms, and a prolonged session at the butts strained and caused even my calloused, hardened fingers to bleed.

Some days, we took time away from plucking the yew and went to seek material for bow staves and arrows. The great bows, which were six feet or longer, were best made of yew wood. The master bowyer who sought, chose and shaped the staves – most yews lack straight grain, so are not suitable for longbows - made them in a 'D' section, flat on the front, rounded on the inner side. The natural creamy white sapwood surface of the yew tree with the bark removed forms the flatter outside and is elastic under tension while the inner part, the belly of the bow, is solid pink-brown heartwood, stiff and stubbornly unyielding. Together, the different types of wood, which show as thin stripes in the finished weapon, make a heavy bowstave that is flexible at the ends, rigid in the centre.

After he finds a straight-grained yew and cuts the rough staves, the bowyer cures the harvested wood for up to three years before shaping it, trimming the sapwood, rounding the heartwood into a D section, and fitting and gluing the stave ends with deer horn nocked to hold the bowstring. He uses hemp to whip a grip or tightly laces a leather wrap around the belly where it would be seized by the archer's left hand, often after gluing a thin strip of cork in place under it as padding. Lastly, the bowyer will waterproof the bowstave with resin, wax and good tallow.

The whole process takes up to four years to complete but when the archer who has hauled the bowstring of the finished weapon to his ear releases his grip he also releases the stored energy in the yew. The heartwood springs out of compression, the flexing sapwood leaps back to shape and their combined power dispatches a clothyard arrow hissing across a killing field to slice through metal, leather and flesh to likely claim a life.

I was musing on the lethal power of simple staves of wood when Master Andrew chided me: "And, don't forget to wear a cap," I probably looked puzzled. "You keep a couple of spare bowstrings under it, to keep them dry," he explained. "A wet bowstring stretches and is no good. Now, let's consider arrows…"

The longbow was not used just for war. Hunting with it was

important, too, and we made arrow heads specific to our prey, be it wolf, rabbit or deer. War arrows were made in thousands with heads that ranged from the bodkin spike that can pierce thin armour or mail through the flesh-slicing broadhead to small barbed blades that inflict deadly wounds. They all come in sheaves of two dozen, their shafts a clothyard long, made of poplar, beech, yew, ash, hornbeam or elm for preference. Any small deviations from straightness could be corrected by heating the shaft, then rolling or stressing it on a grooved stone, and we took care to store our precious arrows in linen bags kept open with willow withy sticks that also separated the missiles, to avoid crushing the fletchings, for which grey goose feathers were most favoured.

Those feathers were glued, tied and so set as to make the arrow spin in flight, keeping it stable and accurate on its way to the target. We also learned to allow for windage and for the natural drop at distance by calculating the arrow's weight, fletching and the bow's power. We would stab our spare arrows in the ground in front of our shooting positions, enabling us to retrieve them swiftly. This had the side benefit of inducing infection in an enemy wounded by a dirty arrowhead.

The arrowheads themselves were usually of iron heated to an orange colour, beaten into a shallow spoon shape then formed into a socket to fit the shaft before being ground razor-sharp as either a bodkin, shaped like a narrow, lengthened pyramid, or as a lethal triangular broadhead. Most archers marked their arrows and would walk a battlefield when the fighting was done to retrieve their own, straight and true missiles, but in the heat of conflict when that was not possible, boys would run up from behind the lines, delivering fresh sheaves in their linen bags to replenish our supply.

Master Andrew cautioned us: "In battle, don't shoot at your maximum rate all the time. You'll strain your fingers, you'll exhaust your shoulders, back and arm muscles and you'll run out of arrows.

"At the beginning of the encounter, you'll be ranging arrows high and long, firing into a mass of men and raining down a battering hail of sharp iron. For them, it will be like being in a storm, only it won't be frozen water that hits them in the face. Later, as the enemy gets closer, you'll be better able to pick your targets. Take your time and aim true. Don't forget that a knight whose horse is killed under him is well disabled and if you or your comrades capture him, a fat ransom could come your way. So, if you have only broadheads to hand and he's in plate, shoot the horse right through its trapper. That's usually only cloth or perhaps a bit of leather across the chest. At close range, the broadhead will do the job, and even if it doesn't kill the beast, the pain will often cause it to unhorse its rider."

Master Andrew paused to think. "Ah, yes, in battle you will usually be alongside men at arms who will be formed in schiltrons, or divisions. The front ranks will be pikemen and soldiers with shields and axes or swords. The pikemen will form a war hedge behind their shield wall, from which they project a line of spiked weapons with a hook and also an axe head at the end of a very long pole. The length keeps horsemen at bay, the hooks can be used to pull a rider down, and an axe, well, you know what a pole axe can do. If you don't, go to a slaughterhouse and watch one being used to kill an ox.

"The thing is that the archers can fall back behind this bristling wall of steel if the enemy knights get too close. Your job is to shoot them down before they arrive, but some will survive, and it will be up to the men at arms to deal with them while you slip in behind the defensive line and shoot them from there.

"If the nobles have chosen the battlefield well, you'll sometimes be positioned on a slope behind the infantry and can fire over their heads while they protect you. Just don't shoot your own men, they don't care for that very much."

Chapter 5 - Plotter

Biter, my late father's destrier, was snorting with pleasure so loudly while the ostler worked on him that I did not hear my tutor Sir John Westwood come into the stable. Only when he spoke to the groom, curtly ordering him out of the stall, did I realise he was present. I'd just come from an hour working with Biter in the lists, charging down a quintain that was a sort of crucifix with a wooden shield and sword at opposite ends of the horizontal arms.

The whole thing pivoted smartly when struck and the idea was to gallop in fast, hit the painted face or chest with your lance point, then be away before the sword swung around to clout you in the back. That day, I'd escaped without bruises because my lance had been accurate and I'd hit the painted paynim's face on the upright. I'd even been showing off my sword skills, vaulting off Biter at the half-gallop and swinging back into the saddle to turn him sharply in a mock attack on what would have been the rear of a surprised opponent.

"Oh, John! I didn't hear you," I said, unnecessarily. He grunted and scanned the stable with care. "Nobody else here?" he asked. "No, master," I shook my head. "Only this fellow" – a nod to the warhorse – "and he wants this apple." John didn't grin. "I have news of import," he said quietly. I nodded, impressed into silence. John was a man without pomp, and to hear him sound solemn was a rarity. "Do not speak of this, on pain of our lives," he warned. I nodded again, "Of course," I murmured. "What is happening?"

"Our earl is involved in statecraft," he said in a low voice. "and we are to help him. We are to seize the upstart Mortimer and restore your friend Edward to his rightful place as ruler. We are to toss the cuckoo from the nest he has assumed. It's a matter of urgency, for one of Isabella's maids whispers that the queen is with Mortimer's child. If she has his bastard, they'll likely try to do away with Edward and put their child on the throne."

This was dangerous talk, I knew. Mortimer had been

increasingly high-handed of late, making policy, plundering the nation and treating the landed nobility with arrogance and contempt. He knew that the magnates wanted to depose him, and he was suspicious and on his guard.

Only a day before, our king Edward had told me something similar: "Sir Roger has been secretly acting against me, without my mother the queen's knowledge. Certainly, his spies have been reading my correspondence and now Philippa has given me an heir, I fear the usurper may kill both my son and myself to legitimise putting his own by-blow on the throne of England. "

"What do you propose, your grace?" I had said, unconsciously acknowledging Edward's role as my king, not merely as my friend. He shook his head. "I think we must take Mortimer and dispose of him." Now, Sir John was setting matters in motion. Two days later, we slipped away from York and rode south, for spies had reported that Mortimer and the queen were in residence at Nottingham Castle, but were hunting from the lodge at Bestwood. They told us that the couple returned to the castle each evening and were mindful to have a strong escort at all times. "The king says to go," said Sir John, his eyes sparkling with excitement, "he feels he can take them at the castle, he has some plan of his own." Therefore we went to lie up secretly for two days at a royalist's manor house less than a league from Nottingham.

It was a frosty October night, when we finally moved on, armed and mailed under our cloaks and hoods, and we rode like ghosts to smoky Nottingham. The city was as usual so wrapped in sulphurous, yellow sea-coal fumes that even in daylight it was hard to see more than fifty paces. By night and in drifts of foggy smoke, we were nigh invisible, but we even booted our horses' hooves in thick leather to dampen their sound.

At the head of our troop rode the king and his close companion Sir William Montagu, Lord of Mann. It was Montagu who had secretly gone to Pope John in Avignon to explain how Mortimer and Isabella had taken over the monarchy. To assure His Holiness that he was indeed dealing directly with the young king, the Keeper of the Privy Seal had agreed with the pope a secret signal to authenticate any correspondence. The code was *'pater sancte'* – 'holy father' – written in Edward's own hand.

Nevertheless, someone had intercepted and read the missive, and although it was written with caution, Mortimer had sniffed the wind and smelled conspiracy. "He had the impertinence to have me brought before him and interrogated me, saying I was conspiring against him. It is unconscionable that he tries to control me. I have to act," said Edward, as we rode out one afternoon in the royal chase of Peak Forest. "but I want the papal blessing on what I must do. Will says it's best to eat the dog before he eats you, so I need the Pope's approval, for I may have to send Sir Roger to the headsman and I do not want mortal sin on my soul."

Montagu was less concerned about killing than was our chivalry-conscious king. "The bastard Mortimer interrogated me, too, accusing me of treachery against him. Against him? A jumped-up franklin who got his lands through his marriage? He has the gall to question me? I'll run him through once opportunity occurs."

That October night, the opportunity seemed likely, for Edward had the papal blessing and we rode to capture Mortimer. Edward had chosen our group of ten carefully, a small troop but each one trained to war. By default, the leader was William de Clinton, whose family had a long tradition of royal service. He was a fierce champion in the lists and melees and rode just behind the king and Montagu, who were stirrup to stirrup. Next came Earl Henry of Lancaster, who at 48 was the oldest man in the group, but still carried a deadly lance and had survived more conflicts than his number of years. There were some other young knights, a few men at arms and towards the rear of the troop I rode on Biter, with my father's sword at my hip. The king was not yet 18, a year older than I, but even though I was the youngest of our band I was still taller and stronger than he was, thanks to my archery training.

Ahead of us on the forest track John Westwood, whom Edward had raised from squire to knight, rode like a wraith, guarding us against ambush; behind us two young knights trailed our group by a quarter mile to protect the rear.

"We are to meet William of Eland before we get to the castle," Earl Henry said quietly. "He is seneschal of the castle and a loyal king's man. He says he can get us inside, but we must approach with caution as Mortimer has kept half of the garrison on the walls and on watch." Eland was true to his word. He met us a mile from the castle, emerging cautiously from a copse of birch, then led us quietly through Sherwood, which surrounds the city and would shield us from watching eyes, if anyone could see through the darkness and smoke.

Our guide brought us through the Broadmarsh safely, and there were no guards on the Trent bridge. We forded the shallow Leen by the fishponds, where we left our horses under the guard of two bowmen, one of them my archery tutor Andrew. Further east, Eland told us, lay the wharves and piers where trade came and went from the castle. "The warehouses will be guarded. Stay quiet," he urged. Above us, where was what little we could see, loomed the dark bulk of the castle rock, with a few flickering torches showing along the battlements and a burning haybale over the massive gate. I heard the bells for Compline, the day's last prayers, which in winter meant only an hour or two before bed. We'd trap our prey in his chamber, I thought.

Now, a quiet order to halt was given and we found ourselves by the stables of a half-timbered house, and a man hurried out to meet Eland and whisper with him. Edward muttered something then told us in a calm voice to put aside our cloaks and unsheathe our swords. He followed Clinton, who seemed to know the route and we ducked into a low cave that had steps cut in the rock leading down to a tunnel.

Edward halted us once we were all inside. "There are steps and an arched door at the other end. It is not locked, and we will be inside the bailey when we emerge. It's less than fifty paces from here. Make sure your swords don't clatter, don't talk and only these two men will have lights. And, when we leave with our man, make a lot of noise. We want to intimidate the guards with the sound of a large body of men. A few seconds' hesitation before they summon courage to take us on could mean we escape cleanly."

We filed slowly and quietly under the curtain wall, trod carefully up fifteen or twenty steps and heard the heavy door creak open to reveal a dimly-lit area that was the middle bailey. "This way," I recognized Clinton's rumble of a voice and we moved along the foot of the wall, cloaked by the dark, crossed a small area of cobbles and stepped inside as one of the raiders opened another door.

A rushlight in a wall bracket revealed that we were in a small guardhouse where two men were slumped at a table, dozing in front of a charcoal brazier. One of them started, probably alerted more by a draught from the open door than by any small noise we had made, but Clinton was on him instantly, clubbing him across the head with the hilt of his sword and lowering the unconscious body to the filthy reeds that covered the floor. The second man never knew his death. Sir John almost casually clamped one hand over the fellow's mouth while with the other he pushed a punching knife into the left side of his neck. The man writhed like a landed fish and bright arterial blood pumped out in astonishingly large gouts, but the dying man made no sound other than some low groans.

Eland gestured: over there. In the corner of the chamber was a spiral stairway, a newel stair. "The solar," said Edward. It was the first word anyone had spoken since we stepped out of the tunnel. Eland led the way, gesturing to us to stay a short distance back. I guessed we were climbing to the chamber of the lord of the castle, doubtless now occupied by Mortimer, and I also guessed there would be guards at his door. Again, Clinton was at the head of our group, but he was staying out of sight, around the curve of the stairwell as Eland arrived at the head of the steps.

I heard a man say in surprise: "My lord William! Is something wrong?" Eland responded with something inaudible, then Clinton and I burst into the open, there was a brief and furious clattering and we were all pushing into the chamber of the solar where Mortimer, in an embroidered nightshirt, was scrambling across a great bed away from us, trying to conceal himself behind a wall hanging. In the corner, Queen Isabella, who was seated at a small table where a maid had evidently been dressing her hair, began screaming. Her hands went to her throat, the maid cowered against a wall.

Edward stepped forward. "Be quiet, mother," he hissed. Isabella gulped audibly and shook her head. "No, Edward, not this!" Clinton and I were at the fore, and we seized Mortimer. He struggled, Clinton fell back, clutching his chest and I saw the bloodied knife in Mortimer's hand. He was turning on Edward when I grabbed the regent's hair and banged his head hard against a bedpost, stopping him dead. Then I had my knife at his throat. Mortimer went still, blood trickling from his forehead. Edward, pale at his escape, turned to him, and I glimpsed the hard-set rage on his face. He levelled his sword at the regent. "Resist, and I open your guts," he said. "I'll be your executioner, right here."

Isabella went to her knees: "Edward, my son," she was sobbing, drawing in great gouts of air like a donkey braying. "Have pity, have pity on him." Edward gestured with his sword at Mortimer who stood white-faced and mute. "Get him out before we have the whole garrison in here." A man at arms handed me some leather straps that I recognized as a hawk's jesses, and we lashed Mortimer's wrists together in front of him. "You'll not fly from me, my pigeon," Edward said grimly. "Out, out of the door."

We deliberately made much noise as we stormed down the stairwell, shouting challenges, cursing, bellowing like cattle. Then we were into the courtyard of the bailey, several crossbow quarrels fired from the ramparts above clattered near us without effect and we were through the arched door of the tunnel, slamming and bolting it from the inside even as several missiles of some sort hammered against its exterior.

Mortimer, barelegged and still in his nightshirt, was bundled along without ceremony, shoved down the steps, pushed along the passage and prodded and hauled up to the open air. We were still only a short distance from the castle, and I could hear the slow clank of the pawls as the portcullis was raised but could see nothing in the foggy dark. Now we went with stealth, and I stuffed a piece of cloth into Mortimer's mouth to keep him silent, but the man seemed shocked and unable to resist.

It seemed only moments before we were at the fishponds and the half-timbeed house where Andrew was looming out of the dark, arrow nocked. Behind him, our tethered horses were stamping and restive. It was the work of seconds to shove Mortimer up onto a mount, lash his ankles together under its belly and loop his bonds to the pommel before we moved out in disciplined silence.

Through the still night I heard the crash of the drawbridge a few hundred yards behind us, but we were again wraiths and we melted into the foggy darkness with our captive, unseen and exultant. I reflected that Edward had been a lunge away from death, but somehow, I'd stopped that, and I was not unhappy.

Chapter 6 - Trial

At the house where we had laid up, we tied Mortimer to a carriage and took him south and east through the winter darkness, heading for the Great North Road at a steady trot. We were on good forest tracks and level ground, facing the climbs of only one or two ridgelines and blessed, now we were clear of smoky Nottingham, with the good light of a three-quarter moon. We had no fear of brigands, armed and many as we were and after a couple of hours, the king slowed our pace to rest the mounts. He sent the word down the column: "We have friends waiting, by the time it chimes for Terce we should be with them."

"Edward knows his business," said John, as we rode stirrup to stirrup. "He sent out messengers ahead of us while we rested outside Nottingham. There should be fresh mounts at Melton and Stamford, and again further south. No pursuers will catch us."

John was right. At Melton, the royalist Sir Rodney Brooksby was waiting with a dozen fresh mounts. I was reluctant to give up Biter, but John assured me he would be taken on to London and would be there within the week. "Best we move swiftly, and we don't want to kill our steeds," he said. We broke our fast with a hasty meal of cheese and apples while grooms moved our equipage from tired horses to fresh and the king himself checked Mortimer's bindings as the carriage horses were replaced but he was not released. I patted Biter's neck. "He'll be fine," John saw my action. "The mounts are being taken just down the road to the leprosarium operated by the monks of St Lazarus. Nobody will seek them there, they'll be fed, watered and rested and will follow us, only slower."

Ourselves hastily fed and refreshed, we remounted and moved on at brisk pace, arriving at the hostelry of the Knights of St John in Stamford after a fast journey down the Great North Road. Again, horses were waiting, but the king said that because it was after sunset and we had been on horseback for almost a full day, we could take relief. "We will rest here and leave after Matins," he commanded "We've ridden nearly 20 leagues and my mother cannot yet have organized a pursuit that could catch us."

We ate heartily, slept in the hospice and rose with the monks before dawn to say our prayers. When we readied to leave, the king showed how well he had planned the capture. "Saddle the new mounts the monks have readied, and prepare to lead the horses on which we rode in." So, with fresh beats and spare steeds for a swift change of mount, we set off down the fine Roman road with our disconsolate captive still held fast in his rumbling carriage.

For the next day and a half, we rode hard, our tunics as lathered with horse salts as were the weary beasts themselves, but we finally clopped through the gates of the Benedictine abbey at St Albans just as the friars were readying for Vespers. Several fled in alarm at the sight of our small column of armed horsemen, but a stout porter stood to challenge us. Lord Clinton practically rode him down. "Go and get your abbot – and doff your cap to the king!" he ordered.

So it was that King Edward met the remarkable abbot, Richard of Wallingford, the orphaned son of a blacksmith who had been educated by his prior at Oxford, and who had reformed a choir of St Albans monks given to carnality, disobedience, property holding, simony and other sins. Despite being beset by leprosy, he rescued the abbey from debt, repaired the property, replenished its stores and frustrated an attempt by the nuns of Sopwell to break away.

When Abbot Richard came to greet the king, though, Edward was tired, dusty, hungry and short tempered. "The south side of the church needs repair," he said brusquely. "Are you neglecting your duties?" Richard said humbly that he had been much concerned with making an astronomical clock which would link the abbey with the heavens, and the king scolded him for such folly.

The abbot responded that after his death his successors could always find builders to restore the church, but if he left the clock unfinished, it must remain so. Edward, at first thunderstruck by this defiant answer, suddenly began to roar with laughter and clapped the monk on the shoulder. "You're the fellow who sent books to my tutor, Richard de Bury, aren't you?" and all the tension ebbed away.

The next morning, as we readied for our last day's ride to London, Abbot Richard had his choir file outside to sing a *'Te Deum'* to the king as he mounted up in the stable yard. I noticed that although the abbot blessed all of our group he pointedly turned his face away from the scowling, bound Mortimer.

In a matter of days, the man who would be king had been imprisoned in the White Tower, charged with treason for the murder of Edward of Caernarvon and for assuming royal powers unanointed. Edward commanded the sheriffs of every county to announce Mortimer's downfall and to declare that the king would now rule justly.

In a matter of days, Mortimer was brought before Parliament and charged with the murder of Edward's father the king, He was condemned to be hanged like a common thief despite his noble blood and was paraded to Tyburn Hill and executed unceremoniously before a jeering crowd. His vast fortune and huge estates were forfeited to the Crown and his body was contemptuously left hanging on the gallows for several days.

His fellow conspirator Queen Isabella was banished to Castle Rising in remote eastern England and was forbidden ever again to take part in political activity but was not imprisoned. Instead, Edward allowed his mother to live in splendor and to move with her considerable retinue between her several residences.

His authority re-established, Edward settled to the management of the realm, and celebrated with feasts, tournaments and hunting expeditions. On one of these, I met the love of my life.

The king and his household had moved for the harvest feast into the great rectangular tower of Bristol castle, called the 'flower of English great towers' by the chronicler Robert of Gloucester, and it was an imposing sight: 70 feet high, as tall as the cathedral at Canterbury, with four corner turrets, one of them taller than the other three. It dominated the landscape for miles around and its gates, barbican, bridge and chapel made formidable fortifications.

But what made me gasp when I saw it was the royal entourage. Edward and Philippa were enamoured of chivalric romances and of Arthurian legends and had chosen to visit Glastonbury, whose magical properties are famous, and to view the great earth castle at South Cadbury, a place built by the ancients and which was believed to be the site of Camelot, Arthur's brilliant court. "Even the local river is the Cam, and the village is called Queen Camel," said John Westwood.

He was telling me how Philippa had given the king a precious illuminated copy of the Tale of Fauvel, a poem that mocks hypocrisy, avarice, envy and other faults through the eyes of a foolish donkey, and the couple had vowed to restore the values of King Arthur to their court, to encourage faith and chivalry and gallantry, but I hardly heard him..

I was entranced by the sight of the glittering horseback procession that approached across the stubble fields. Knights and ladies, they rode horses adorned with gaily-coloured trappers, a few even of cloth of gold, some with small plates of polished silver sewn on harness and trapper to wink and flash in the sunlight. To make the procession look even more of a unified body, the ladies, who must have been some of the most beautiful in the realm, all wore red velvet tunics and caps made of white camels' hair.

I did not properly take in the knights' appearance, for a lovely girl of about my own teen years had caught my eye and smiled gaily at me as she rode by. I made my best leg and doffed my cap to her, half-ironically, half seriously, and she fluttered a hand at me in return. I resolved to find her at the feast that evening. And I did.

My enchantress was called Marian de Trafford, only daughter of a baronial family with lands near Manchester and she was comely and shapely, not tall, with auburn hair and green eyes under long lashes. Her face was shaped like a heart, her hands were white and slender, her soft lips stood before teeth like pearls that broke into a smile to dazzle me. I was smitten, she was awed by the glamour and romance of the court and we both had ardent spirits. It was inevitable that we became lovers.

That happened on a golden autumn day on the Feast of the Holy Cross and we felt it was the perfect day for our pure love to be consummated, for how could such be a sin? The days that followed were a mad, intoxicating whirl of tender love and discovery, of promises made that we could not keep and earnest vows we desperately wished to fulfill but that I secretly feared we might never see attained. And it ended too soon.

Perhaps her family suspected something. Certainly my tutor Sir John had noted my elation and asked me one or two direct questions, but there was neither warning nor farewell from Marian when the de Traffords departed abruptly from court and a stony silence followed.

I must have moped for a while, I recall the misery and jealousy of not knowing where my lover was or what she was doing, or even if she had a new love, but I could not travel to find out, for King Edward kept us busy for months with tournaments and melees that were not just for pleasure or distraction. He was training his fighters for war with the Scots and winter slipped into spring without word from Marian and she eased from the front of my mind.

It was in the tourneys that I was finding my own inner peace. I thrilled to the conflict, to the joy of the contest and to the control I had over the maddened fighting lust that sometimes tried to swamp me. Instead, by controlling it, I entered a state where all my senses were heightened, where time seemed to slow and I could read and parry my opponents' strikes even before they were fully formed.

Despite my youth I was as big and strong as any man, for my archery training, which I exercised every single day, gave me power and precision. I did not neglect my swordplay nor my horsemanship, for these were important to any would-be knight and what was in my thoughts was war. Another spur to encourage me in my dedication was that I was ever closer to the king, one of his personal conroi of eight young squires and knights, all under the tutelage and leadership of that valiant warrior Henry Grosmont.

We trained, ate and hunted together, we fought side by side with the king in tournament melees and we drank together as we planned tactics, strategies and campaigns. One day when we were in the stables, grooming our destriers, for Edward held that a knight must take care of his own weapons and horses, not entrust them to others, I asked about the raiding Scots who were devastating our border lands. "They have the numbers, they're confident in themselves. Can we beat them anyway, your grace?" I wondered.

"The Scots put us to shame at Bannockburn," Edward said thoughtfully, "and they eluded me when I took our army north. I am resolved to crush them, and I think our best tactic will be to use massed archers. They allow us to kill the enemy before they can grapple with us hand to hand. One archer can easily kill several hostiles, at ranges from 50 paces to 300 paces, all without being imperiled by infantry or cavalry.

"It didn't work well at Bannockburn because our bowmen were left without protection and the Scots cavalry were able to race through their fire and butcher them. If we can protect the archers, our longbows will be doing the butchery. We will form our phalanxes like a bull's horns: the head will be a shield wall of infantry with pikes to hold off cavalry, the horns will be bowmen protected by infantry and sharpened stakes or pikes and they will pour in death from the flanks. I want you, Thomas, to be my captain-general of archers. I want you there in the field directing an arrow storm that will cut down our enemies like wheat stalks before the scythe."

Edward told me he had a missive from Henry Beaumont, a rebel who had supported Edward Balliol's claim to the Scots throne and who had lost his lands as a consequence. Beaumont had persuaded the king to support Balliol against the infant King David of Scotland and Edward was willing so to do.

"The problem," the king told me, "is that by treaty, I may not send an army across the Tweed." "Then don't cross the Tweed, go around it," I said. "Send the army by sea! I'll help to lead them, your grace." Edward looked at me thoughtfully. "Yes, that would obey the letter of the treaty, and that would not break our word."

We fell into a discussion of tactics and agreed on a formation to defeat the Scots' schiltrons. "Establish the archers, have them protected by infantry, as we discussed, safely set behind a war hedge of pikes that themselves are behind a series of pits and sharpened stakes. I can trust you to carry out that plan, Thomas. You know as well as anyone that if our bowmen are protected from their cavalry, we can cut them into ribbons. But there's another consideration. Balliol won't countenance a mere squire in command of things. I'll have to make you a knight."

Three days later, I was kneeling in vigil in the chapel of St George at Windsor, clad in white except for my hose and shoes, the whole cloaked under a red robe. The white symbolized purity, the black was for death and the red was a sign of nobility. I attended the altar for ten hours, heard Mass, was joined by my comrades for a long sermon on the duties of a knight. Next, I swore allegiance to Edward and took oaths that forbade me to traffic with traitors, to respect and defend a lady, to attend daily Mass and to observe abstinences and fasts.

Eventually, Edward presented me with my sword and shield, then administered the colee, or dubbing, with the flat of his sword on my shoulders. I was almost in a daze as my sponsors girded my sword and spurs on to me, and I arose from my knees, Sir Thomas Holland, knight. I shook my head to clear it of all the emotions flooding through me and my gaze fastened itself on Edward, who was grinning widely. "Congratulations, Sir Thomas," he said, bowing ironically. I must have grinned back like an idiot, for his own smile widened. "Death to your enemies, your grace," I murmured. I was ready to go to war.

Chapter 7 - Dupplin

We must have made a fine sight as we converged on Sandal Castle in Yorkshire, where Edward Balliol had made his headquarters, a couple of thousand armed men with their horses, banners and blaring brass. Ahead of us was the steep-sided motte and impressive bailey with the drum towers that overlook the Calder river below. We had hurriedly rallied about 1,200 archers and 800 men at arms after word came that King David's guardian had died. Now was a good time to strike the leaderless Scots and we were arriving to do just that.

The Calder was not navigable at Sandal so we could not sail for Scotland from there so some of the force mustered downriver on the Humber estuary at Goole. Others, including a contingent of Frisian and German cavalry gathered at Hull, and the main body of Cheshire and Welsh bowmen were ordered to take ship at the fishing port of Grimsby. In all, we had 80 or so cogs to transport our small force, and we would meet near the mouth of the Humber before we sailed north in convoy. The weather was July-rainy but the sea was calm and the wind fair and we sailed and landed in Fife without incident, then marched to the River Earn, just outside Perth.

Henry of Beaumont commanded our force and at a war council informed us that the new regent of Scotland, Donald, Earl of Mar faced us from across the river, and was camped on the heights of the moor at Dupplin. He commanded more than half of the total 10,000 men the Scots had put into the field. The other half, under Patrick, Earl of Dunbar was approaching from our rear. "Too many of the plaid rogues," said Beaumont. "We can't wait for Dunbar to get here. We'll slip across the Earn by night – we have a fording place. Mowbray, you take a picked force and get across the river. Be discreet, don't take Mar for granted, he's killed more men than the plague."

The Scots were carousing noisily upwind of us and their sounds came clearly. It seemed they had no inkling of our movements and a cautious survey suggested that had not posted sentries along the river to watch us. Mowbray moved out quietly shortly before dawn and we heard his attack as we were getting the rest of our army across the river behind him. As wolf light gave way to daylight, we saw that Earl Mowbray had mistakenly attacked the Scots' camp followers, not the army, but by then almost all of us were over the river and we took up a defensive position on high ground at the top of a narrow glen. "Excellent spot," gloated Beaumont. "That slope will slow them down, make them struggle uphill to meet us, but before they can get here, we'll put down such a rain of arrows on them that there won't be any of them left to fight. Just kill 'em before they get close. All we have to do is tempt them to come to us."

Horsemen brought word that Dunbar was fast approaching, so we did not delay. I formed my archers in echelons, staggered at the flanks to give every man a line of fire. A phalanx of men at arms under Beaumont formed the centre of our force and had dug some trenches in front of their pike wall, set with sharpened stakes against horse attack. I established a defensive screen of stakes; pits and pikemen in front of my archers, who, being higher up the steep gradient of the glen could easily fire over their heads. Only a few Frisians and Germans in our army remained mounted, and they held the rear, high on the glen's ridgeline.

At Beaumont's command, our trumpets, pipes and huge goatskin drums struck up, and our men began bellowing insults. The Scots responded promptly with shrieks and pipes of their own. I expected we'd have some contending noise and mutual shouting for a while, but suddenly everything changed. Unbelievably, the clansmen's kilted schiltrons swarmed out of their fine defensive positions on the opposite slope and came flying downhill in a bare-legged, ragged disarray, hammering their spears and axes against their shields and yelling hoarsely.

Galloping their tough little Highland ponies at the head of the charge were Donald of Mar and Lord Robert Bruce of Liddesdale, the bastard son of the onetime king. Both of them were easily recognisable in unvisored helmets called sallets. Later I found they had quarreled, insulted each other's courage and, inflamed to anger, had impetuously set off to spite the other. "Hold fire, hold until I shout," I commanded my bowmen, "then skewer the bastards!"

The Scots forded a small stream at the foot of our sloping glen and began to climb towards us, dramatically slowing the foot soldiers' progress but the small squadron of cavalry separated themselves, riding on ahead regardless. Clods of earth flew up from the thudding hooves of the leading ponies, spattering those who followed, and I clearly saw Donald of Mar standing in his stirrups shouting as he waved a flanged mace that I knew could pierce even good armour. I hoped my archers were sighting him clearly, it would be good for our troops to see the enemy leaders shot down.

Realising my very thought, the two noblemen among the first flood of oncoming cavalry were suddenly on stumbling, curvetting steeds that were staggering and crashing down. They had been spitted by our archers, whose reloading and releasing was so fast there were two or three killing shafts from each bowman hissing through the air at any one time. It made a dark cloud of hammering death so fearsome that to avoid it the Scots swerved away from the archer-heavy flanks, to hide themselves in the milling crush that was the centre of their own battle line.

Many of the wounded infantry were lightly-clad Highlanders who had been hit in the upper body or face by our showering arrows, blinded either from eye injuries or from the sheeting blood that always follows a scalp wound. Those disabled fighters were shoved and penned by their own comrades' impetus. Unbalanced, shocked and bloodied, they hampered their comrades' efforts to engage our line and were helplessly pushed forward onto the sharp stakes, shields and long pikes of our war hedge.

Even unwounded clansmen were stamped underfoot by their fellows when they slipped and fell on the steep, blood-slick slope to be trampled or suffocated. Almost the entire first four or five ranks of the mob – for it no longer was an organized attack - were so confined, crushed and pinned they could not even lift their arms to use their weapons. As the foremost ranks were shoved against the blades and points of the English shield wall, they fell and made obstacles for the next wave, turning the schiltrons into piled heaps of dead and dying, and still the unrelenting pressure came from the urgent, onrushing rear. Panic-stricken clansmen tried to escape by scrambling over the mounded dead and dying, only to attract the deadly arrows to themselves and make the heaps higher.

I spotted one big, half-naked, shaggy, red-bearded villain who was wielding a huge pole-axe. He used it as a staff to help him clamber over the mounded dead then swung it with devastating effect through a cluster of our men-at-arms who opposed him. Two went down at once, heads smashed, and a third staggered away, his neck spurting blood. The clansman drew back his axe for another slashing swipe and I levelled, drew, willed the arrow to its mark, and loosed. Before it was even halfway to the target, I'd snatched up another shaft, nocked and bent, leveled, drawn it to my ear. I paused to mark more accurately, the first arrow struck Redbeard in his exposed armpit as he raised his axe, causing him to stagger. In that instant, I loosed again, grabbed for another shaft and raised my eyes in time to see his head lower like a stricken bull at the abbatoir. I even witnessed my second arrow strike his forehead. It was bodkin-pointed and it buried itself deep in his unhelmed skull. The impact did not drive him backwards, for he was leaning into the fatal missile, but he dropped to his knees. The slashed scalp sheeted blood down across his whole upper body. In his last instants of life, he raised his great shaggy head and seemed to look directly at me through the cascading blood before toppling forward to snap the shaft as he fell face down into the mire.

My next arrow was already on its way and passed over him, to strike a following clansman in the thigh, spinning and dropping the fellow where he stood. I reached forward, caught up another arrow and nocked it. Like a man under a sorcerer's entrancement, I nocked, bent into the horns, leveled, marked, drew, loosed and repetitively snatched up another arrow and yet another, and another. My mind was blank to the day, with a snatch of the drinking song 'I saw many birds sitting in a tree' going around and around in my head.

For all the cheery scrap of music inside me, the slaughter went on in a stench of human dung and sprays of blood while the mounds of dead and wounded kept growing, forming near-impassable barriers. The place reeked like a butchers' shambles, the sound was one unending blur of screaming horses and groaning, shouting men. "Pour it on, fellows," I was bellowing myself hoarse, "shoot them flat!" Our bowmen nocked, marked, drew and loosed with dedicated intensity, plucking arrow after arrow from the rows of shafts they had stabbed into the ground in front of themselves, following the repetitive drills of notch, level, draw and loose an iron sleet into the packed horde of enemy struggling uphill just 50 paces distant. I recalled the memory of Andrew my archery tutor and heard his voice once again: "The supply of arrows is more important than the accuracy of our bowmen. The side that runs out of missiles must lose, unless the infantry is invincible."

I looked around, my fingers bleeding from the scores of shafts I had loosed, to check that the young boys who brought linen bags of fresh arrows were racing up with more missiles. Around me, the steady thrum of released bowstrings and the hiss of speeding arrows was all I could hear. No archer was shouting, none showed anything but grim, silent concentration on sending shaft after iron-tipped birch shaft thudding into the struggling crowd of humanity that was being pushed from behind into the arrow storm and onto the end of our foot soldiers' pikes.

Finally, a horn sounded and a Scots nobleman on horseback waved a yellow standard, trying to call off the shattered attack, but pages and squires rushed up the English horses and I saw Beaumont mounted, leading a ferocious, slashing charge to surround and chop down those who did not kneel in abject surrender. Few could escape our cavalry, for the horse-holders at the rear of the Scots army had realized the size of the rout and had fled, releasing the horses, which fled with them.

In many places, the heap of dead and writhing wounded was as tall as a pike and the gore-spattered English knights and men at arms who finally went forward to take sword and spear to the Scots had to stumble for footholds as they waded through the mound of bloody meat that had so recently been onrushing clansmen. I saw one pile of dead and dying fully 12 feet high, with English soldiers standing atop it, hacking down and stabbing with swords and spears to kill any survivors.

In less than an hour, all was over. I half-expected Dunbar's army to attack from the south, but they never came, even though we were weary. In readiness, I sent archers and the pages out onto the killing slopes to gather arrows, and we prepared to repel any new threat, but it did not come.

In time, I released our infantry to scour the field, collecting weapons, armour and any booty they could find among the discarded jupons with the telltale insignias that would have marked their wearers as soldiers, not innocent civilians. So it was that the surviving Scots vanished after discarding the evidence of their rebellion.

I myself turned up a fine punching knife that one dead rogue had carried secretly at the nape of his neck, and I relieved his carcass of it. I came across several who had strapped a knife inside the wrist, and took one of those, too, but did not don it. Several of us acquired some mail shirts and even helms and breastplates from lairds and grandees who no longer had use for them, but I was most grateful for a pair of excellent pleated woolen plaids that were warmer and more waterproof than anything I had. The blood would wash out, I supposed.

Later, wrapped in a dead man's plaid, I visited the pavilion tents where our wounded were being treated, for I had heard that Sir John Westwood had received an arrow wound. He was lying on a litter on his side. The missile had entered above the hip and from the front but seemed not to have struck anything vital. The only way to remove it cleanly was to push the whole thing through – a painful experience for the wounded man. I gave him a sip or two from a small silver flask one of my archers had taken from a dead laird. "Got some ardent spirits, water of life, they call it," I muttered.

John gestured at the grey-robed nun, a Benedictine. "Canoness Joan the Palmer," he said. "A sister who has travelled to the Holy Land and who has learned much Arab medicine." I saw that the nun had pinned to her habit a small palm leaf woven into the shape of a cross, and guessed it was a symbol like the sea shells of Santiago de Compostela, a token of one who had made a particular pilgrimage. She smiled at me but did not speak as she laved her hands in a bowl of water, then gently sponged the entry wound in John's side. She let her fingers run around the wound, sensitively feeling where the arrowhead had lodged, then looked up at John with a small gesture. "There is no bone in the way. The path is clear," she said.

The canoness-physician set about her preparations, first readying a poultice of yarrow, barley and honey which she chopped small and mixed with vinegar. This she set aside, covered with a clean muslin cloth. Next, she put a flame to a small dish of thyme. "To prevent infection in the chamber," she smiled at me as fragrant smoke curled up from the tiny leaves.

From her satchel, she took a slender, shaved-smooth stick, plastered it with the poultice and put it to one side, covering it too with the muslin. She turned back to John, carefully clipped off some of the protruding ash shaft and tied to the end of the shaft a cloth which she soaked in turpentine. I noted that she seemed to make an exact measurement of the birch shaft before cutting it shorter. She gave John a small leather pad. "Bite on this, save your teeth," she said. Then, working with confident speed, she began the extraction, pushing the shaft in deeper to force it through.

John swore through gritted teeth and sweat burst out of his temples. I clasped his shoulder. "Nearly there," I said, seeing skin and muscle in his lower back begin to bulge. The nun was breathing hard as she pushed once more and the point of the leaf-shaped arrowhead broke through John's skin. At once, she took up a pair of pincers, seized the arrowhead and tugged. John's body rocked against the pull. In a rush of blood and fluid, the arrowhead came clear, bringing with it a small plug of linen and leather, fragments of the clothing the missile had pushed ahead of itself as it penetrated its victim.

John groaned again as the shaft and its turpentine-soaked cloth was pulled through the wound, cleansing it, then he fainted into silence. The nun muttered in satisfaction and carefully pushed the shaved stick with its coating of poultice into the oozing wound and drew it too all the way through John's body. "That will keep the pus of infection from forming," she explained. "It's good that the soldier fainted, it's best he not feel the prodding and poking." She bound up the wound after applying a liberal coating of the poultice to it and set down a small stoppered glass flask. "A tincture of rosemary," Canoness Joan explained. "Let him drink it when he awakes." I sniffed, scenting the pine-like perfume. "The flowers are blue because the Virgin dried her cloak on rosemary on her way to Egypt," she said. "It is a gift from heaven for healers."

I may have sounded croaky as I thanked the nun, and once I stepped from the tent I wiped cold sweat from my forehead and took a long swig from the dead laird's flask. I'd rather have been arrow-shot myself than have to witness my friend's suffering.

In Beaumont's pavilion that night, we ate sparsely of oat bread and cold beef and drank from a butt of thin red wine we had captured from the Scots' baggage train. A chamberlain reported that we had suffered 33 deaths among our knights and men at arms. "The clansmen did worse," he said. "Their lairds and their landlords died with them. The Earl of Mar's body is on the field, with those of Liddesdale, Moray, Menteith and Fraser," he said, "and so are about 9,000 of their tenants."

Beaumont turned to me: "Those bowmen rogues of yours are damn killers," he grinned. "Seems that archers and foot soldiers acting in unison can stand up to anything. And you, my lord, how does it feel to be preparing to sit again on the throne of Scotland?" This last was directed at the morose Edward Balliol, who sniffed that there was much more to be done, alas.

It turned out that Balliol knew of what he spoke. His 'reign' as king of the Scots lasted a dozen weeks before he was driven out and even Edward's victory at Halidon Hill could not restore him, for the Scots despised him as Edward's puppet and David would become their accepted king.

But that was in the future, and now the battle was done, I was eager to cross the spine of England to visit my lover, Marian de Trafford, of whom I had no news for many months. John insisted on sending three men at arms with me, and I was glad of their company across the wild moorlands, where the first autumnal frosts came early. We followed the old Roman road from York to Chester, turning aside at the bow-shaped hill which gave Bowdon its name and, in great excitement as I neared the end of our journey, came near Cnut's Ford, and then to the hamlet of Mobberley, where Marian's father's manor house was sited.

The men at arms tactfully halted short of the house, indicating with grins that I should meet my lover without being under their gaze, and I cantered Biter up to the building with the metallic taste of nervousness in my throat.

A serving girl came to the door, bobbed demurely and asked my name. I wondered if she paled a little when I told her I was Thomas Holland, but she bobbed again and disappeared into the house. I waited, cap doffed, at the doorway and heard a familiar footstep on flagstone. My heart was thumping so loudly I felt Marian must hear it before she even saw me. Then she rounded the corner into the hallway and faced me, the blood almost visibly draining from her cheeks.

"Thomas?" It was a question. My eyes were locked on hers. "Marian, Marian, I am so sorry for such a long separation," was all I could say. "I have…" my voice trailed away as a woman followed her out into the hallway. It was a wet nurse and she was carrying a small child. My Marian was the mother of a child.

All I could do was to blurt out a stupid question: "Why did you not tell me?" Then I asked another, even more stupid question. "It is our baby?" She nodded. "Of course." She sounded utterly calm. I suppose she had lived this moment a hundred times before it happened. I had to ask again: "Why did you not tell me? How old is it? When was it born?" She answered the second question first. "He is Hugh, a boy, not an 'it.' He was born last summer, he is beautiful and healthy, a fine son."

She looked piercingly at me with those dazzling green eyes. She looked angry. "He is my son, mine alone, for I will not marry you." I felt as if the wooden Saracen of the tiltyard had come to life and struck me in the chest. I had not yet proposed marriage, but Marian, my Marian, had already turned me down. "I was going to ask you, I truly was," I said, sounding sullen. "How else will you live?"

She had everything decided, for she had had months to consider matters. "He will not be a burden on the parish or on anyone else. Father has money, I am his heiress, and I have my own income. I do not need a mantle child. I will acknowledge you as his father, but I shall bring him up in my way, not in yours. He will not be a warrior who would rather be away fighting than be here with me."

So that was it. My absence and ignorance had given Marian time to consider how she wanted to live, and she chose not to be left alone while I was away fighting for the king. Nor did she wish to send her child to war. I had a son, but he would not follow me as a soldier. I bled, inside.

Chapter 8 - Conroi

Marian called our child Hugh of Mobberley in defiance of her father the baron, who wanted to make a de Trafford of him, for Marian was a tigress unafraid of a family storm, and by happenstance the boy was even born on the Feast of Saint Vitus, protector against tempests.

That may have helped me, for I had to weather the outburst that came from Marian's parents. Eventually they understood that I was eager to marry their daughter, but she was unwilling to be married. "I have a son and I am content," she said, although she did agree that I could visit the boy at frequent intervals. And so I trailed away back to Windsor, dismissed with only the promise of occasional times my small son.

Those visits were less frequent than I would have liked, for I was called upon to spend much time in attendance on the king at court. It was not an unpleasant duty. Edward and I were good friends and our small conroi was close and dedicated. The young king was eager to learn, eager to be a good monarch and when I returned to Oxford, I found he was also eager to be a good father, for his queen, Philippa of Hainault had given birth to a prince, another Edward.

Edward of Woodstock was born on the same June day of the Year of Our Lord 1330 as my son Hugh and his father the king was determined that he would be properly trained as a warrior. "My father taught me no military skills, Thomas," Edward confided, "because he had none of his own. Our humiliation by those ragged Scots at Bannockburn has burned on me. The safety of our nation was imperiled, our subjects were plundered and raped. At age ten, I myself was almost captured by Scots raiders far inside our kingdom at York; not so long afterwards my mother took up widow's weeds, mourning the betrayal by my father of their marriage.

"But she did not act in my best interests, she was not called She-Wolf for no reason. It was degrading to be reliant on her and the odious Mortimer. You yourself helped me regain my crown when we captured the usurper regents. Now that I have control and the kingship, I vow to be different from my father. I shall be faithful to my wife, I shall restore chivalry to my court and I shall make England into a military power. And I shall properly train my heir in kingship and military matters."

I had never seen my carefree friend so solemn. "You have good advisors, Your Grace," I said quietly, "and you have faithful followers. We can help you recreate King Arthur's ways, and the rest will follow." Even today, I am unsure how much I wanted to restore Arthurian ways and values, but the king wanted to hear it, and to my shame, I complied.

So we worked at our military skills, spending hours at horsemanship and swordplay, recruiting and training men, improving our weapons. Edward and I, with our conroi, set to learn about smithing and weaponry. Nor did we neglect our pleasures, and we were led in them by Henry Grosmont.

Heir of the Earl of Lancaster, Henry was famed for his jousting abilities, and was a skilled and enthusiastic fighter. In his elegantly-wrought armour he was always to be found in the thickest melees, while away from the tournament fields he was a dazzling dancer and ladies' man entranced both by the silks and scents of the noblewomen and the warm acquiescence of commoners. I once asked him if he was wealthy. "Yes, I am. I'm a member of the royals – Crouchback was my grandfather and Edward is my cousin." Henry demonstrated his wealth when his royal kinsman needed funds for some adventure or other. The earl pawned seven of his coronets and eleven gold circlets and I happened to be there when the moneylender came to exchange the payment for the regal hoard.

"Women love these things," he said casually, gesturing at the treasures, "but they like these," turning to display his rounded calf muscles – "more." I laughed at him, but he shrugged. "Watch at the lists next time we prepare. I stretch out my legs in the stirrups as I stand, and swooning ladies gaze mistily upon my wondrous limbs and yearn for me." He laughed in self-deprecation.

For all that, Grosmont was a fine and honourable companion at dining table or fireside storytelling, a tough ally in a tournament and a skilled tactician in battle. Edward recognised his qualities, making him a campaign captain and would one day appoint him to rule Scotland as his own trusted lieutenant.

In his role as a household knight, Grosmont commanded a cavalry force ready at short notice to deal with any military or civil emergency. As a member of those *familiares* I was paid an annual fee and also received pay for the number of days I was in attendance in the household. If required, we were expected to call up military forces and to oversee the garrisons of certain castles – we were a military organization which also orbited around the king.

His household was more than that, though, it was a government, not just an army, and it travelled with the monarch. The most powerful barons inhabited the upper reaches of the court, but officials held powerful sway, too. The chancellor and his clerks and scribes were responsible for the King's Seal, a disc the size of a man's hand which showed on one side an image of Edward armoured, on his destrier. On its obverse the monarch was shown enthroned, holding the Orb of Christian Sovereignty. This seal was to prove the authentic, royal endorsement of any document to which it was affixed and was perhaps the nation's most valued possession.

Other important officials, some with lesser royal seals, included the treasurer and chamberlains who oversaw the king's money and possessions; then there were the customs officers who provided much money for Edward's expensive military campaigns, demanding duty on exports and imports, with wool, skins, leather, wine, wax, lead, tin, butter, cheese and lard the chief revenue sources, while there were still others, the steward for instance, who might be delegated with important tasks either political or military

The king's travelling household of officials, courtiers, jesters, musicians, squires and pages was swelled even more by traders, petitioners, constables, courtesans, clergy and scores of hangers-on of all stripes. Too, there were the domestics: larderers and butlers plump from secretly sampling the king's food and drink; cooks red-faced from working over hot fires; smocked carters, pack horse drovers in their distinctive leather leggings, grooms, stablemen, falconers and huntsmen all with the individual marks and dress of their trades. There were proud heralds in tabards, laundresses with arms red to the elbow, weather-beaten verderers, drovers and herdsmen; brawny smiths with burn-scarred hands and arms, brightly-clad minstrels and horn-blowers, leather-aproned nakerers hefting their great goatskin drums, even the keeper of the king's bed, who bore no obvious signs of his office but rode in comfort on the wagon which carried the royal couch. All had their duties, and many knights who performed courtly duties also acted as local sheriffs in their own demesnes.

The next day, after admiring Grosmont's legs and laughing at him, I was visiting Sir John, who was recovering well from his arrow wound. "They put a horsehair into my side," he confided. "They say it will keep the wound open and allow the noxious humours to drain so it will heal more quickly. At some stage, the physician – he's Arabic, you know – says he'll pull the horsehair out, and allow everything to heal. I'll be back to fighting form in a few months, he says. It's expensive – these physicians charge what they think you can pay, and I'm not a poor man."

The whole thing was stunning. I had no idea anyone could survive such an arrow strike, much less be healed and well so quickly, but if you were at court, and had the king's own physicians ... what other marvels could be achieved? "John," I asked, "how many people are there here, dealing with things?" He shrugged. "There are vast numbers, but even so there's an upper limit during times of peace. The king must make regular progressions around the kingdom to reinforce his influence and at the same time, in a different way, to reduce that same influence," he explained with a small smirk. "It makes more sense for the king and his entourage of 1,000 or more to visit the regions where food is grown and to enjoy the hospitality of the local magnates than it is to have those supplies carted to the king in his current seat, be it London, Windsor, Oxford or Winchester. "

The miles-long royal train would leave for a progress around the country to remind the local magnates of their loyalties, often devouring in a week a nobleman's entire annual harvest, while removing the burden from the royal household in London or Windsor or Oxford. Wherever it went. Edward took with him the spirit of Camelot. He called them Round Table tournaments, and I went along, to enjoy the festivities of feasting, dancing, amours and best of all, jousting, although Edward insisted we fight only with blunted weapons.

We knights dressed in costumes that identified us as legendary gallants like Tristram, Lancelot, Percival, Gawain and Lionel. I was assigned the role of Bedivere, who returned the sword Excalibur to the Lady of the Lake. The king chose for himself the role of Galahad, the 'most perfect knight' who was noted for his purity and gallantry, and was a highly popular figure when he called a Round Table celebration to honour a wedding, a knighthood or a victory.

But the tournaments were not mere playacting. They allowed younger knights an opportunity to sharpen their battle skills, for even with blunted swords and spears, wounds would be given, men would be forcibly unhorsed and blood made to flow. There were contests in the tiltyard, in a massed melee and in hand to hand combat between warriors.

Apart from enhancing our fighting skills and offering the chance to win costly prizes, the tournaments were vital at building camaraderie. "We eight of the king's conroi are brothers," Grosmont intoned. "Even the ancient Romans understood it, and made their basic military unit a group of eight men. Men in a small group will bond and will fight better, for they will fight for each other."

And fight for each other we did. A typical Round Table event was a splendid exhibition of magnates, knights, noble ladies and beautiful young women, all attired in finery and jewels. There were martial contests, feasting, dancing and singing and illicit love affairs which caused the clergy to fulminate futilely against wickedness and debauchery.

Over it all, Edward shone like a star. On the Feast of Saint Hugh he introduced his three years old son Edward to the court as the new Earl of Chester, clad in an elegant new suit of clothes.

As the applause rang out, I realized with a pang that I had not visited my own toddler son Hugh for more than a year. A short while later, I approached the king to ask permission to be released from court so I could travel to Cheshire to see the boy, and he took me aside to urge me to stay at his side.

"A soothsayer tells me of a prophecy that I am to fulfill," he said eagerly. "It is that a 'Great Bear' like King Arthur will arise again and subdue England's enemies. The seer said that I had furthered chivalrous Arthur's aims with the Round Table festivities that honour him, and he smiles down on me, so that if I were to set out against England's foes, I shall prevail. I think we are ready to make an expedition into Scotland, Thomas!"

I could only agree. It was early spring, soon we could be moving north on good, dry roads. There would be seasonal fodder for the beasts, fair weather for the troops. Best of all, after the archers' triumph at Dupplin Moor, we knew we had a weapon that could defeat any Scots army. We had the longbow.

Chapter 9 - Escalade

Edward banged his fist on the table, a fiery-eyed young man of only 20 years demanding silence from his grizzled, battle-hardened elders, but they listened. We were at a war council in Bamburgh Castle, a dominant fortress on the sea coast of Northumberland that the young king had chosen as a rallying point for his army.

"Our first priority is to take back Berwick," he said, moving his gaze from face to face around the table to measure each of his listeners in turn. "The Scots have held that city for too long and I want it back. Seizing it will make them face us in the field, and then we shall crush them. They are overconfident, for they took advantage of English errors at Bannockburn and on the Weardale campaign."

Inwardly, I flinched at the references, for Edward and the rest of us in his conroi had spent hours analyzing and debating those humiliations and planning how to avenge them.

At Bannockburn, where the Scots had destroyed us, our cavalry had crashed disastrously against a war hedge and spiked pits, and our archers had been left unprotected against rampaging Scottish cavalry. In the Weardale campaign the bowmen had advanced too far, had again been left exposed and were cut to pieces by the mounted knights. I remembered the scene in Edward's chamber when the two Henrys, Grosmont and Beaumont had leaned forward across the table and used chessmen to illustrate their plan.

"It's what we did last summer at Dupplin Moor," said Beaumont, placing pieces here and there to show the dispositions of the army. "This was a small glen with rising sides, we used the terrain - so - we kept our archers - here - safe and we shot the clansmen down into heaped drifts of dead before they could even reach our wall of pikes."

"And we were the smaller force, your grace," I said. "The key is the archers. Give them a field of fire, protect them while they send an arrow storm, and find a way to impede the enemy to keep them where you want them while you shoot at them. It will work again." The plan could be a success, but there was one vital fact: the clansmen had killed more of their own than our archers had shot dead.

The onrushing Scots surging from behind had trampled their own men underfoot as they were compressed in the bottleneck of the narrow glen. More hapless Scots had suffocated or been stamped into the ground by their kinsmen than had been killed by our weapons. If when we came to battle we could not engineer a similar choke point, it could be a fatal flaw. If the enemy failed to oblige by repeating their error, or by being forced into it, we might well fall to their overwhelmingly-superior numbers.

Edward brushed aside the objection. "We're where we were before Bannockburn," he told the assembly. "Then, we went to relieve the siege of Stirling. Now, we will reverse matters and put the Scots into our old position. We will besiege Berwick and they will have to come to its relief. We will choose the place where we fight them, and we shall create a killing ground. Henry, you have the infantry, Thomas, you must gather for me a formidable force of archers."

So I went into Cheshire and Lancashire to recruit bowmen while a siege train rumbled north to Berwick under command of Edward Balliol, whom King Edward openly recognized as ruler of Scotland. We of the royal conroi were busy, sending men to survey and repair or reinforce the roads and bridges before the heavy siege engines rolled over them; recruiting carpenters and foresters to locate, cut and shape lumber for bridgeworks and for the engines we would construct on site.

The woodworkers would also be needed to make targes to shield our archers as the engineers sapped towards the walls, they would build mangonels, catapults, galleries, tortoises, rams, ramps and siege engines including at least two covered belfries from which archers could fire down across the walls at the defenders. They would also make a few dozen scaling ladders as well as camp structures for stores, cooks and smiths, and in one grim note, build a gallows for the day we broke into Berwick, should the citizens not first surrender.

More court officers were delegated to locate long carts and oxen to move big timbers, for the huge rock-throwing engines would require six or eight long carts each, plus oxen teams to draw them and drivers to control them. Other men went to bring quantities of expensive rope from Cambridge and Lynn and Southampton's rope walks as well as cow hides to make replacement slings from which the great stones would be hurled. An engine could wear out two or even three slings a week, and we would need saddlers to shape, cut and sew the leather.

Then there were the questions of food supplies and gathering crops to feed our troops; of herding animals to be slaughtered, of finding grain and hay and nearby grazing lands to feed transport mules and oxen as well as war horses. A victualling fleet was organized to land supplies at the port of Tweedmouth, a mile downriver and on Berwick's opposite bank. To it would come wine from St Ives and Cambridge, food stores and animal forage from Kent, Hertford, Northampton and Nottingham and crossbow bolts from royal armories at Corfe and Oxford, among others.

There also was a need to find blacksmiths to create weapons and to forge parts and iron missiles for the engines we would build at Berwick. Those smiths would in turn require supplies of iron ore and charcoal, all of which had to be located and brought to the siege.

Some harried chamberlains were sent to locate a source of stone and to recruit quarrymen and stone cutters, who would be needed to cut and shape the half-hundredweight missiles the engines would throw, and to supply hammers, wedges and chisels to do that cutting and shaping. We would also need harness, animals and carts to transport the shaped missiles, which would be hurled at a rate of 200 or so each day at Berwick's walls. The first shipment of 700 shaped stones was to be transported from Hull.

Edward ruled that if the city walls did not quickly crumble under the assault of hurled boulders, they would fall another way when miners dug beneath them and collapsed them into caverns dug beneath them. Privately, I doubted that. The river and the moat would flood most workings, I was sure, but the king was not to be denied. Men were dispatched to recruit skilled miners from the slate quarries of Wales and the coal pits of the north. These too would need specialist supplies, from pick axes and steel-edged wooden spades to sturdy wooden pit props that would hold up the cavern's roof until they were fired and burned through to collapse the fortifications above.

But the greatest need was for weapons. Edward would take an army of 9,000 men, and most needed proper swords, axes, pikes and above all, arrows for the archers and iron quarrels for the crossbowmen. These latter posed less of a problem, for the royal armories at Corfe, the White Tower, Dover, Oxford, Northampton and York could provide 30,000 bolts.

Arrows for the vital archers were more of a problem, but Edward solved it in an efficient manner. He ordered the sheriffs to send sheaves of arrows, each sheaf to contain two dozen missiles. From London alone, wagons brought 200 sheaves – 4,800 arrows - and similar supplies came from Huntingdon, Nottingham, York, Lincoln and a score of other places.

So the administration began, Balliol set off in March with an advance guard and surrounded Berwick. He dug trenches and cut the city's water supply. He defended the land approaches, confident that Edward's fleet, based on the Tyne, controlled any approach from the sea. He also devastated the surrounding region, destroying habitations and stripping the fields to fill his storehouses with Scottish crops and cattle and deny those supplies to any possible relief column.

And Balliol did it all virtually unopposed. Bruce's heir, nine years old King David of Scotland was managed by a regent, Sir James Douglas, Guardian of the Realm who gathered a national army but did little to help the commander in Berwick, Sir Alexander Seton.

So the situation at Berwick was fairly quiet. Balliol was settling into the siege, no relief column was approaching, the king was sailing north and I was on my way to York, having used my recruiting drive in Cheshire to visit Marian and our son Hugh. With a pang or two of regret at leaving them, I rejoined the tail of the king's army as it marched to Berwick. Following in the train of 9,000 men and probably 20,000 horses, plus a few herds of sheep and cattle was a grim experience.

Normally, I would ride at the head of the column, behind the scouts, pickets and engineers who guarded and prepared the way, but in the vanguard leading the royal household cavalry who themselves were just ahead of the main army. Behind the troops would come the baggage train, animal herds and the rearguard and behind them in turn would follow the ragtag mob or stragglers, laggards and hangers-on.

Approaching from the rear was a much less pleasant experience. The ground was trodden into foul mud, dunged by thousands of beasts which had also stripped all the edible vegetation, and churned into a morass by the wheels of a thousand carts. After slogging through a few miles of this, I opted to ride far to the west of the trail on cleaner ground, all the while keeping my fellow travellers in sight. The rear of the column was made up of a horde of camp followers, pedlars, preachers, runaways, prostitutes and the like.

Most of the animal herds were driven ahead of this group, and followed a phalanx of cavalry that in turn shadowed a cavalcade of ox wagons and pack animals bearing the equipment of smiths, armourers, slaughterers, tenters, hunters, scullions, wainwrights, fletchers, kennel varlets and their hounds. These in turn trailed a large force of infantry from Kenilworth Castle, a body of Welsh and Cheshire archers, some slingers and the factors of the royal household at Oxford.

Only after passing by these assorted groups did I begin to near the head of the vast procession where the nobles of the household cavalry led the way, ahead of a band of mailed and armed magnates with their knightly attendants. They in turn were accompanied by a bench of bishops in silk who displayed an array of holy relics and were themselves surrounded by retainers lofting a thicket of their fluttering, brightly-coloured episcopal banners, pennants and swaying oriflammes.

Clerks and stewards danced attendance on these princes of the church, while more humble friars, stewards, jesters, pages and chamberlains surrounded the wagons that carried the king's great bed – no room for that on a sailing cog – and guarded the three sumpter wagons filled with barrels of wine, sacks and boxes of provisions, candles and clothing exclusively for the king and queen, who would be reunited with their goods at Bamburgh Castle.

No royal goes to war without his comforts, I thought jealously, and the siege of Berwick promised to be a long one. That promise would be kept as I feared it would be from the moment I set eyes on the town walls.

***

Berwick sits on the border between England and Scotland, on the coast where the Tweed empties into the North Sea. It is Scotland's gateway to the northeastern marches of England and is also the port through which the lucrative wool trade passes and was Scotland's richest burgh. Some of those riches had gone into fortifying the town, which has two miles of stone walls, all recently rebuilt to the height of more than three tall men. Imposing towers and the river itself provide more defences for the town, which is entered over a stone bridge and through a strong barbican.

The castle itself stands west of the town, and looms ominously behind a broad moat, making both the walled town and moated castle into separate strongholds. This would not be an easy place to invest, although Balliol's forces had laid some foundations for the siege by cutting off its water supply and beginning trench works.

John Westwood and I had scouted the devastated lands around the town – those crops were safely in our hands now and were at Tweedmouth - watching the first of our troops and some shaped-stone missiles being unloaded when the king's ship arrived. Edward had left his queen safely inside Bamburgh Castle and was eager to attack Berwick before he Scots army arrived, but first insisted on sending heralds with a formal demand of surrender.

"We must treat them with chivalry, although I fear they would not respond to us that way," he said. Remarkably promptly, two heralds rode to the city gates and called out their terms, which I assume were 'Open up and let us in, and we'll be good to you,' but were met with disdain and a few hurled buckets of slop, which did not reach them. They were soon back to Edward's pavilion tent with the negative news, but the king seemed oddly exhilarated. He waved the guards outside and gestured for us to come closer. "We can take these Scots and then get on with our primary cause, forcing agreement in Paris over Aquitaine," he said quietly.

"I have maintained a correspondence with my indecisive cousin Philip of France and sent embassies to negotiate with him and keep him focused on other matters. Instead of attacking me while we are busy with the Scots he is dreaming of great deeds on a Crusade. He's had the nerve to raid our Channel islands at the exact time he's been inviting me to go on Crusade with him but I have ignored the insult and have indicated an interest in joining him.

"Meanwhile, I've locked the south coast against him, I've improved our great stronghold at Dover and other fortifications there and I've instructed our sailors to offer no provocations to the French. They'll stay quiet while we put chains on the Scots, and then we can deal with Cousin Philip."

Grosmont, Westwood, who was now recovered from his arrow wound, and I were listening eagerly. Edward continued: "Our forces are by no means complete, and those inside Berwick know it. They also know that the Scots are raising a big army, but that won't be here for weeks. They are in no hurry, and spies tell us the defenders are relaxed because they feel nothing is going to happen soon.

Edward glanced around to ensure again that we were not being overheard. "I think we should attack tomorrow, before dawn." My eyebrows must have shot up into my hairline, and I heard Grosmont rumble a protest but the king was smiling at Westwood. "Tell them Sir John," Edward said. "It was your idea." "Thank you, your grace," said John. "Just a simple thing. There's no moat or ditch outside the town: those Roman walls could fall to an escalade." He went silent and Grosmont and I looked at each other.

Westwood cleared his throat. "No waiting about, no trenches, no sapping slowly forward, no siege engines, no battering a hole in the wall. Just a dash across to the wall, plant ladders and swarm up them. Archers and slingers will lay down a covering fire to keep the defenders' heads down, then it's swords and axes as the attack party goes over the parapet and captures the gate.

"We'd have another force waiting to storm in as the barbican is taken, and we'd be inside the walls and eating their food weeks before Douglas arrives with his reinforcements." We all stood mute for about 30 heartbeats, each of us silent, contemplating the plan. With surprise, it could work. The walls, I recalled, were not insurmountably high, about three times the height of a man. Two hundred men, a dozen ladders, a hundred archers … there would be a butcher's bill, but it could be much cheaper than months of siege, with its concomitant plague, bloody flux or other diseases that invariably ravage an encamped army … and it could be done long before a relieving army arrived.

"I'll pick an escalade force, your grace," said Grosmont, "and I'll lead it." "My archers will be at your disposal, your grace," I heard myself saying, "and I would be honoured to lead an attack." Edward was grinning. "And me," said Westwood. "After all, it was my idea."

So, an hour before dawn, on a night barely lit by the merest sliver of a moon, I was huddled in bracken and shivering with unseasonable cold. Probably, I cursed myself, I should have brought one of those warm plaids I'd acquired after Halidon, but it would have meant abandoning it once we moved to attack and I'd rather be cold for an hour or so than lose such a useful garment. I was fairly lightly clad and protected, for I'd need to be unimpeded to swarm a ladder and fight my way onto a battlement, so I wore only a Jack Coat of stout leather under a mail shirt, with my helm, a banded sallet firmly strapped to my head. The brim would give some extra protection against missiles from above and the openness of it would give me clear vision in a fight.

We were about 400 paces from the town walls, crouched in the dark, with wool or linen scraps tied tightly to muffle our weapons. Here and there along the town walls I could see the dull glow of a watchman's brazier, and very occasionally a shadow as a sentry passed before it. We were downwind of the town and once or twice heard a murmur that must have been a sentry's challenge, but otherwise the night was still, but for the harsh, scratching shriek of a barn owl quartering the ground as he hunted. Edward had promised to hang any man whose careless noise betrayed us, and his edict was working. A group of poachers and hunters skilled at moving quietly had crept about 200 paces closer to the walls than where we were hiding to stash escalade ladders, concealing them under piles of brush and bracken before returning to our waiting force. At the approach of first light, we would creep forward, take up the ladders and rush them in silence the last furlong or so to the walls.

The waiting took an eternity, but finally, a thin glow showed in the east. I gulped, for the older soldiers had told me about escalades, the mad charge, the scramble to set ladders against the wall, the desperate jostling as men struggled up the rungs, men falling, arrow-shot, the missiles raining down to break the ladders or sweep the attackers from their rungs, and finally reaching the ladder top to face the defenders' steel, shafts or rocks while you tried to scramble onto the fighting platform even as you defended yourself.

"Wolf light, son," the old soldier next to me murmured. "Be goin' soon." He was right and a rustle of men moving and standing drew hissed commands to be quiet and soon we were moving forward, crouched behind the hunters who led us to the ladders. Somebody swore softly as he jammed his thumb; the unwieldy ladders were on our shoulders and we were trotting towards the walls, grey in the dim light of the false dawn. We were still a hundred paces away when I heard the familiar hiss of arrows spinning over our heads. They came from our own lines and were clattering against the ramparts ahead. The man behind me grunted: "Bloody fools have fired too soon, they're warning the sentries." More thudding paces and the walls loomed above us, the ladders went up, scraping and thumping against the stonework and drawing alarmed shouts from above our heads.

Grosmont's voice was rising above an increasing buzz:

"Follow me, Lancaster and Saint George!' Somebody forced himself onto my ladder ahead of me, I was scrambling, missed a rung and banged my shin painfully. The helmet of the man following me was pushing against my rump, I was climbing with sword in one hand, the other grasping the ladder rail when the man above me gasped and fell backwards onto my head. I pushed myself in against the ladder and the fellow toppled sideways. The weight of the handful of other men on the ladder kept us stable enough, and I pushed on to reach the parapet.

A face appeared above me and something heavy hit the top of my helmet. I struck out blindly with my sword and distantly heard it connect. It made a dull clonking sound like an axe hitting a tree. Head spinning, I threw a leg over the capstones and tumbled onto the fighting platform. The fellow I'd clubbed had a split forehead and his face was sheeting with blood but he vaguely waved his sword and I backhanded him with my blade across his Adam's apple. His eyes rolled up and he fell sideways.

Something thumped hard on my left shoulder, knocking me forward onto my knees and I half-turned to see a spearman levelling his blade at me. From seemingly nowhere a swung sword crunched into his cheekbone and he was falling. The next man up the ladder had struck the defender down.

Still dazed, I was struggling to my feet when three men at arms raced up from the nearby bastion. I turned to fend them off and found I could not raise my right arm though I was still gripping my sword. The last thing I recall was a gleam of steel, an explosion in my head, then just blank nothing.

Chapter 10 - Physician

Brightly-coloured stripes crossed the sky and it took time for my sticky eyes to focus and for me to realise that I was inside a pavilion tent, lying on a litter. For a few hundred heartbeats, I lay still, puzzled to find myself here, but gradually I began to remember the escalade, the ladder and the wall. Trying to raise my hands to rub my eyes and clear my sight was painful, I soon found I could not move my left arm much at all and my shoulder throbbed under some tight strapping. There seemed nothing else to do, so I closed my eyes and drifted off into sleep.

Movements in the pavilion woke me and I found myself looking into the grave, studious face of a turbaned Arab. "I am your physician," he said. "My name is Absalom. Welcome back."

The next few days were a blur of physicians sent by the king, of dressings and salves, spooned soups and soft white bread fed to me as if I was an infant, all flowing dimly by until one morning I awoke feeling clear-headed but weak. I called for my nurse, who hurried away to return within minutes with Sir John Westwood, whose head was bandaged and who walked with a limp. He grinned at me. "I knew you'd come back to us," he said cheerily. I spoke, surprised at the croak that came from me: "What has been happening, John? The last recall I have is of the ladders and getting over the parapet." He nodded. "That you did, and a fine time we had getting you back afterwards. Got a crack on the head, myself, you're not alone."

The story he told was of a failed escalade, of our attack repulsed by the determined defenders of Berwick. They had cost us 180 lives and three times that number in wounded, many of whom could be expected to die of their injuries. I was a lucky one. Edward had been forced to settle in to a conventional siege, battering the town with mangonels, trebuchets and even iron cannons, firing many houses and shattering others with the bombardment of hurled boulders and cannon balls.

"Balliol's been here for two months now, and the Scots have

an army finally on its laggardly way, about 15,000 of them," said Sir John. "They've burnt Tweedmouth, but Edward wouldn't be drawn off. He wouldn't even budge from the siege when they went to pester Bamburgh where the queen is staying, but that fortress is too much for clansmen with no siege engines.

"There was a treaty that they'd surrender Berwick if not relieved by a certain date, and they broke it, so yesterday, the king hanged the first hostage, the son of Alexander Seton, who commands the garrison. It was the third son he's lost. Now they've agreed to surrender the town by Tuesday in hopes of saving the other hostages. Of course, they're hoping for relief, but as we speak Edward is positioning us on a dominant hill just north of here that the Scots can't bypass. We rode out three days ago and Grosmont hand-picked the site. If the Scots fight us there, it will be Dupplin Moor all over again." He licked his lips, hungrily.

Sir John's prediction was as accurate as any soothsayer's. The Scots could not avoid us in the field, the conflict was joined and although I spent the day of battle on my litter, unable to be there, the accounts that my comrades gave to me later told of a disastrous decision by the clansmen. They elected to fight on Halidon Hill, the exact ground that Edward had chosen.

Much later, I viewed that killing field. The Scots really never had a chance, and their own impetuosity destroyed what little hope they had. They had left their positions in their traditional wild charge. It took them down a steep slope, funneled them between some cliffs and left them bogged in a wide marsh that separated them from the English ranks. After slogging slowly through that, all the while under arrow storm, they then had to struggle up steep Halidon Hill to reach us. Just as at Dupplin Moor, the English were positioned with my archers flanking each side of the main phalanx of men-at-arms, infantry and knights, who were all fighting on foot from behind a hedge of pikes fully 16 feet long.

"You should have been there to see it, Thomas," Edward told me excitedly after the battle. "I placed your archers in wedges that projected forward a little, just as Beaumont did at Dupplin, and when the clans came they stepped into a crossfire that looked like smoke, so dense were the showers of arrows falling on them. And they were truly trapped, bogged down in the marsh almost to a standstill, and packed as tightly as thatch in a roof. Our arrow storm was hitting them in the face and upper body so thickly that many of them simply turned away from it and retreated, stumbling and falling in the bogs, taking the arrow strikes on their shoulders and backs."

The Scots right wing made first contact with the foot soldiers commanded by Balliol but were so depleted by the unceasing hail of arrows that their schiltron shattered on the war hedge and men began running away, back down the hill. "Our bowmen were still pouring shafts in from the flanks and the clansmen just cowered away," said Edward. "They were like sheep huddling together, sheltering from a hail storm, hiding behind the dead bodies of their comrades, and then they broke and ran."

Only one Scot, the Earl of Ross, rallied his Highlandmen and resisted the rampant English, but when that schiltron was inevitably overrun, Edward and his knights mounted up and hacked into the fleeing army. They left the Guardian of Scotland dead on the field with five other earls and about 8,000 common soldiers. "We lost 14 men," crowed Edward. "Fourteen! They had us outnumbered two to one, and we crushed them with our longbows and swords!"

Edward was ruthless when it came to those he saw as rebels, and had no mercy to offer the scant 100 or so clansmen who surrendered. They were paraded out the next morning and beheaded. "Treasonous vermin," he said, turning away. He left for London the next day.

I stayed in a comfortable chamber in Berwick's battered town while I recovered my strength. I had been speared through the shoulder just before being knocked cold by something I never knew and had leaked considerable blood but would recover well, said Absalom, the Arab physician of Edward's court who attended me. Unlike the friars and clerics who often acted as physicians, he did not regard illness or fever as a punishment from heaven. "I do not subscribe to the notion that astrology or numerology is involved in curing you. This is a simple injury caused by a weapon, it is not a curse from the gods."

He cleaned the wound with a concoction of wine and egg whites, applied a salve and some spiderwebs to encourage the wound to heal, then bound it up in bandages hardened with a mixture of flour and eggs. "Immobilising the joint for a while will help it heal," he explained. "Be grateful I'm not one of those bonesetters who use smelly animal fat in the mixture. Some of my colleagues use lime from crushed sea shells to set the bandage, but that's much harder to remove, when you wish to refresh the dressing." He himself changed my dressings every third day, fed me potions of barley water mixed with honey, liquorice and figs and told me to eat pulverized almonds. He checked my urine, sniffing it and examining it for cloudiness, which he said would indicate infection in the body and after more than a week of treatments, bade me farewell before he returned to his court duties.

I was well along with my recovery when a grubby priest slid into my chamber. "I administered Extreme Unction to you," he said accusingly. "You were dying, and on the eve of St Lawrence I gave you the last rites. Although you are recovered in body, in the eyes of the Holy Mother Church you are as good as dead, and you must act accordingly. I would also appreciate a donation for my services." He fingered a greasy leather purse that hung at his waist.

"What?" I raised my voice and he immediately shrank away. "The Church says," and he pursed his lips piously then licked them, "that since you have had the holy last rites, in its eyes you are deceased. You must spend what time remains on earth in fasting, you must go barefoot and you may never again enjoy the pleasures of the flesh with your wife. You may not even amend your will."

I stared at the man. I did have a vague memory of halfway surfacing from sleep to consciousness when someone dropped cold oil on my forehead, someone whose wool clothes held the stench of human grease and stale sweat the way this god-botherer's brown habit stank. Then the arrogance of his words sank in.

"Get out," I snarled. "I'll give you a fee that will take a long time to heal. Bloody nonsense. I'll decide when I'm dead, not some ragged hedge-priest!" I remembered that Prince Henry once thought he was dying and had himself dragged with a rope around his neck to rest on a bed of ashes between two gravestones. That expression of deathbed piety was misplaced.

I said aloud: "The king's own son was anointed by bishops but survived to swive and feast for years to come and no snivelling churchman condemned him for it. And that is what I shall do, priest. Go and grasp for money elsewhere!" I half-rose from my seat, looking for a club to beat him, but the cleric scuttled for the door in alarm and I heard someone laughing a familiar laugh.

"Sir John!" "Well said, Thomas," he spluttered laughing, "though your immortal soul may be a bit blacker now." "John," I said, "these superstition-mongers need to be brought to heel. Anyway, I have royal precedent to quote: King Louis of France thought he was dying and to express his penitence for his sins had himself laid on a hair cloth and ashes, ready to exit. He lay there and gave such a speech about mortality that half his court were in tears. But then the bastard recovered, was hale and well and went off to fight on Crusade. And I bet he didn't spend his life fasting and celibate, not touching his wife and mistresses." John laughed heartily. "You'll probably break a few commandments yourself, and soon," he said. "The priests won't hobble you."

Two days later, I was astride Biter and riding for London, sore but alive. I was not fasting, and I had in mind a tavern in York where there was a flaxen-haired serving wench with whom I could break a couple of the Commandments.

Chapter 11 - Falcon

Saint Bartholomew's Day was marked in London with a three-day late summer fair at Smithfield, just outside the old Roman wall and the greatest attraction of the event was the jousting. My wound was mostly healed, I felt cheated that I had not been properly present at the fall of Berwick and the victory at Halidon Hill, and I was eager to join in the melee, at least, if not the joust. I felt I could cope with fighting one-handed, with my left shoulder heavily strapped and protected behind my shield.

Biter sensed my eagerness and snorted and passaged about as we rode through the merchants and stallholders who had set up outside the priory in Farringdon Without, selling everything from salted meat to cured salmon, from fleeces, hides, coverlets, furs and cloth to horseshoes, ponies, mares, sheep and goats.

Food vendors offered cheeses and fruits, nuts, wine, breads and smoking meat. The bakers and butchers, mercers, carpenters, weavers, smiths and leatherworkers all had their stalls set up and were working their trades while calling out their wares to attract customers.

I heard a roar from inside the wall and guessed the contenders were already in the lists. These would be the individual challenges, knight on knight. I would only fight in the melee, or *behours* that is the climax of the tourney when I intended to join my companions of the conroi. There had not been such a big melee as this since a huge one was fought to celebrate the wedding of Edward and Philippa at York five years ago. I did not join that combat, being judged too young, but now I was a man and a trained fighting man at that. With my archer's strength, which I kept up with daily training, I could easily fight one-handed. I edged Biter, who was champing and restive, through the crowds and headed for the arena and the lists alongside it.

Jousting is a hard and technical activity. A large man in nearly a hundredweight of armour on a half-ton armoured horse hurtles at you at full gallop and concentrates all his weight and speed onto the swaying steel tip of a lance. If he connects - and he will usually be aiming at your helmed head – he could snap your neck. If he hits almost any part of your upper body, you will likely be unhorsed, and falling from a galloping destrier in heavy armour could easily enough kill or cripple you.

The most skilled knights aim for the head, intending to strike it with the point of their lance for a winning blow. A less-skilled horseman might angle the lance at less than straight-ahead, and hope to duck the opponent's point then sweep him from his high-pommelled saddle with the broad of his own lance. For my part, with all the hours of practice at the quintain and with the extra-long lance of seasoned oak that my archer's strength allowed me to wield, I had enjoyed considerable success in the lists and had only once been unhorsed.

The fact was, the spear head of my overly-long lance reached my opponent about an arm's length before the point of his lance could reach me. He was already thrown backwards, lance askew, before he could touch me. That is, it would happen thus if I was accurate in my aim from the jolting back of a large, fast steed. But my injured shoulder meant that this St Bart's Fair would not see me in the lists. I would, however, be in the great charge and melee at the side of my king.

His pavilion was easy to find: a great gaily-striped blue and white canvas castle over which flew the royal standard of the three Plantagenet leopards. I found the king in a temporary mews where he was speaking with his falconer. He brightened when he saw me and embraced me and gave me the kiss of peace. "How is your wound, good Thomas?" he asked solicitously. "I am fine, your grace," I told him, "I shall be at your side in the melee, that's how fine I am." He laughed and turned to the falconer.

"Broggers, be so good as to show Sir Thomas my new peregrine." The hawker gestured and a boy approached. "Fetch Edith," he said. I must have raised an eyebrow, for the falconer smiled at me. "The boy's my cadger, he'll bring the cadge with the king's new peregrine." A minute or two later, the boy reappeared with a wooden frame – the cadge - strapped to his shoulders. On it rested two hooded birds, one much larger than the other.

Broggers, a large and powerful man, showed unusual gentleness as he unfastened from the bird's legs the leather jesses that held one of the raptors to the frame and slipped a long length of twine onto her. "The creance," he said, unecessarily. I knew what that tether was for: he could exercise and train the bird on the wing while controlling her. Drawing her back by hauling in the restraining tether was known as 'reclaiming the hawk.'

Next he knotted the jesses that dangled from her legs and looped them around his little finger. "She's a longwing, have to control her properly. Well, now I have her wrapped around my finger." With a flick of his nail, he chimed the two tiny silver bells that adorned her legs and touched the silver bands called tyrrits that fitted over his finger to secure her.

Broggers looked critically at the thongs, straps and rings to see all was well, then gently removed the soft red leather hood from the bird's head and offered her his upraised, gauntleted forefinger. The tethered peregrine hopped onto it. "They always seek the highest perch," he said, clamping down on her talons, "and when she does, I have her under my thumb."

I admired the bird's bright intelligent eye and knew that this handsome, blue-barred predator was the fastest queen of the skies, a blur of speed when she stooped on her prey. Only the eagle and the gyrfalcon, largest of its species, both of them birds allowed to be kept only by kings and emperors, could compete. Those great predators could kill bigger fowl like geese, cranes or herons, but in a stoop, the peregrine was the champion for speed.

"She'll knock down ducks, songbirds or bats as they fly," said Broggers. "She'll dive on them, kill them and catch them in midair. She's loyal – they mate for life – and a fierce defender of her territory. I think she's the best of the raptors." Edward spoke up: "What about the saker falcon? Lots of knights hunt with them." Broggers paused, seeking a tactful response. "Well, I admit to your grace that he's a big bugger, but he has blunt wings and he's just not as fast. He's a better bird than the lanner, though," he said helpfully. I knew the red-headed lanner was a less-regarded bird relegated to squires' use.

"What's the other bird on the cadge frame?" I asked to distract, for I caught Edward's small frown at being corrected. "Ah," said the falconer, "That's a windhover, a kestrel. He's a gallant little bird, the sparrow hawk. He's used mostly by lesser clergy and he's a killer of small mammals. He's so skilled in flight he can hang motionless while he searches for his prey. I've seen one in a tithe barn, hovering silent and still as he looked for mice then stooping and falling like a stone on one."

Edward, I saw was over his moment's pout and looked on interestedly as the cadger dug into a pouch at his hip and pulled out a furry, bloody lump of something. "Quail, with feathers and fur," explained Broggers, offering a scrap to the peregrine Edith. "She needs more than just meat, she requires roughage. It cleans her crop and she spits out a casting like that -" pointing to a round pellet of something grey lying nearby.

"You should feed her on the fist to get her used to people. We call it 'manning' and the bird soon understands if she comes back to the fist, she gets food and attention." As he spoke, the peregrine stirred uneasily and began beating her wings. "She's bating because she's hot," Broggers said unconcernedly. "Soon sort her out." He swiftly hooded the bird then strolled, the hawk still flapping on his fist, to a granite water trough for horses. Although the water was full of green animalcula, he dipped a leather cup into it and poured it over the peregrine's hood and back, soaking and cooling her.

Almost immediately, she stopped bating and Broggers settled her on a rail of the cadge, tying her jesses to keep her in place. Then he slipped off the hood and began feeding scraps of the quail to the eager hawk. Edward stepped forward: "Let me do that." He took a piece of the bloody meat and was about to feed it to the peregrine when Broggers stepped forward. "No, your grace, use this," handing over the leather gauntlet. "She would have had your fingers, your grace," said the falconer. Edward nodded. "He's more used to horses," I said. "When will she be ready to hunt?" the king asked, ignoring my jibe. "Maybe in a fortnight," said the falconer, hastily adding: "Your grace."

"Well, I'll look forward to that, once we have done our fighting here," said Edward, gesturing at the bannered arena where we could hear shouts and the clank of metal on metal. "I'm going to walk her over there myself, your grace," said Broggers. "Get her used to crowds and noise." "Don't lose her," said Edward. "It's more than your two pence a day is worth."

He looked at me and shrugged. "Better get ready for the lists, sorry you won't be fighting there." I grinned at him. "I'll make enough of a mark in the melee, you can have all the glory to yourself in the tiltyard."

Back at the king's pavilion, I was mildly surprised to see Queen Philippa, and I made a leg and bowed deeply. She posed a few solicitous questions about my injuries and when the king and two of his pages joined us, she turned to one of her waiting women and nodded. The woman bustled away and returned holding a toddler. "Look who's come to see his father," said Philippa, smoothing the boy's hair. It was the young prince, Edward of Woodstock.

"Give him to me," said the king, who tossed the boy into the air, eliciting squeals of joy. "Start you early, teach you about warfare, my fine son," he said. "Watch your daddy on his big horse. One day, you'll have a horse like him, eh?" The boy, wide-eyed, went to chew on his fist but his father stopped him. "Warriors don't suck thumbs," he scolded gently. "Oh, Edward, he's just a baby," said the queen. "He's nearly three years old, madam," retorted Edward. "He's the Earl of Chester, no less. Can't have one of my earls sucking his thumb at court!"

I laughed aloud and Edward turned to me, grinning. "I was just thinking that my lord Henry of Grosmont might find it nourishing," I said, and at the thought of that doughty magnate ever acting childishly sent us both off into guffaws. We were still smiling when servants brought in Edward's armour. "I had some amendments made for my jousting harness," said Edward. "The armourer put a heavier plate on the cuirass and helm, on the rerebrace and pauldron on the right side." It was a shrewd decision: you did not need battlefield mobility in the lists, so the armourer had bolted on extra metal to the breastplate and helmet, and to the right arm and shoulder that were not hidden behind the shield and where Edward might reasonably expect to be hit.

"Look at the helm closer," the king urged me, as happy as a boy with a new toy. The visor seemed odd, so I put the helmet on and realized I could see out only by leaning forward. "If you sit more upright just before impact with your opponent's lance, your eyes will be absolutely protected," Edward explained. "Sensible," I murmured. It was not unknown for a splinter from a broken lance to enter the visor and blind or even kill a knight.

I looked over the breastplate and plackart that would protect Edward's chest and belly, both of them heavily padded against any hammer-blow of an opponent's lance. "I've even had Stamper's chanfron padded," he said, referring to the iron shield that protected the horse's head, "and his caparison is lined inside with mail right across the chest."

The powerful, warm-blood destrier was well worth protecting, costing as he did the equivalent of several good farms. He was trained to do more than maintain the smooth pace of the amble, he could also bite at an opponent's face, jump and kick rearwards if he detected an attack from that direction, and would respond to the pressure of his rider's knees, enabling the king to fight with a weapon in each hand, standing in the stirrups or while jammed securely between the high pommel at the front of his saddle and by the tall cantle behind him.

The destrier's amble was especially critical; by eliminating an uneven gait, it allowed the rider to more precisely aim his lance, and the fact that the destrier was typically twice the size and weight of a warmblood charger gave a devastating power to any impact from the rider's lance. Edward had one other trick up his gold-threaded sleeve: "I like to stand when I fight, especially if I use a sword, morningstar or flail." I looked at the array the squire was putting out: Edward's war sword was two-edged, with a blade as long as a clothyard; his morningstar was a long-handled spiked ball and the flail also employed a similar lethal orb, only on the end of a chain with a handle. In a real fight, the king also carried a rondel at his waist, a slim foot-long blade with round hilt and pommel much favoured by foot soldiers who would ease it through a visor's slits to finish a downed knight.

A thought occurred to me. "You like to stand to fight from the stirrups, your grace," I said, "and I once saw a Pole who did that. Because he extended his legs, his spurs hardly reached his mount's ribs, so he had some long-necked spurs made." Edward shook his head. "Stamper responds so well to pressure from my knees that he'd be indignant at me if I spurred him when he didn't expect it." He looked mock-thoughtful. "He'd probably throw me off and flatten me."

Our conversation ended quickly, as Edward was diverted by a giddy troupe of young noblewomen who were shockingly dressed like men and cavorted into the pavilion. They all wore multi-coloured tunics divided like a harlequin's with long-tailed hoods. Each flaunted a knife, worn dangling suggestively in front of her waist, suspended from a belt of gold or silver.

Edward had a lively eye for the women but I noticed that his confessor, a Cistercian monk who happened to be in the pavilion, turned away in disgust. The visitors swarmed around the king, who laughingly pushed them away and I glanced around to check that Queen Philippa was not present. Then I joined in the merriment. It was, after all, a tournament.

Chapter 12 - Salvation

Edward had a fine day in the lists and carried Philippa's silk favour, which he tied to the back of his helm, to victory. His principal combat was against a Teutonic knight of great size whom he fought with lance, axe and sword in three separate engagements. In the lists, Edward unhorsed his opponent at the first pass, but had a much closer contest with the battle axe, only defeating the giant after a blow to his knee took him down. The third joust, with swords, was one-sided as the big man could hardly move and Edward soon forced him to yield.

In a fine Arthurian spirit of chivalry, he helped his defeated opponent to his feet, settled him alongside the royals in their viewing stand and served him wine with his own hands. I noted the Teuton's eyes, though. He was humiliated and angered at his triple defeat and although outwardly gracious, seemed to be simmering with a resentment that Edward's courtesy had not defused. I resolved to be alert to the fellow, especially in the melee that would follow in two days' time. I made note of his heraldic insigna, a simple black cross on a white ground. His name was Johan von Endorf and he had murdered his own order's Grand Master, although we did not know that then.

Edward was exultant over his triumphant day's jousting and proposed that the royal *familiares* make an excursion with him to watch the king's blacksmiths working at the White Tower. "I have some ideas for my jousting armour, and I have a surprise for you, dear Thomas," he said.

We clattered across the drawbridge into the barbican of the Tower in high spirits although some of the conroi showed bruises and wounds from the previous day's encounters. As we passed through the great walls, the gate guards snapped to attention when they saw him and his gold circlet. Edward was riding slightly ahead of us and spotted something that caused him to signal us all to halt. He slipped from his horse and waved to us excitedly, gesturing for quiet, then led the way to a half-hidden gate. To my astonishment, four burly men were passing though it with a huge white bear on a chain.

"She was brought here from Woodstock," he said in a low voice. "We had all sorts of animals there, gifts from kings and emperors. Those fellows -" gesturing at the bear's attendants – "are taking her fishing in the river." Edward had ordered a long thin chain made so the bear could get some exercise, swimming and fishing in the Thames while still under tether.

"You kept her at Woodstock, your grace?" I asked. "Oh, we had all kinds of things there. My grandfather was given three leopards by the Emperor Frederick to salute the arms of England, and because the chase at Woodstock is so contained – King Henry had a seven-mile wall built around it – he let them loose in the park. There were lions and lynxes in there, too. The gamekeepers told me that big cats only attack from behind you, so they wore masks on the backs of their heads when they worked in the woods and nobody was ever attacked."

We stood quietly by the wall and watched the huge bear swimming and then fishing, standing quietly in the shallows, pouncing and swiping up some large fish. "We call her Boreas, after the north wind, because she came from the icy north," said Edward. Finally, we left the bear to her fishing and followed the king back through the gate and into the courtyard.

He led us to a short line of buildings that were wreathed in sooty smoke. At the first, as we ducked through the low door, we came upon a metalworker scribing a design into a tourney helm. The man stumbled to his feet at Edward's entry, but the king waved him back to his workbench under a window space, examined the half-completed helmet, praised the man and we all moved to the next hovel. There an armourer was working, finishing a batch of flanged maces. "Not expensive, and a deadly weapon," said Edward, moving on.

The third building, a smith's forge, was open on one side and was dimly-lit so the smith could see the glowing metal more clearly. Edward was plainly well-known to the smith, who merely grunted a greeting and gave a minimal nod as sign of respect. I eyed the man, ready to reprove him for his lack of courtesy, but Edward, sensitive to events, gave a near-imperceptible shake of his head. "Robert here is a fine craftsman, a valuable man to me, aren't you, my friend? Look at the sword he has made for me." He nodded to the smith, who silently lifted down a sword from a shelf. It was unfinished, awaiting work on the hilt. The blade was fine steel with some faint decoration like smoke and bore an inscription 'Eduardo de Woodstock.' The sculpted crossguard had a Celtic design, the groove was deeper than usual and the pommel was wheel-shaped and ready for a jewel to be inset. "A fine piece, Robert," the king said.

The burly smith, bare-chested behind a leather apron, hardly responded. "Aye." A pause. "Your grace." He turned to use pincers to draw a red-hot length of iron from the forge and placed it carefully on an anvil before tapping it with a small hammer. This indicated to his apprentice, who was acting as striker, where he wanted the next blow, and the youth swung a heavy sledgehammer down on the indicated spot. Robert turned the metal and tapped it again and the apprentice smashed another precise, heavy blow. Only then did the smith turn and push the iron back into the glowing charcoal of the forge.

He straightened up and eyed Edward. "Aye, your grace," he said, "And I'm a fine fellow." Edward laughed. "Tell my friends here what you're doing." The smith sighed. He jerked his head to the apprentice, indicating that the youth should withdraw the iron from the forge and set it aside for now. It seemed that Edward had interrupted his work more than once before.

"Well, my lords," he began, "we get blooms of iron like this from ore smelters in the Kentish hills." He indicated a rough lump of pitted rock. "That's iron ore that was buried in a pit with a drain. The smelters put down layers of ore and charcoal then fire it and seal the pit with clay and dirt, trapping the heat. In time the molten ore flows down the drain and congeals into this bloom of iron which has some carbon in it, and that's what makes it into steel. It's all about adding a bit of carbon and quenching it to turn iron into steel."

The bloom was like a sponge, containing a network of channels full of molten glass from the ore's impurities. To clean them out, Robert reheated and hammered the bloom in his furnace, turning it with long tongs while the apprentice worked leather bellows to heat the lump to glowing heat. "Red, orange, yellow, white, they're the levels of heat," the smith said gruffly. "Every time you hammer it, you heat it more with the energy of the blow." Time after time, the two men dragged the mass out of the forge, broke off a largish piece and began hammering it into the desired shape, every blow superheating the malleable mass, friction-welding it together and driving out impurities.

"The best blooms come from one particular spot in the Weald and make good weapons; other ore from different places is only good for casting because it melts easily but it's brittle. This bloom is good, and with enough hammering and reheating I'll shape the iron into rods. After that, I will twist them into a braid – that makes a faint pattern down the blade when it's finished."

He took a swig from a water skin that hung from a rafter, stepped around the table-high forge and produced a pair of rods he had readied. They were longer than a clothyard, and about as thick as my thumb. "Five of these make a blade. You heat them, twist them together and hammer them flat. Then you fold and hammer them again. And again, over and over. You can lengthen the bar by beating it with the peen side of the hammer or by using this tool, called a fuller. Either way, it makes a series of indentations or 'waves' along one side. Then you reverse the hammer and flatten the iron, one 'wave' at a time, which stretches the whole thing.

"Braiding the five bars gives the sword strength and when it's flattened into a blade, makes a pleasing, swirling pattern down the whole length of the sword. When that's done, I grind a channel down the centre, reducing weight and making it all stronger. It also helps break the clinging suction when you've pierced an opponent's body and want to withdraw your weapon."

The next stage, he explained as some of our group listened with mouths agape, was to file the cutting edges to lethal sharpness. Then the blade, reheated until it was glowing hot, would be tempered by plunging it into a bath of salts before being quenched in oil, which the smith said cooled the steel evenly. He told us his secret for tempering the blade so the edges were harder, to hold sharpness, while the rest of the weapon remained flexible. "I use layers of clay to coat the blade – except for the edges, which are tempered hard to hold an edge. The clay slows the cooling and builds that vital flexibility I want. A good sword bends a little, a bad sword is too brittle and will snap under pressure. I keep my swords flexible."

Robert looked around the forge and picked up a sword in process of being finished. He pushed a steel guard over the shoulders of the blade, snugged it firmly with the hilt and locked all in place with a heavy pommel. "The pommel is more than just a counterweight to balance the length of the blade, it's an offensive weapon, too. Use it as a club."

He looked around, grimy but proud of his skills, and saw we were all impressed. Edward coughed. "Robert?" The smith grinned at his king. "Your grace, certainly," he said and moved around the forge to pick up a leather-wrapped object which I deduced from its shape was a sword. He handed it to Edward.

"Thomas, step over here," Edward commanded. Puzzled, I did as I was ordered nd Edward, grinning broadly, handed the package to me. I stood like a fool, until the king said: "Well, man, open it! It's tradition on St Bartholomew's Day to hand out knives and cutting tools. You've earned it!"

Inside the leather was a sword, and what a sword! I took in a rounded bronze pommel, a knobbed hilt ridged for the fingers and fitted with a ring. This secured and protected the digit as the swordsman pulled back from a thrust. The crossguard bent gently towards the blade, which was long, about an arm's length, and had a subtle dark line called a 'hamon' where the harder steel of the cutting edge met the softer, more flexible steel of the spine. The point was tapered and both cutting edges of the blade were slightly curved.

I hefted the weapon, more than three pounds' weight, I judged. I lifted the point and the whole sword seemed to flow in my hand. "Counterbalanced to the weight of a silver penny," boasted Robert. "And, see the ricasso – there, unsharpened." The blade just below the guard was left without an edge to allow the swordsman to wield it two-handed - useful for its length. The hilt was wrapped in perforated leather retained at pommel and guard with tightly-drawn wire overlaid with ferrules of beaten gold. I marveled at the whole weapon then noticed a word stamped into the steel before it had been tempered. It said 'Salvation.'

Edward was still grinning triumphantly. "It's time you acted like a proper knight, and stopped being a common archer," he said teasingly. It was our oldest joke. He knew the value of archers to the English army and he admired my skill with the longbow, and from the hours I spent daily at the butts, he knew it was a serious matter to me. "Use this, and you can bring Salvation to our enemies, Thomas. May this sword protect you – and save them!" I had unmanly wetness in my eyes at his gesture. "May it always be at your service, Sire," I said fervently. "As will I." My chance came the very next day at the closing event of the fair, the massed melee.

Chapter 13 - Melee

Dust hung in the air like a smoke cloud, churned up from the hard-trampled ground by grooms exercising their masters' chargers and destriers. The sharp smell of wintergreen stung my nose as I entered Edward's pavilion. The king was seated on a stool, allowing a squire to buckle his body harness in place over the quilted gambeson that cushioned the royal self from its steel carapace. I wrinkled my nose. Edward nodded: "Wintergreen and olive oil, to ease my bruises and warm my muscles. It's the scent of battle, Thomas."

Privately, I thought the scent of battle was human dung and blood but kept my tongue still. A king could become snappish even when he was your friend. "How are you, Thomas?" Edward was in genial mood. "Tired, your grace," I said. "I hardly slept for thinking of Salvation." He looked puzzled. "Have you sinned?" he said. "I meant my fine new sword, your grace." "Ah," and he laughed. "You'll bring Salvation to our enemies, eh?" Now it was my turn to laugh. "This very day, my lord."

The squire was finishing fitting the monarch in the two dozen pieces of armour that would protect him; a page arrived carrying the oak lance, striped red and gold that would be Edward's largest weapon, another page brought the king's great sword and belt, yet another squire was leading Edward's huge destrier Stamper towards the pavilion and even another page held the king's shining helm with its plume of madder-dyed ostrich feathers..

It was nearly past time for me to get myself ready for battle, but I was waiting for the Arab physician Absalom to bind and immobilize my wounded shoulder. He appeared and soon the strapping was done and I could don my armour. My left arm was bound tight to my body from the elbow up, which meant I could at least hold a shield or my horse's reins.

Eventually, all the straps were buckled, I was readied from comb to sabatons, Edward was gallantly fastening a silk favour from Queen Philippa to his helm and we were assembling our force on a field adjacent to the enclosure. Edward, who was dressed in some Arthurian costume I assumed was that of his favourite, Sir Galahad, joked with me that I should stay off the field and simply shoot arrows at our opponents. I had to bow in mock-despair: "Can't even hold a longbow, your grace," I said. "I'll just have to use inferior weapons, as you do." He grinned and shook his head. "After you, Sir Thomas," he said, bowing ironically. "You should have costumed yourself as Tristan." I had no idea what he meant.

Then we were trotting out, 40 horsemen and 60 men at arms in each opposing schiltron. We rode past a row of refreshment tents – armed, steel-clad warriors incongruously riding out to do harm and passing through the food smells of a fair's homely atmosphere. There was an attempt to limit the violence, though. Under a statute of arms laid down 40 years before, we could not use the deadliest weapons: swords, clubs, maces or daggers with pointed ends. Like the king and most of our battalion, I had capped my lance with a crown-shaped knob in place of the point. I also had the armourer fit a guard on my new sword Salvation to blunt it but discarded the sheath and opted to use another sword, as the extra metal altered the balance and ruined Salvation's wonderful feel. Besides, there was always the chance that the temporary guard might come off, and I'd inadvertently stab someone.

Edward had appointed a court of honour to settle any disputes and made specific orders that only our own squires, properly identified in tabards that carried our heraldic insignia, may help a fallen knight to his feet. He was so determined to follow Arthurian principles of gallantry and virtue that he threatened any squire who cheated with three years' imprisonment and the forfeiture of his horse, body harness and weapons.

Sir John Westwood had snorted when he heard that. "What does it matter who helps you up? You're probably only half-conscious anyway. This isn't a tourney of peace. People are going to be killed or knocked silly. I'd let anyone help anyone else to his feet to take more punishment." But, mindful of Edward's eagerness to be chivalrous, he said nothing to anyone else.

Now we were moving out to the arena and the heralds were scanning the riders, to announce them. Their task was to identify the various insignia that sometimes were the only clue to an armoured, visor-down knight: who was the man inside the anonymous carapace of steel? I heard a red-faced herald bellow out the name of the Earl of Warwick and saw the familiar ragged staff and rampant bear of his coat of arms, then there was a blast of trumpets – everyone knew Edward's royal insignia, and he had his visor open, too.

He stood in the stirrups and waved his sword over his head, then we were lining up, cavalry to the front, infantry behind us and we were gazing across a furlong of greensward at our rival body of knights and men at arms, a large contingent of whom seemed to be under the command of Johan von Endorf, the Teutonic knight whom Edward had three times defeated in single combat two days before. The crowd in the stands were buzzing, then a herald strode out importantly and dangerously, I thought into the open ground between the opposing schiltrons. He shouted something I could not hear, a blare of brass-throated trumpets sounded and I was digging my heels into Biter's ribs as we surged forward.

The younger knights mounted on the lighter chargers sprinted ahead of those of us on the slower, heavier destriers and Edward was bellowing for them to maintain line, but the teenage hotheads were bent on glory as were the younger knights fighting against us. A spatter of torn-up turf hit me on my closed visor and surplice, I lowered my oak lance with its green and yellow stripes and focused on the possible targets ahead.

Horses galloping en masse sound like drumbeats. Our relatively modest charge of 40 cavalry still made a blood-stirring noise, especially to those of us who had experienced what came next: the split-second choices, the clanging crash, clatter of tumbling men and horses and thrilling ring of steel on steel.

I'd chosen a knight with alternating yellow and black chevrons on his shield and leaned forward into the impact, couching my lance confident in my strength of arm and core, exulting in the pounding ambling weight of my big horse, watching the tip of my lance circling to the rhythm of Biter's thumping hooves as I aimed for the pauldron that protected Yellow Chevron's right shoulder. His crowned lance point was an arm's length from Biter's head when my own blunted point struck him. He went abruptly backwards under the oncoming power of my bigger horse and his lance went harmlessly up into the air. One of his armoured feet flew up, the other was caught in the horse's trapper or perhaps in the stirrup and Yellow Chevron spun sideways and backwards, out of the saddle and over the high cantle that was supposed to keep him seated. He crashed to the ground headfirst and I judged he had a good chance of being knocked unconscious.

For myself, the impact had little effect. It is always that way if you win the contest: your opponent absorbs the force and you remain rock-solid in the saddle crammed between pommel and cantle. I had the advantages of the bigger, heavier mount and of the tremendous upper-body strength my archery had earned me. My first opponent was on the ground, motionless. No time to pause, I kicked Biter on and into the second rank of oncoming knights, who trailed the first line by about 20 paces.

There was just time enough to shift my grip on my lance and re-couch it, to make a hasty choice of target, swerve around a riderless horse and aim at a knight in rusty mail who had made the error of dropping his lance and swinging a battle axe. "He expects to be in among a broken line," I thought even as Biter closed on him. I should have simply speared him, but mindful of the new chivalry Edward nobly expected, I dropped my own lance. Too close now to draw a sword and anyway I was fighting one-handed. Use Biter, quickly, now. One swift jerk on his reins, painful to my left shoulder, that, a kick of the spurs and a shout to my intelligent horse: 'Up, boy, up!"

As he had been so painstakingly trained to do, Biter reared and lashed out with both forefeet. One caught the opposing charger squarely on the forehead. Protected by iron or not, it was a crashing blow and the horse staggered. His rider was almost unhorsed, snatched at the pommel to stay on his mount and dropped his axe. "No second chance for you," I mumbled, reaching across my body to draw my blunted sword. Rusty Mail had two hands on his pommel, fighting to stay seated as his stunned horse began to sink to its knees. Biter was back on all four hooves, still moving forward and I levelled my sword forward, pointing across his head and thrust hard.

Rusty Mail shrieked at the blow, which hit him with blunt force in the gorget protecting his throat. His hands left the pommel and went to his head. I was almost past, going by on his right side, but had time for a backswing of my heavy blade which took him across the nape of the neck and he was slumping, falling with his horse. And I was among the men at arms, trampling, stamping, swinging and thrusting, horse and man acting in unison in among a storm of cavalry that was shattering the Teuton's orderly line into a mob.

The tide of fighting went back and forth, flowing across a tidemark of downed men, ebbing back as one side or other countered. I saw Edward, visor open, a bloody stripe across the bridge of his nose, beating at the shield of a cowering baron whose insignia was so battered it was unreadable.

After what seemed like a short lifetime but was probably less than an hour, I eased out of the battle line to water Biter and to sluice my own parched throat, then we move back into the fray, passing a crocodile of injured and weary men who were easing off the jousting green. Edward's tall red-gold plume was prominent in the thick of the scrimmage, and I urged Biter forward towards the king and the rest of our conroi, though I noticed it was severely depleted, and seemed to be down to just three or four knights.

A glance at the marshals' stand showed there was no sign of them bringing in heralds to call a halt, so I deduced that the fighting was to continue for some time yet. Edward and our conroi companions were at the centre of a semicircle of opponents, facing them like a bull faces the dogs, when I witnessed a swirl in the crowd of men at arms behind them and realized that a big knight in white surplice with a simple black cross was forcing his way forward, directly at the backs of the beleaguered king and our comrades.

Biter responded to my kicking and surged forward towards

the Teuton Johan von Endorf, for it was the knight Edward had decisively defeated in single combat two days ago. Then, I had seen the hatred the German had for his conqueror and made resolve to mark him this day, but it had slipped my mind. Now the fellow was seeking vengeance and was about to cut down from behind the unaware Edward, who was battering at two opponents to his front..

A knot of infantry was shielding von Endorf from me but gallant Biter stormed into them, ignoring several hard blows on his chest and muzzle as they retreated from his teeth and hooves. One man screamed shrilly as he went down under those iron-clad feet, a shriek unusual enough that von Endorf turned to see what caused it. He saw me, sword raised. I was about to wipe him from his saddle when a man at arms seized my foot and tipped me sideways. I only had one hand with which to grab on, so I dropped my sword and caught the pommel with my good right hand. Something banged across my gauntlet and the hand went numb but I hung on, struggling to get upright in the saddle again.

Biter bucked as someone's pointed knife – illegal, I thought – stabbed my horse in the shoulder and he curvetted away. An eddy of fighting men separated von Endorf from the unguarded rear of the king's conroi and I heard him swear as he tried to push his horse through. I was back in the saddle, enraged and in the familiar cold fury where the world sparkled in bright colours, where time went slower and my opponents all seemed to move as if in deep water. My lance and sword were gone, but I had a morningstar looped at my saddle. It was the work of a half-second to snatch up the handle, another fraction of a heartbeat to shake loose the iron ball at chain's end, a moment more to raise the whip-like thing and whirl it over my head.

A squire on horseback rode at me, I swung the heavy iron ball round and up to catch him under the chin. I heard his broken teeth crunch as he went off the opposite side of his charger and my way was clear to von Endorf, who had risen in his stirrups and was about to swing his sword at Edward's back..

Instinct told him I was attacking and he ducked in the saddle so the whirling iron ball whizzed over his helm. He backswung his great sword two-handed and it crashed across my shield, making me call out in pain as it splintered the leather-faced yew and jolted my wounded shoulder. The shield took the brunt of the blow, but the sword tip cut me above the eyebrow and, as with most head wounds, even minor ones like that, it bled profusely, half-blinding me. The shock to my injured shoulder made me sick and dizzy and for a few moments I was vulnerable. Biter was not. He jumped vertically and lashed out his rear hooves at some attacker who was trying to slash my mount's hamstrings and the man fell, face crushed and horribly lopsided. The destrier's movement saved me, for von Endorf's sword whistled harmlessly past my face.

Biter moved inside the arc of the huge sword, I had no room to swing my morningstar and I was knee to knee with von Endorf. He struggled to get the sword pulled back for a killing stroke. I dropped the morningstar, stood on my stirrups and leaned forward, grasping and balancing with my knees, to backhand the Teuton with my armoured gauntlet's spiked knuckles. It was a last-gasp blow of desperation and I leaned every part of my archer's huge upper body strength into it. It could not have been a harder hit if I had used a club. He probably never saw it coming: his visor was closed and the blow came from his side.

My gauntlet's knuckle spikes actually dented the side of his visor and Von Endorf's head flew back, his brain rattled into stupor. He slumped sideways, I leaned down to his stirrup, seized the sabaton that guarded his foot and heaved upwards. The unseated Teuton flew skywards and toppled out of sight on the other side of his charger.

Now I was in a crowd of opponents, unarmed, dizzy and bleeding from my reopened shoulder wound. Using only knee pressure, I turned Biter in a tight circle, and the men at arms who surrounded us stayed cautious, well aware that even if his rider seemed vulnerable a trained warhorse like this would rip off their faces. I still had my shield and used it twice to fend off questing spears until the pressure eased, the ring of iron expanded and I became aware that Sir John Westwood and another knight I did not recognize were hacking and stabbing a space around me. John took a moment to throw me a mace, blunted according to tourney rules, and I swung it at a pair of ruffians who were trying to unhorse me when suddenly Edward was at my side. With four of us hacking and thrusting we broke clear of the swirling melee just as a rush of Edward's knights and the battered remains of his personal conroi tore into the flank of von Endorf's schiltron. In minutes, it was over, the heralds were blowing their 'Cease' commands and we were exultant victors, bloodied but masters of the field.

Chapter 14 - Feast

Edward called for a great feast to celebrate the successful Windsor tourney, and his chamberlains spent a week preparing Westminster Palace for the event. The almoner laid in several hundred pounds of candles, more than 20 times what would usually be consumed in a couple of days, and the master chef ordered 500 cartloads of good, dry firewood and a barn full of coal to be made ready. The vast kitchens that would need this fuel were manned by a hurrying legion of bakers, cooks, sauciers, butchers, larderers, scullions, carvers and squires.

In the smoky hall's centre there was also an open fireplace where food preparers roasted fowl, beef, mutton, pork and venison on spits that ranged from small enough for a single bird to large enough for an ox. The red-faced, perspiring cooks carefully collected all drippings to baste the meat, or to use in sauces. Ovens adjoined the fireplace, and in them bakers made pies in a huff paste of suet, flour and hot water. This stiff coffyn was almost inedible, and was simply a container for the stew within. I knew that on less grand occasions, poorer magnates would serve the coffyn, which soaked up meat juices, to the servants, just as they would allow the poor to consume the stew-soaked trenchers, the hollowed-out loaves that had been used as dishes.

On this feast day, the High Table was set up on a dais at one end of the hall, and was covered with a fine linen table cloth; stepped buffets were set up along the sides of the hall, covered with rich draperies and equipped with the king's finest gold and silver plates. Dishes were displayed on this series of shelves. Servants selected, carved and delivered meals from them to the distinguished diners at the top table who cut their meats, then delicately ate them with their fingers. Lesser mortals on the lower tables helped themselves, hacking off great smoking lumps of meat before eating them from the knife point.

In the great gallery above Edward's head, a choir sang, while at intervals, minstrels took over the musical duties as they strolled around the hall. Tumblers, jugglers and several dwarfs performed between the trestle tables that were set along the length of the hall, coming from time to time to the top table for gifts of silver. All around, servants waited on the guests with towels, bowls and ewers of scented water for them to wash their hands between courses. Other servitors waited by the buffets to cut and present the food on a staggering array of silver vessels, many of them gilded. Silver candlesticks and spoons were arrayed ready, more humble chargers, platters, dishes and saucers of pewter were also piled up for use. A constant swarm of pages ran to and from the buffets, collecting and delivering dishes to the diners at table.

On the High Table where the most distinguished guests ate stood a boat-shaped golden container called a *nef* that held utensils, rare and expensive spices, precious fresh white bread and a flagon of wine, but even the humbler trestle tables for the common herd each bore a large platter of valuable spices.

The chamberlain had set up a centrepiece below the High Table, a green linen to represent a field around a pastry castle that was fully a clothyard high, with baked battlements, fighting platforms, inner and outer baileys and even a cunningly-made lattice of a portcullis. Small flags bearing Edward's insignia of three leopards flew from its gilded turrets and wisps of steam escaped from its roofs because the whole building was filled with venison. This meat had been salted overnight then cooked with a loin of veal and several roast hares. A moat of red wine enclosed the castle and at each end of the 'lawn' stood a huge pie whose crust was silvered and gilt.

Each was surrounded by smaller pies, and all together formed the shape of a crown. One of the two huge pies contained lampreys baked in vinegar, the other contained a ragout of heron. The smaller, surrounding pies were filled with eels, capons, salmon in syrup and halibut in a galantine of cinnamon, ginger, vinegar and stock.

The king stood to welcome the guests, made some compliments on the tournament to his fighting men (I noted that the Teuton was not present) and to laughter, took his sword and sliced a turret off the pastry castle, releasing a gush of aromatic venison stew. The whole hall buzzed in approval and all settled down to enjoy the feast.

After the first course, hurrying servants brought in a 'subtlety' of fruit, nuts, pomegranate seeds and gilded sugar plums to please the palate before the second course arrived. This arrived to loud acclaim and calls of 'Praise our good King Edward!' and was a complete roasted wild boar with gilded tusks, carried in shoulder-high by four serving men in royal livery. Roast chickens covered in a plum sauce followed, then came a dozen large pies filled with the flesh of a whole roe deer, plus the meat of goslings, chickens and rabbits. Two dozen hard-boiled eggs flavoured with cloves and saffron made a sort of stuffing for each pie, and all were brought triumphantly in by a procession of servants.

While all this was being delivered to table, a whole stag was being turned on the largest spit of the hall's fireplace. It was larded and roasted to crispness, then quartered, doused in pepper sauce and served to the diners, many of whom had stopped to admire the spitted roast as they left the tables to relieve themselves and to wash their hands in rose-scented water before returning to the feast.

More courses kept coming from the kitchens' copper vats: a rare sturgeon cooked in parsley, loins of crisply-roasted pork, stuffed capons, boiled ox meat from the castle's supply that was kept salted as basic rations. Roast kid, two roast herons and dishes of jugged hare also crowded the buffet shelves and were served from there, but some on the lower tables simply hacked off great smoking lumps of meat from the joints as they came from the spits.

I noticed that the queen was hardly eating, even of the pike and bream that were Edward's personal favourites, though she was cutting up delicacies for her husband and serving them to him. I watched as squires brought two elegantly-farced dishes: a swan and a piglet. Each had been skinned and dressed, its body shape preserved (and in the case of the swan, its wings, too) and the meat ground fine, spiced and stuffed back into its skin in the shape of the original creature. The swan's beak was gilt, the piglet had a spiced apple in its mouth. All at the high table applauded, but the queen, tall, dark-haired and regal, was the only one not to take a morsel of either dish. I mentioned it to my table companion, Henry of Lancaster.

"She's staying delicate and neat, she doesn't want to stain her clothes. Eating's messy," he said, helping himself to another dish of salmon in rich sauce. "The ladies like to eat in private, even the farced dishes. You know, 'farcing' comes from the Latin *farcio'* meaning 'I cram.'" It was like Henry to exercise his knowledge, and I smiled fondly, for he was such a good fellow. He was still churning on: "It might be well to cram a duck's body with spiced meat, but the only stuffing for those ladies is the kind they get in the bed chamber." I now smiled only thinly, aware that the king would not tolerate unchivalrous bawdy talk. Henry, for all his royal blood, was on dangerous ground. I changed the subject.

"See them?" I said, nodding to a table below us. "You can put a jaw rope on a biting mule but our clerical brothers would chew right through it." A group of monks eating at a lower table were determinedly tucking into everything. "They're not so concerned about privacy," I said. "Ah, the good brothers," said Earl Henry. "They're all fat trenchermen. They claim that they follow the rule of St Benedict, who said they should live plainly. Their idea of that is to restrict themselves to a flagon of wine daily, but there's no restriction on beer, and most slosh down about a gallon a day. They're allowed half a dozen eggs, two pounds of bread and two pounds of fish or meat daily – about twice what a peasant doing heavy manual work gets.

"The Church absolutely forbids consuming the flesh of four-footed animals for about 100 days a year but the clever clerics have found ways around that. Offal, bacon, which they call collops, or other prepared food is adjudged to be exempt from the ban on meat, as are marine animals, so roast barnacle goose, beaver tails, puffin breasts, oyster and conger and even dolphin, seal or whale meat are all on the clerics' list during meat-free days."

"Monks have served me fake eggs made from fish roe flavoured with almonds, or faux ham and venison on fast days. I've even dined on beef and roe deer with the monks during

Lent, because they say the dietary restrictions only apply to the refectory where they normally eat meals. Eat elsewhere and God turns a blind eye." I laughed, and the old warrior grinned back at me. "Here comes another course," he said, and being the younger man, I dutifully carved some lamb for him, as is etiquette, and we shared our beaker of wine.

Several hours after the feast began, pages brought in the finishing courses: jellies, cream cheese, strawberries, plums stewed in rosewater, some sweet pastries and an assortment of pears, apples, nuts and cheese. Much of it was wasted. A good number of the guests, overcome by the huge meal they had washed down with wine and floods of cider or cinnamon and juniper-spiced beer were slumped, head on folded arms, asleep at the tables.

The king had left with his queen, a brawl had broken out between drunken pages at the foot of the table, guards were hurrying into the hall and I opted to slip away. My shoulder ached, my head buzzed from the wine and the sword cut I'd taken, and my gut was uncomfortably full. Time to retreat.

Chapter 15 - Cadzand

Over the next months, my wounds healed, and I was able again to draw my bow to the fullest. I worked hard to recover that strength, spending hours a day at the butts and working with our weapons master. A year, then two, went by and I kept recruiting and training my Cheshire archers and had built a formidable force. Too, I visited Marian several times, but she had little interest in me now, although we both enjoyed our time with our son Hugh, a sturdy, merry six years old.

Marian did agree with my idea to introduce him at court – he was after all the same age as Lord Edward as they even shared their birthdate – and that had gone well. The king had handsomely rewarded all of us in his conroi and we were a practised tournament cadre now. Some of the group entered wholeheartedly into the king's obsession with Arthurian principles and playacting, but I was less enthused.

We did have an expedition of sorts to the polder lands of the Low Countries, but that first excursion was political, not military. It all began with the enthronement of a new pope, who took the name Benedict XII. The so-called White Cardinal was a rotund imbiber who made popular the phrase 'To drink like a pope,' but he was financially scrupulous, and when he found that his predecessor had accumulated chests full of gold intended for even more magnificent buildings at the papal palace in Avignon, he used them to fund a crusade.

I heard that the king wanted us to visit the Low Countries, but was unclear about all the conniving, until John Westwood cleared it up for me: "Edward, knowing that King Philip of France is about to go off on crusade has dusted off an old Lancastrian claim to Provence on behalf of Henry of Grosmont. He has also demanded the return of England's demesnes in Gascony. He expects that Philip will shrug and go to the Holy Land, so we will take an army and invade in Philip's absence. Right now, Edward plans to recruit allies in the Low Countries, to defeat the French and claim the throne in Paris."

Our king acted too quickly. The pope heard of the English claims and did not want England and France at war and imperiling his crusade. He told Philip that peace in Europe must come first, that the French had misused the papal funds for a crusade and the whole thing was cancelled. Philip decided to deal Edward a blow and while we were on an expedition against the Scots he attacked Guernsey and Jersey and moved his great crusader fleet from the Mediterranean back to the Channel ports.

Edward mustered the English navy and lavished honours on his warlords and money men. He created seven new earls, including Henry of Grosmont and turned the vacant earldom of Cornwall into a duchy, of which six years old Edward was made England's first Duke. The child was also equipped with a small suit of armour as token of his regal status and of Edward's intent to train him as a soldier.

Edward's once-humble archer, me, Sir Thomas Holland, son of a murdered rebel baron, was also given land grants and gold to sustain the fighting force I had built, and Edward made me a quiet promise: "It will soon be titles, dear Thomas. For now, I have only a certain supply to award and first my older fighting men must get them." I clasped his hand. "For you, my liege, the only worthwhile honour is to serve you."

"Well," he said, "I have a task for you and my conroi." Briefly, he wanted us to take gold to the Low Countries and use it to smooth alliances on which the English could draw for a land invasion of France. Edward was well aware that the Hainaulters resented the French and was resolved to make a coalition with them and other Flamands. He planned to move to the region for a while, appointing in his absence his small son Edward of Woodstock as Guardian of England.

As for making new allies, he advised: "You can persuade those who resist gold by suggesting we might not be supplying wool for their clothmakers," he said gently. It was a good argument. Weavers facing ruin because of interrupted supplies could bring a lot of pressure on their rulers. It was classic Edward: carrot and stick tactics. We would land a small army, and hire mercenaries and Germans, too. The Flamands and

Brabanters would reinforce us to win back from the French the stolen towns of Douai, Lille and Bethune. Or we could strangle the Flamands' trade if they chose not to cooperate.

About 40 of us dashing young courtiers, who had been encouraged first to polish our French phrases, sailed with several earls and four great iron chests of gold. In a stroke of genius inspired by Grosmont, we all wore a silk patch over one eye, a distinguishing and to the locals an intriguing identifier. The plan worked, and in a month or so we made alliances, some of them discreetly with lovely locals, some equally quietly with regional barons and magnates.

We secured promises of help, roused old enmities against the French and persuaded the Flamands to blame their Gallic neighbours for the wool boycott, causing demonstrations by angry clothworkers. The local overlord, Count Louis of Flanders blundered when he attempted to put down the protesters. He cut off the head of a popular leader and was forced to flee for his life to France.

One of our bishops agreed trade and military terms with the ruthless burgess who took the throne vacated by the count and another treaty was also agreed with the Holy Roman Emperor Louis of Bavaria. For much gold, he promised to provide troops and ordained King Edward as Vicar of the Holy Roman Empire to give him the authority he needed over his allies.

When our negotiating bishop and his companions sailed for home, the French planned an ambush. Edward's spies sniffed out the plot, and our ships trapped and defeated the attackers, capturing two ships full of Scots nobles, French soldiers, treasure and horses en route to Scotland.

Edward was furious at the French plot and authorized Sir Walter Mauny, admiral of the northern fleet, to retaliate. I knew Mauny well. A fine and bold fellow, he had come to England from his native Hainault as a page with Queen Philippa. He was appointed keeper of her greyhounds and held post as her own personal carver of meats at feasts. He had been knighted after fighting with distinction at the battles of Dupplin Moor and Halidon Hill. I was at Dover Castle and saw him after he had just received his commission to goad the French, and he greeted me affably. "Want an adventure, boy?" he said. I bristled. "You're only a few years older than I am, Walter," I said. He grinned. "Come with me on this one and beard the French. I'll look after you, sonny." I punched him in the arm. I was 24 years of age and no child.

He winced obligingly and laid out the plan: Edward wanted to goad the French into action and he'd start with an easy victory to enhearten our troops and demonstrate what we could do but the king was not yet ready to embark his main army. Mauny was to go first, establish a beach head and sweep across the island of Cadzand and its hinterland in a small *chevauchee*, a raid to destroy the countryside and inflame the French. The island was a miserable place of marsh and fishing villages containing no plunder, but it stood close to the wealthy port of Sluys, which was considered Europe's finest harbor. A destructive raid on its region should tempt that town's garrison out to repel us, and we might get inside the walls without a siege.

"I'll give you command of the archers," Mauny offered. "How many?" "Enough." "Where are we going?" "To Hainault. I'll put together a vanguard of our army – English archers for you, with a force of Saxons, Rhinelanders, Brabanters, Flamands, some Genoese mercenaries, a few thousand men. We'll tweak King Philip's nose, attack his holdings in Flanders and by the time the French have mustered some troops together, Edward of Windsor and our whole army will have landed and we'll give the French a thrashing they won't soon forget. We'll recover Gascony and Aquitaine, take wagon loads of plunder and go home rich with a whole lot of new, French mistresses.

"All you have to do is shoot that bloody great black bow I see you with all the time and for that simple task, you'll not even be able to lift all the loot you collect."

***

So it was that on a chilly October day we sailed from Dover for Hainault, met and marshalled a mixed body of troops, arranged supplies with the new count, William II, who also ruled Zeeland and Holland (by the by I made much of being

Thomas Holland, to his amusement) and began preparations to gather long wagons, beasts to pull them and artisans to make siege engines. Count William also arranged for a flotilla of barges to be gathered together to transport us to the island of Cadzand, adjacent to the well-defended port of Sluys. There was little in the way of crops on the island, so I arranged parties of mounted archers and men at arms to scour the hinterland for supplies and fodder while Sir Walter and his men rampaged across the region, burning, looting and raping.

The French did not come out from Sluys, although the plumes of smoke across the whole of Cadzand advertised what was happening just a couple of leagues away, so Mauny parlayed with the military commander of the town, Sir Guy the Bastard of Flanders, an illegitimate son of Count Louis of Nevers but could not persuade him to surrender. Both sides settled down to a siege before a shot was fired.

We were waiting for the English army to arrive, Sir Guy was busy reinforcing his defences and all was quiet, so I suggested to Duke Henry of Grosmont that we go to hunt one of the island's small deer, or at least kill a few fowl for our supper. Henry had just returned from a patrol and was in full armour, but I wore just a Jack Coat of heavy leather and took my huge longbow and a quiver of good straight arrows.

We rode into the marshes, where I shot a goose and started to clean it while Henry rode on, looking for swamp deer or otters. Later, I found that he had come to a fishing village, found a short bridge across a deep inlet, crossed it and had ridden south not realizing he was on a small peninsula.

I finished cleaning the goose, threw it over my pommel and set off in the direction Henry had taken. Soon, I spotted him on the other side of the waterway. We shouted back and forth and I was preparing to head to the small bridge – the water seemed deep and there was a tidal current running – when I spotted movement in the direction of the village he had told me about. A glint of steel told me more, and I soon spotted four men at arms trotting their horses towards Henry, who was now cut off. I yelled a warning and slid from my horse, stringing my bow and grabbing my quiver. Henry was about 70 paces away from me, with the channel making an impassable barrier between us. He seemed confident, and he was armed and in full armour. "I'll ride through these Frenchies," he shouted. "I'll meet you at the bridge," I called back. As I turned to remount my horse, Henry's horse screamed.

An *arbalestier* had fired his crossbow with admirable accuracy from more than 100 paces and struck the horse in the great vein of its neck. The animal was gouting blood, pumping out its life in a stream that steamed in the crisp air. Henry slid clumsily from the saddle as his horse buckled and I heard him swear. His armour so weighed him down that he was ankle-deep in the boggy ground. Even as I looked on, a quarrel glanced off the pauldron armour at Henry's shoulder, unbalancing him so he staggered heavily. "Are you hurt?" I shouted unnecessarily. I could do nothing if he was. "Can you swim it?" Henry shook his head. Obviously not. There was the problem. By the time he'd taken off his armour, his enemies would have gutted him.

I eyed the oncoming French, planted six arrows in the ground before me and nocked a shaft. Drawn, released, it flew true and struck the leading horse in the chest. The second arrow followed eight heartbeats later and also hit a horse square in the chest, the third shaft, following 20 heartbeats after the first, slammed into the shoulder of the third steed as its rider pulled it around. The *arbalestier* was out of the picture for a moment. He had dismounted to make his accurate shots at Henry and he was now scrambling to remount.

My fourth arrow hit him in the back of the neck, the best shot I'd so far made. He slid forward over the pommel of his saddle and fell to the ground. His horse trotted back the way it had come. The first and third horsemen were coming, but separately, for the horse I'd wounded in the shoulder had swerved away and his rider was taking time to control him. The second horse must have been hard hit for he was standing shaking. His rider slid from the saddle and advanced on foot towards Henry, who was moving stickily through the mud to meet him. He was still a distance from the Englishman, so I turned my attention to the pair who were still riding.

I had an arrow nocked and fired it at the leading horseman.

who ducked. The arrow clattered off the broad-brimmed bascinet that protected the soldier's head. I plucked the last of my standing arrows and fired it, lower this time. Alerted by the whistle of its arrival, he ducked and moved right into it. He took the missile full in the face. The impact threw him off his horse and, I guessed, out of the fight.

Now the last mounted man was almost on Henry and I had to fumble at my quiver to withdraw a couple more arrows. I need not have worried. Even hampered by the boggy ground, de Grosmont in fighting mode was a match for any mounted man. As the fellow kicked his horse forward, Henry stepped aside and swung his longsword into the animal's muzzle. I even heard the crunch across the water as its teeth shattered and watched in awe as it reared up and fell backwards, trapping rider under beast. The high pommel struck the Frenchman square on his sternum, crushing his ribcage, and he screamed just as the horse also screamed its agony, the two declarations of pain joining together.

Arrow nocked, I turned away from watching Henry. The man at arms who had been advancing on foot changed his mind and moved to catch the bridle of the horse that had carried the dead *arbalestier*. He scrambled clumsily, but the unhurt horse halted at his command and he caught its reins. The horse was facing Henry, the man scrambled to mount from the left side, lurched and momentarily was sprawled over the animal's back. My seventh and eighth arrows arrived six seconds apart and hit the man in his arse and neck, driving him right over the horse.

Henry was stumbling forward, the horse stood still. "He's still holding the damned reins," Henry shouted, stamping on the man's head with a muddy, iron-clad foot. Then he somehow heaved himself into the saddle despite the weight of armour on him and kicked his mount forward, towards the bridge, where I met him. "That was a damned good horse I lost back here," he said. "You and your stupid ideas of going out to hunt game!"

Chapter 16 - War

King Edward arrived the next day. Eager to gain a swift, easy victory, he opted to try again what had succeeded at Berwick and ordered a surprise escalade to capture the town. It was quickly detected and cost us a two score of men at arms. However, the king ordered the depredation of the region to continue and as he predicted, Sir Guy the Bastard could not ignore what was happening virtually under his walls. The Flamands came out to fight. We were ready.

Guy's men, a body of Italian, French and Genoese, thought to surprise us by crossing the channel before dawn, using a fleet of commandeered fishing boats, but Sir Walter Mauny had anticipated such a move and had paid spies inside Sluys. They lit a fire in woods a short distance from the town walls, an agreed signal of warning. Days before, Sir Walter had also made contact with a renegade Devon man who commanded a small force of mercenary routiers, the so-called Free Companies. These lawless, brutal soldiers fought for any man who could pay and their mindless savagery had been condemned by the pope himself at a Lateran council.

Many of the nobles who might have employed the mercenaries refused to do so, resenting the ascent to high office of low-born fighting men who cared nothing for the principles of chivalry. "They're godless criminals and misfits, Thomas," said Sir John Westwood. "They're freebooters who'll ransack a monastery or a village then demand payment from the locals for protection against other routiers, or even from themselves. They'll take a castle, use it as a stronghold from which to pillage the region, then sell it back to the noble who owns it. It can make vast fortunes for their captains and even the commonest man at arms becomes wealthy enough to buy himself some rank and lands, but they are without honour."

The Free Company captain with whom Mauny was doing business was an Englishman called Celvin Barnstaple, who, despite his questionable past – he said to be a refugee from murder charges in London– was a splendid fighting man. His eye for tactics had brought him victory after victory against Flemish and French militias sent to suppress him and his cohort of Gascon brigands. On being told of our arrival, he and his routiers had sailed a roundabout way to Cadzand, avoided detection by the forces from Sluys and landed in darkness on the opposite side of the island from the beaches the Flamands would use.

Mauny greeted him heartily, nodding when he was told of the invaders. "Knew about them, thanks," he said briefly. "Heard about you, glad you're here, there's plenty of work to do." The duo settled terms and discussed the upcoming conflict. "Grosmont and his men at arms will hold the centre, young Thomas has the right wing with his Welsh and Cheshire archers," I bristled obligingly at the 'young' epithet and Barnstaple grinned. "Your *cottereaux* can take the left with our javelineers and slingers," said Mauny. I didn't understand the French term, and Barnstaple must have caught my puzzlement. He slapped the long knife at his right hip. "Our blades. Good as any sword," he said, "especially if you have a spear, too."

I sized him up, a compact, sturdy man in light harness of mail over his lanolin-greased leather Jack Coat. He wore leather trews, riding boots with the hilt of a punching knife peeking out of the top, a heavy-pommelled medium sword at his left hip, and a steel sallet with a broad band to protect his head.

He looked to be a rogue, a ragged scar across his eyebrow, one gold earring, a spade beard, and a quick smile although his bright blue eyes were wary and seemed constantly to scan the area. He changed to crude French to address his henchman, a swarthy Gascon who was missing several fingers on his right hand. "Guillaume says we'll be happy on the left," he said shortly. "What horses do you have?" I spoke up. "I have 380 mounted archers." Mauny interrupted impatiently. "We have enough of everything. You just concern yourself with holding the left wing," he told Barnstaple. "We'll shoot them flat, then send mounted men in to clean up."

Soon, the discussion became animated and plans were also made to burn the fishing vessels and trap Sir Guy's men on our island. "No ransoms this time, we want to catch and kill them all, to frighten others in future conflicts," said Mauny. And we settled down to iron out just how we would spring the trap.

The Bastard of Flanders and his force arrived even before wolf light showed in the east, but their 'surprise' approach was clumsy and noisy. He had brought a few horses, but unloading them was problematic, and the 1,800 or so men at arms splashed ashore onto their beachhead careless of secrecy. Unloading took time and daylight had been with us for several hours before the invaders formed up and began tramping inland.

I watched them go, assessed the score or so Sir Guy had left to guard the fishing boats and gestured to the squad of Cheshire archers who were hiding with me in the sandhills. A dozen of them moved east, across the trail taken by the invaders, I stayed to the west with six others. The guards never had a chance. Our ambush had full surprise and the first they knew was when their comrades began to fall around them, arrow-struck.

Four or five were still writhing on the ground when we went in to finish them, and it was the work of less than an hour to cut rigging, place tinder and set fire to the fishing fleet beached on the sand. Soon, the flames began to flicker, then roar as ship after ship turned into a torch belching a plume of sparks. The wood was old and dry, and burned fiercely, although the tarry rigging sent up much smoke that could alert Sir Guy's men, but by then the whole fleet was being destroyed beyond salvage. We slipped away quietly, circled around the enemy force and joined our own army.

We did not arrive too soon, for both forces were drawn up and readying to clash. Henry of Grosmont greeted me cheerfully. "About time you came back from your adventures," he said. "I've been doing your work for you, you scamp. Your archers are more or less emplaced, on our right wing, and I have the centre." I thanked him, making a deep ironic bow and hurried to my place in the battle line where my archers were busily setting up, stabbing arrows into the ground in front of themselves, stringing new bowstrings and putting a couple more under their hats for swift replacement should they be needed.

Pages and servants were hurrying to set up behind the lines

numbers of linen bags filled with supplies of arrows. Those bags were reinforced with willow withy sticks to hold them open and prevent the fletchings from being crushed. To our right, at the extreme end of the crescent-shaped formation and atop a sand dune, Sir Henry had ordered constructed a timber emplacement that anchored the edge of our line. The fortification was within 50 paces of the water and would prove to be almost impassable.

Our archers were mustered in ranks along the front face of some dunes, facing slightly inwards and above a screen of dug-in infantry over whose heads they had a clear field of fire. The dunes levelled out somewhat towards the centre of our lines, where Grosmont's men at arms had established an excellent defensive position, with deep holes and trenches dug in front of them against any cavalry attack. I noted that the pits were lined with sharpened stakes and that Henry had ordered caltrops scattered about to halt any cavalry charge.

Our preparations were complete and I had ordered food delivered to my formation when there was a stir in the enemy ranks and a pair of heralds came out to parley. Mauny, Grosmont and I rode out to negotiate, turned down the peremptory demands to surrender and I was back among my archers before my stew had gone cold.

The battle that followed was just as short and sharp. Sir Guy threw his skimpy cavalry force at us first, they were halted by our defences and as they hesitated at very short range, were quickly shot down by the flanking archers and slingers. Guy should have backed away at that point, but he hurled his men at arms into the fray, threading them between clusters of fallen, thrashing horses only to see them, too, halted at our defensive lines and shot down by our arrow storm.

Suddenly, it was a rout and the French began to throw away their arms and armour to run from the killing field. We had few cavalry for the pursuit, but the French were trapped anyway – their retreat had been cut off when we burned their ships. Our men at arms slowly closed the ring of steel that surrounded the enemy, and no mercy was shown. Guy and his nobles were taken for ransom, but his soldiers were trapped on the beach and put to the sword. A few splashed into the channel in forlorn hopes of making the long swim back to Sluys, but a dozen or so of our own boats manned by mercenaries under the renegade Barnstaple got in among the fugitives and clubbed and speared them like fish.

Within a matter of a day we left the gutted, smoking island and went about ravaging its hinterland, undisturbed by the remains of the garrison at Sluys. Our uncontested depredations brought hatred on the English, but undermined the authority of the French king, Philip who took no action to defend his holdings or his people. It was the result we had sought and Edward sported his new banner of leopards and lilies and declared himself king of England and of France.

Back in England, things were changing. The king's younger brother, John of Eltham, who had fought at Halidon Hill, died of a sudden fever. Edward was distraught, beset by nightmares and decided that the young prince, Edward of Woodstock, would assume the duties of his dead uncle. "Edward is going to give the boy estates to enlarge his Duchy of Cornwall, he's to have his own household and won't be staying with his mother any more. The boy might only be seven years old, but Edward is determined to make a warrior of him," said John Westwood.

The young prince was also being groomed as a diplomat and was furnished with glorious garments of purple velvet, a pearl-encrusted hat and a ribbon belt adorned with more than 200 pearls and three dozen enameled ornaments. Thus accoutred, he met a peace delegation comprised of a brace of cardinals sent by the pope, who hoped to broker understanding between England and France. In the child's entourage was a new playmate: Hugh of Mobberley, the son Marian had given me after our short passion. Her father, a de Trafford, had influence at court and noted that both boys shared their birthday, so had presented his grandson at court with some generous gifts and young Hugh became a royal page who shared Edward's weapons training.

The boys became friends, Marian was appointed to lady in waiting to Queen Philippa and settled to life at court, where Edward planned a voyage to Flanders.

"King Edward has no illusions about peace with France," said

Westwood. "He's off to Hainault to wine and dine the Germans, Flamands and Brabanters and gather forces against Philip while his son acts as Guardian of England, but really it's a couple of earls and the archbishop of Canterbury who'll be making the decisions back at home."

The king's efforts in Flanders were slow to pay off, and the allies he wanted dragged their heels, made excuses and wasted time. At last, in the autumn of 1339 he began to devastate the region around Cambrai to goad Philip of France to meet him in battle. It nearly happened, but then Philip changed his mind, dug a defensive position, considered matters then quietly slipped away.

Edward had declared himself King of both England and France, pitting the Plantagenets against the House of Valois. To underscore his claims, he displayed the arms of the two nations, lilies and leopards, on his banners in the market square of Ghent; swore on Saint George to his claim and contracted his son Edward of Woodstock to marry Margaret of Brabant, ensuring an alliance of forces and an influx of desperately-needed funds. Meanwhile, he was assembling a war fleet of more than 100 ships in eastern England, on the River Stour.

John Westwood was involved in gathering the fleet and spoke with me in worried tones: "Even the young prince knows his father is in great danger. The king is insisting on sailing in cogs converted into warships by constructing wooden 'castles' at bow and stern so the archers can have firing platforms. The problem is that the cogs are sluggish merchantmen and the French know we're coming.

"They were planning to attack our herring fleet at Yarmouth, but were scared off by Sir Robert Morley. Now, they have a great navy of warships harboured at Zwin and our spies report that a squadron of Genoese galleys have just reinforced them. If they catch us at sea, we'll likely be out-sailed and out-fought. On land, the French can't stand up to our troops – they've been battle-hardened in Scotland – but the quality of their ships is far superior to ours and they'll out-sail and sink us."

I went hawking with the king and bluntly asked if he had doubts about the respective qualities of our fleet compared to the French one. He was adamant: "Every advisor except one says we can't face them, but our sailors know about fighting, most of theirs do not. I have ideas on how to face them and I'll fight them in ways and places where I have the initiative, Thomas. Have faith: I'll not let my ship be sunk!" I had to smile: Edward had named his flagship 'Thomas' in a generous compliment to me. "Don't send me under the waves, your grace," I said in mock supplication. "I am not a good swimmer." He grimaced, and I recalled his statement that one advisor seemed to think we could face the French at sea intrigued me. "Who has faith in our navy, your grace?" I asked, before hastily adding: "Except me, of course."

Edward smiled. "You know him well. He fought with us at Berwick, Thomas." I must have looked puzzled, for the king added: "A Zeelander." Then, I understood. John Crabbe, a Flemish merchant, soldier and pirate had preyed for years on English merchantmen. He'd seized a countess' treasures, Newcastle merchants' wine and wool and had even kidnapped sailors. The old king had spent years trying to get reparations out of the Flamands, but wily Crabbe had based himself in Aberdeen and was protected by the Scots until he was captured, fell into Edward's hands and changed his coat.

Five years ago, Crabbe took command of a fleet of ten English ships for his new master and kept the sea lanes to the Low Countries clear of pirates so Edward could send English wool there to finance his war on the French. "I've given him command of 100 archers, 70 sailors and a double handful of men at arms," said Edward, "and he's keeping an eye on the French." Crabbe carried out his orders, and in early summer reported that purpose-built Castilian and Genoese war galleys were being mustered to join the French fleet at Zwin, a port in Flanders. And so, we readied for war. I was eager to fight but I had a pang at leaving my new lover.

She was young, fair and stunningly beautiful, a Plantagenet called Joan of Kent, and her cousin Edward, my king, introduced me to her at a ball. We fell at once, were both ardent, I was her first love and we spoke of betrothal, but I had to go to war. There would be time for marriage later, but we went through a private exchange of vows. For now, it was best we keep our love a secret. I carried two tokens of Joan's love. The first, a silken scarf, I kept pressed against my heart, the other, a small silver ring, I wore on my smallest finger. I had never felt such passion in all my ironclad life.

Chapter 17 - Sluys

Sir Robert Morley came from the north, but was first to arrive at Holbrook, the English navy's rendezvous on the River Stour, with 50 ocean-going, square-rigged cogs, all of them larger than the French vessels, but slow to manoevre and deep-draughted where the French ships were nimble and could operate well in shallow water. "We don't have an actual fleet of warships," said Sir John Westwood gloomily, as we rode ahead of the royal entourage, "and neither do the French, but they have somehow persuaded the Spanish to send their galleys and they've paid the Genoese for theirs. They'll be a problem for us, they're swift and highly mobile."

"The king is not impressed," I asserted. "He plans to meet them on our terms, not on theirs, and he has expressed great confidence in Master Crabbe, who told him that the French sailors have little experience."

We stopped speaking, taking in the view that had suddenly opened up before us as we emerged from woodland on a small hill. The low-lying terrain around the Stour let us see the bustle and provisioning traffic around the small port: drovers herding lowing cattle into rough pens set up by the army, for soldiers needed beef and shepherds from the wolds brought in the walking mutton they also required. The herds of beasts were interspersed with mule trains carrying grain and great nets of forage, and with convoys of creaking wagons laden with barrels of salted ham, cod and pork, Spanish olive oil, twice-baked bread, beer, wine and salt. Long wagons carrying the timber, rope and iron that would be constructed into siege equipment creaked along ahead of the disassembled catapults and trebuchets which also lurched along the sun-baked, rutted tracks. They in turn followed leather-covered carriages that carried bundles of javelins, sheaves of arrows, stacked piles of shields, breastplates and helmets and rope-tied bundles of spears, pikes, crossbow bolts and poleaxes.

Close to the water, we saw the smoke from low buildings that were evidently smiths' forges, and piles of timber showed where carpenters were constructing crows' nests for the single sturdy mast each blunt-bowed vessel boasted. The same carpenters built fore and after castles to be mounted on the cogs. From these fighting platforms archers and crossbowmen would pour down fire and huge rocks on the enemy before boarding parties were launched.

John nudged me as we sat our mounts, taking in the bustling scene. "See the catapult mounted in the bows of that cog?" he asked. "Master Crabbe had something similar on his ship when he took a Hollander with 160 wine tuns. It throws an iron bolt as long as a man is tall, and can pierce inches of oak. Master Crabbe said that many ship's captains would surrender after just one or two bolts went through the hull. It's a deadly weapon!"

It was hard to pick out one cog among so many – I later learned that we had about 80 ships in the fleet – for they were clustered like bees in a hive. I spotted at mastheads the arms of the earls of Arundel and Huntingdon, who had brought fleets from the west country and from the Cinque Ports and saw Baron Mauny's standard fluttering above a green-and-white striped pavilion set as far as possible from the stench of the cattle pens and the smoky forges of the smiths.

We rode down to the tent lines, passing a dozen decrepit sailboats with smashed decks. They seemed abandoned, although they were packed with brushwood that stuck up through the open hatches and broken decking. John caught my glance and once again had an answer: "Fire ships," he said briefly. "They'll not be readied until the last minute. The thing sailors fear most is fire, and one here would be disastrous."

I spotted a horse herd corralled at a distance from the cattle and thought that another thing sailors feared was the threat posed by soldiers' mounts. I'd seen the damage a panicked war horse could do to a gunwale as he was swung aboard, and wondered how many chargers would be shipped to Flanders in these cockleshells. I just hoped there would be none in the vessel in which I sailed. Three dawns later, I had my answer when I went to the harbor to board my transport. Just one destrier: the king's mount, Stamper was swayed aboard the

Thomas, but the cog was full. Not only was Edward and his entourage aboard, but Queen Philippa and a dozen of her ladies went along, too. One of them, Lady Viginia Glossop acted as a secret go-between and brought me a passionate letter from my Joan, to which I responded with an equally-ardent missive, promising to make our love public once this campaign ended.

Joan mentioned that she had been present at the celebration of the tenth birthday of King Edward's son Edward, who was named as Guardian of England in his father's absence. He was, she said, in London, safe in the Tower. First, though, the boy had made an offering at the shrine of St Edmund, praying for his parents' safety, and had himself rowed out to the Thomas to make his farewells.

"The word is that Philip of France has a great fleet waiting for us at Zwin, in Flanders," John Westwood told me, "but Edward wants to push up that waterway to Bruges to meet his new allies. The chancellor isn't happy. He says our ships are inferior, our numbers are fewer and he'll resign if Edward doesn't wait and reinforce our fleet." I was incredulous. "What does a churchman know about fighting a naval battle?" I asked. "He might know a lot," said John grimly, "but Edward is determined to go now and Sir Robert Morley and his fleet are with the king."

When I saw Edward later, I asked him about the archbishop's advice. "He's come around to it," said the king. "I told him for all that their pirates roam the Channel, the French are not experienced at sea battles, and our archers will win the day. It's important that I am the one to determine how and where we fight, we'll not take on the French on their terms."

So we sailed from the Stour at midnight on a brisk northwesterly wind and our fleet made a brave sight under a bright moon, with banners flying, men at arms cheering from every hull and even the lantern-lit bright silks and jewels of the Queen's lovely entourage to encourage us as we breasted the moonlit summer waves. At dawn, all in the king's conroi were in harness, mail and plate gleaming, swords buckled on, our jupons bearing the quartered arms of England and France in support of the king's claim. "Truly a chivalric, knightly sight," said Edward, his eyes glistening with emotion, "truly a brotherhood of courage and gallantry."

I wasn't too sure about the courage and gallantry of some of our knightly brethren, in fact I knew that some of them were outright cowards, but if the king wanted to indulge his dreams of Camelot, I knew enough to stay silent.

We sailed until the waters became cloudy with runoff an unseen river, gulls flew screaming around our mastheads and the low coastline came into view. At that, the steersman made a small correction of course and our fleet wheeled with us. A half hour went by and we saw the enemy's yards and masts, but no sails were set.

Edward swore a mild oath, then apologised to Philippa. "Your pardon, my lady," he said courteously. The queen merely smiled. "They are very close together," she said. The words were hardly out of her lips when a sharp-eyed young sailor in the crow's nest shouted down, his voice crackling with excitement. "They're fastened together, masters," he called. "It looks like a floating castle with wooden walls!"

Edward called for reduced sail and we crept closer. "God's beard!" he swore again, but this time did not apologise to the queen, for he was utterly focused on the enemy line. He gestured at the big merchantman. "That's the Christopher! The rogues stole her at Southampton and now use her against me! We'll anchor here, time to talk with our captains."

Scouts in heavily-manned skiffs that were too fast and too nimble for even the Genoese war galleys went closer to view the French fleet. What they reported made Edward smile. Philip's flotilla was ordered tightly, chained together gunwale to gunwale and anchored in three lines across the three-miles-wide estuary of the River Zwin. They looked impressively intimidating, a forest of bare poles above fortified bows and decks crowded with armed men, but Edward slapped me on the back. "That goose is cooked, Thomas," he chortled. "They think they can fight a land battle on the water, but they've wasted the two rear ranks because their front line blocks them from the fighting.

"We'll get close enough for our archers, slingers,

crossbowmen and catapults to do their work and destroy them one rank at a time. St George has smiled on us!"

So it was in the mid-afternoon, with sun and wind behind us, we sailed at the front rank of the French fleet. Edward ordered our trebuchets – we had three of them mounted on our biggest cogs – to the right flank of the French line where the curve and current of the river would make the water deeper and allow our ships to edge closer to the locked-in-place anchored enemy. He then ordered a strong screen of archer-laden cogs around them to defend against the galleys that were the only mobile ships in the enemy force.

Our artillery ships manoevered into position unchallenged, keeping Cadzand to our right and a dyke lined with armed Flamands to the left. We sailed on an incoming tide that had pushed the enemy line closer together, impeding themselves even more. "Admiral Quieret is cautious," remarked Edward, "but Signor Bocanegra is at last beginning to move his galleys." On cue, the first of the Genoese warships edged sluggishly from its position behind the second rank of cogs.

Before it could clear the French formation, our vicious trebuchets opened up with boulders on the main target, the St Denis, a royal warship with 200 men aboard. The artillerymen fired down the length of the tethered line of shipping and could hardly miss. All our they had to do was aim straight, high and not too long. The big rocks were hurled skywards and plunged down near-vertically to smash through the bodies of hapless men and shatter the hulls of their immobile ships.

Our artillery crews loaded boulder after boulder, rounded river rocks brought from mountain streams in England and Wales and flung them up into the air above the locked line of the French flotilla. Down they smashed in a remorseless, deadly rain of rock that spattered blood, entrails and brains and made jagged splinters fly to wound more men, puncture the hulls and panic the survivors. There was nowhere to run, the cogs were chained together, and as the rocks rained down, we poured our deadly clothyard arrows onto the French like a winter hailstorm.

It all went on to the accompaniment of agonised screams from crushed and dying men, and we watched in awed horror as enemy soldiers began jumping from their ships' sides to escape, only to sink under the weight of their own armour. When the moment was ripe and the enemy were shot to ribbons by our missiles, our men at arms grappled onto the French line and swarmed aboard to hack the survivors into bloody ruin.

While we took ship after ship with arrow storm and pikes, the terrible artillery bombardment continued unending on other parts of the locked-together line. Finally, the only ships moving on the enemy side, the galleys began to row towards our artillery ships. At their approach, our own cogs interceded with a deadly hail of arrow shafts, crossbow bolts and the slingers' leaden bullets. The missiles smashed into the crowded benches of unshielded rowers, killing scores in just minutes. The wounded and dying oarsmen broke stroke, but the whistling rain of iron-tipped ash and birch shafts continued to beat down on them. Archers in our cogs' fore and after castles skewered the rowers, while from the looming crows' nests above, our most accurate longbow men aimed for the steersmen and officers on their afterdecks. It took just a few hundred heartbeats for the deadly arrow storm to kill or cripple almost all of them.

Unprotected men could not withstand such punishment and the Genoese in their open galleys shrank away from the missiles. Some turned away to avoid receiving a quarrel or clothyard arrow in the face, only to have one thump deep into their neck or shoulders. Men scrambled to huddle in any shelter they could find to escape that death storm, but in only minutes after each galley came under fire, it was crippled as its oarsmen died or cowered in hiding, some of them seeking shelter under the bodies of their dead comrades.

With all but a few galleys out of the battle, Edward waved forward our reserve cogs with their archer-packed castles. He sent them in threes, two packed with archers, the third with men at arms. They were ordered to grapple the artillery-battered enemy vessels, so the archers could pour in fire at close range and soften up the enemy before the soldiers boarded them. The trios sailed briskly downwind, and the king signaled them closer to the French line where frantic serjeants were trying to unchain their vessels from the ships on either side of them. It was all too late and what Admiral Hugues Quieret had seen as an impregnable line of oak and iron became a deadly trap and killing ground.

The French were as pinioned as a wolf in a trap and while our archers punished their soldiers, our trebuchets pounded their ships into wreckage and our catapults thumped long, iron bolts through the knots of humanity huddled in their scuppers.

Some of our cogs closed on the battered French too quickly, attempting to board their enemies' vessels before they were properly subdued and the French resisted ferociously. Now began a phase of brutal hand-to-hand fighting that saw ships taken and re-taken as desperate men armed with axes, pikes and swords trampled the wounded underfoot as they scrambled to kill or be themselves killed. No quarter was given by the English for the French had flown the oriflamme which announced that it was battle to the death.

Over all the bloodshed and clanging noise of metal on metal came the occasional boom of one of the English guns, punctuating the constant cacophony of screams and moans of the wounded and the unceasing, fizzing zip of the arrows that brought horror and death.

Something caught my attention, maybe it was the unexpected scent of wood smoke. I turned from my post at the after-castle to look and saw a familiar group of ruinous-looking cogs under full sail bearing down on the second French line. Several of them were being towed by longboats as well as moving under sail, boosted by the stiffening wind. Their speed through the water was creating a feather of foam under their bows, so rapidly were they moving. They looked like wolves loping down to a sheep fold.

As I watched, the oarsmen in the towing longboats hastily cast off and sheered away. That was when I saw the curls of smoke and flicker of flames rising from the open hatches. The following cogs, under sail alone, were each trailed by a tethered rowboat and the few men on each of the burning cogs hauled the small boats in and scrambled down into them.

"They'll have tied the steerboards in place, those fire ships will go right into Quieret's line," said Edward, snarling with anticipation. He turned to the Thomas' captain. "Go closer, but for the Virgin's sake, stay upwind." I could no longer stand and watch. "Your grace," I asked, "may I join the archers?" Edward looked at me blankly, his mind on every action of the conflict. "Yes, whatever," he dismissed me. I retrieved my great black longbow, paused to strip off my constricting jupon with the royal arms on it and turned to clamber up the rigging to the crow's nest, where I took a place among the half-dozen archers crowding it.

One man was busy hauling up linen bags loaded with sheaves of arrows, another was directing fire on the enemy captains and steersmen, but the galleys that were our targets were already almost hors de combat.

Our fire ships were bumping into the bows of the line of chained French vessels and, as our sails flared like giant candles, he French rigging began to burn. Near one end of the line, a French mast toppled, blazing, onto its neighbor. I saw men in full harness leap from a burning Pisan round ship, splash into the sea and vanish, never to surface.

Below me, on the after deck, Edward was shouting encouragement and waving his sword. All eyes were on the burning French line and I felt the Thomas list as our men poured to the gunwale to watch their enemies die. The archer next to me gave a startling gurgle and slumped against me, gouting hot blood on my neck and shudder. I hauled him upright but the man was dying and I saw protruding from the archer's neck the short, iron quarrel that some *arbalestier* had fired from his crossbow.

A heavy thump struck the timbers of the crow's nest as another bolt hit home and I glanced sideways to see that somehow a high-prowed Genoese galley had grappled onto the Thomas and its men were swarming in relative silence over the gunwales. No Englishmen appeared to have noticed. Edward was intent on the battle in front of him, as was the small crowd of men at arms, and the enemy soldiers were climbing aboard behind their backs.

I yelled a warning which went unheard and knew I had to be at Edward's side or see my king captured or killed. I swung through the glory hole in the deck of the crow's nest, and slid down the rigging, burning and tearing even my calloused, horny archer's hands before I jumped the last eight or so feet to the deck, where at once a Genoese boarder stabbed at me with a pike. My descent and crashing arrival saved me and I lurched, causing the pike to pass me. I seized the shaft, pulled two-handed and deflected it downwards into the deck. The soldier was still moving towards me, my hands were occupied, so I head-butted him, hearing his nose crunch as he went backwards, knocked unconscious.

Behind me, I heard a rallying cry as Henry of Lancaster saw the danger from the French boarders. I seized a fallen pike and swept it across the knees of an axeman who was coming at me. The shaft broke but the fellow went to the deck, bellowing in pain. I grabbed his axe and ran at a small group who were skirting the main rally to attack Henry. I still had half the pikestaff in one hand, and the fire in my blood made the axe feel like a lightweight stick in my other hand.

Two of the Genoese turned on me. I rammed the staff into the teeth of the first and swung the axe at the other just as he swung his sword. The weapons clashed, the sword blade broke and I back-handed the axe head into the man's spine, collapsing him with all my archer's strength behind the blow.

Henry and a skinny, dark Welshman called Ianto had their backs to me and were fighting the boarders. Ianto clubbed one down with his edged mace, but a second Genoese soldier speared him under the ribs in his left side and the Welshman went down coughing blood. Lancaster faced several men at arms, one with a spear, two with swords. I still had my axe and I chopped viciously at the knee of the first swordsman. The weight of my weapon was too much. He tried to parry the blow but the heavy axe head turned his blade aside and crunched into his leg, collapsing the man to the deck.

Something struck hard on the back of my head and the world blurred. I stumbled, saw Lancaster crash his own mace down on an attacker just as a third man ran at him from the side with levelled sword. Somehow I swung my axe. The stroke seemed feeble, but it caught the fellow on the hip and swung him so the blow missed the earl. I was dizzy, could not stand and sank to one knee. The swordsman flicked his blade at my eyes, I swayed aside and jabbed upwards with the axe. It missed and my opponent's sword crashed onto my previously-wounded left shoulder with a blinding flash of pain. He raised his blade for another sweep and I poured every last drop of my willpower and failing strength into a stumbling lunge forward and upwards even as I grabbed at the punching dagger I kept at the nape of my neck.

The hilt was in my hand, the blade came loose of the scabbard, my arm straightened at the exact instant I thrust my whole body at the swordsman, inside the sweep of his blade. He saw the action and reversed to hammer his sword down on my unprotected head but I drove the knife deep into his crotch just as he missed my bare skull but clubbed me instead with the heavy pommel of his sword on the exposed nape of my neck. It was what my fencing master had called 'the blow of two widows,' when opponents each commit to a killing stroke at the same moment.

For me, it was the end of the battle. I awoke in darkness lit by the still-burning wreckage of King Philip's ships, several of which still floated. A man was holding my heavy gold neck chain and was rummaging through the purse at my belt but I felt too feeble to stop him. He started violently when he realized I was alive. "You, you get off me," I whispered. My lips were cracking. He stood and I recognized him, a toady hanger-on at court. His name was Caoler or some such, a treacherous Scots renegade.

"I thought you were French, you wear no insignia," he said defiantly. "You're that archer of Edward's, aren't you?" I was too tired to respond. His rat-like eyes gleamed. "Why are you hiding here, did you think the French would take you for one of their own?" I licked my lips. I was thirsty and hurting. "You're a thief and a looter," I rasped. "I'll have you hanged." "No," he said, his mouth breaking into a crooked smile. "You're a deserter. You are not wearing English colours. I should kill you now."

He stood over me, hesitant, then drew his sword. I cursed my enfeebled self and tried to get up onto one elbow. He took a step back to swing the sword and stopped abruptly. "There's a Frenchy here," he said to the shadowy figure who had just padded up on bare feet. A sailor. "Oh, we'll deal with him," said the newcomer. "One more dropped overboard won't matter. If fish could speak, they'd talk French, they're eating enough of them right now." And the seaman casually clubbed me unconscious. Again.

Chapter 18 - Bruges

Distant voices like angels' roused me, the sound of nuns in choir, all chanting in Latin. A Mass. The familiar words were comforting and I kept still, eyes closed while my mind tried to cope with memories. Blank. Time to see where I was, but my eyes were sticky, opening them was an effort and the light hurt, but I squinted. Whitewashed stone walls, a crucifix. Something was wrapped across my head. I could move my hand, cautiously groped it up to my forehead and touched linen. I was bandaged.

Slowly, memories returned. The fireships, hand to hand combat, the lunge and the shattering blow on my head. The snakelike Scot, Caoler. And the second explosion inside my head. I must have groaned because an old nun glided silently across the chamber. "You are awake, yes?" she said. French. Was I a prisoner? My eyeballs seemed rusted, set grittily into their sockets, it hurt even to roll them sideways to glimpse the questioner. "Are you with me?" she said in English. I began to nod, but the movement brought a wave of nausea. My voice crawled from its cave to croak: "Yes. I am here." Bloody stupid response, I thought, of course I'm here. "Here, sister, here is where?" Even my speech was jumbled. Get a grip, Thomas. "Where is here, sister?" I tried again. "Ah, bon," she said. "Would you like water?" Would I? I had never wanted it more. My tongue suddenly seemed like a piece of wood, glued to the roof of my mouth. Some sort of sound escaped which she took for an affirmative and soon, cool water was trickling its lifegiving way down my throat.

The sister evaporated away and returned in minutes with a younger nun who took my wrist and felt my pulse with a cold hand then issued a short stream of instructions to the older woman. Two hours later, I was sitting propped up, sleepily full of a tasty gruel of some sort and only vaguely wondering about my future. If I were a prisoner, I did not care. I was not drowned, not stabbed, not arrow-struck. My head ached and my shoulder was brutally painful but I was alive and not inspiring the fish to speak French.

For nine days, the gentle nuns in the convent of Our Lady of Aardenbourg brought me back to health, told me with horror how every tide brought in more bodies and how they prayed for the dead of both sides. They even a carter to take me to Bruges to rejoin my army. Where I fell from grace.

Edward was staying in a grand merchant's fortified house and was working to improve the wool trade links as well as to recruit forces and to rest after his famous victory. The city was a bustling, optimistic place as the Flamands grasped at their chance to cast off French rule. I arrived at the royal residence to a gruff reception from the guards, some of whom I knew well enough, but was at last admitted to the king's presence.

"You dare to show your face, my lord?" Edward scowled at me. I bowed, recovered, and said as mildly as I could that I had no idea why he was displeased, if that were the case. "Displeased?" his voice was a bellow. "You ran from the battle, you disguised yourself as a Frenchman!" There was a ringing in my ears, a mist of disbelief across my vision. "I have no sense of what you speak, your grace," I said. Edward stood up from his seat. "You threw off my insignia, you hid among the dead and dying. Did you think to emerge at battle's end, safe and unhurt and claiming to be on the winning side, whichever that was?"

I felt as though he had punched me in the chest with a mailed gauntlet. "Who tells you these lies?" I demanded. "The knight who saved you from being drowned, Sir Brian of Caoler." "Drowned?" The story was becoming even more fantastical. "He fought off a sailor who wanted to loot you and throw you overboard." Only later did I find that Caoler had murdered the sailor because he wanted my gold chains and coins for himself. He had actually started to drag me to the rail to throw me into the sea when another mariner approached and, thinking the wretch was taking me for medical help, assisted in carrying me to a physician.

"He lies, your grace," I said hotly. "You are deceived." "I am never deceived," said Edward, in anger at being challenged. "I was deceived by you, but it seems you are not worthy of your spurs. You are a coward, and I dismiss you from my circle. We represent courage and honour, yours was the deceitful act of a thief. You did not fight for your comrades, you hid in hopes of saving your own miserable skin."

He looked around. "Send for Caoler, you!" This was to a serving man, who scurried away in fear. "You can hear the truth from one who witnessed it, you creature!" I shook my aching head, disbelieving, but the slimy Caoler was sliding like a lizard into the chamber, obsequiously bowing low to the king, secretly sneering at me. Edward reiterated what he had said, that the Scot had saved me, I tried to protest, Caoler was smirking and my Angevin demon blood boiled up in a black overwhelming rage. I took two quick paces, snatched the punching knife from its hidden place at my nape and went to threaten the lying wretch, thinking to force him to tell the truth, but he shrieked, began to back away, stumbled into a stool and fell forward, right onto my blade.

It went in under his breastbone, sliced through wool, linen and flesh and burst his deceitful heart. He bled out in 90 or so pulses and the guards had me pinioned, disarmed and under threat of a blade even before he gasped his last. Three slab-faced soldiers dragged me from the king's presence and pushed me into a heavy-doored cellar which had plainly been used as a prison. "You don't carry arms into the king's presence, and you certainly don't kill his servants," the serjeant told me, punching me in the gut to underscore his words of advice. I doubled up, retching, they slammed and bolted the door and clattered off, up the stone steps. I took it that I was out of Edward's favour.

I spent more than a month in that dank Bruges cellar, but at least it gave me time to heal properly. For a short time, I had a cellar companion, a charlatan convicted of selling poisonous 'medicine' to the locals. I was taken out in chains to watch his punishment, presumably to let me experience some dread of what might be in store for me, too. I noticed that my guards seemed to be paying ghoulishly eager attention to my reactions, so I remained stone-faced.

Outside in the courtyard, someone had left a big wooden wagon wheel lying on the stones. My cellar companion, a

Brabanter called Simon, was chained to the rim at wrists and ankles and a pair of executioners began beating him with iron cudgels, crushing his bones and limbs as he screamed for mercy. One of my guards helpfully informed me that the torture could go on for days. "Last year, in Ghent, a Jew lasted four days on the Breaking Wheel," he said proudly. "That wheel had spikes, too, that pinned him in place. He was a strong man and the executioners finally had to finish him off. They beat his chest and stomach. It was a good spectacle."

The guards tired of watching when the Brabanter passed out and stopped screaming. Observing the executioners beating a limp body was boring, so they returned me to my cellar, gave me a few thumps for luck and left. I made mental note of my chief tormentor, whom I called Cabbage Ear. One day, I would kill him.

Three days later, my tormentor was at my cell door, to chain me and take me up into the manor where a guest was waiting. It was the last person I would have expected: Marian de Trafford, as lovely and fresh as ever. Next to her was her confessor, the Benedictine canoness Joan the Palmer. I was acutely conscious of my own filthy self, stinking of stale sweat, dirt and human grease. Marian's eyes opened wide. "What have they done to you, Thomas?" she said gently. I shook my shaggy head. "Not enough," I said grimly. "I'll survive them all." "Do you need a doctor?" asked Joan, who I recalled was a physician. "I'm fine, thank you, sister," I said. Marian was busying herself with a wicker basket. "We brought you food," she said. "They've searched it, but it's all right." She stared at me as she said it, conveying a message. "Thank you," I said, cautiously. "How is Hugh?" Her face brightened. "He's well, he's at Windsor with Edward, the Prince of Wales as he is since King Edward appointed him." I smiled.

Before I could ask why she was here, so far from Cheshire, she burst out her news: with Queen Philippa's help, she had petitioned the king to take me back to England for a proper trial. "At least the matter will be dealt with in the light," she said. "If you remain here, they'll quietly dispose of you and nobody will know." I agreed, and we made arrangements about an escort, a ship and gold. I was taken back to my cell and I examined the bread, meat and small baked cakes Marian had brought.

The little cakes were the only things in the basket that had not been cut or broken open, so I did it cautiously. One of them contained a coiled loop of wire, a garotte. All it needed was a pair of small handles, and pieces wood would suffice. I looked at the wicker basket and realized that someone had cleverly woven two short lengths of wood into the handle. Each had a hole drilled to receive the wire of the choking weapon. It took two minutes to assemble it and I felt comfortable. I was armed again.

Two days later, the guards came, two of them, and manacled my hands before me. "We're sending you back to England, you pig," said Cabbage Ear. I tried to look contrite and humble and he laughed. We started for the door, and as the first guard started up the stairs, I said: "I need to piss." Cabbage Ear snorted, but I turned back to the stinking piss pot in the corner of the cellar. As I hoped, he came after me to grab my shoulder. "No time for that," he said. They were his last words. I swung around, dropped the loop of the wire noose over his head and fell backwards, yanking hard. His fingers came up to my face, clawing for my eyes but I head-butted him in the face and he reeled backwards.

At arm's length so he could not reach me, I used my archer's fearsome strength to choke him with the garotte. His face empurpled, his eyes stood out, his lips went blue and flecked with spittle and he was dead. I took a moment, slowly reached down and removed the wire from his neck. It coiled easily into my hand, useful in case I needed it again. I savoured the moment, then stepped slowly over his body. "You won't abuse any other poor bastard," I said quietly.

There was no noise from outside, so I quietly opened the cellar door, which had swung closed, bolted it behind me and trod up the stone steps. The other guard was waiting by the next door. "Where's Christophe?" he said. "He had to piss, he said to get moving quickly, something about the tide, and go to the harbor, he'll see us there." The guard, who was notably stupid, shrugged.

His prisoner was manacled, he was going to England, why would he wish to escape? We marched the few hundred paces to the river, and he handed me over to a cog captain eager to catch the outgoing tide. The captain was busily ordering sails hauled, anchor raised, this stowed, that wrapped, the other coiled. A deckhand locked me, still manacled, inside a fish-smelling cabin and I found myself on a captured French cog rushing down the River Reie and heading for England.

Chapter 19 - Trial

King Edward viewed me with distaste. "You were my trusted friend but you have shamed my court with your cowardice. You also transgressed my law and even killed a man in my presence. I want you tried for murder." There was nothing I could say. I had reacted to false charges, the killing was an accident. All I had wanted was to scare Caoler into a confession. Nothing for it, now. I straightened up, gazed steadily at a spot just above Edward's gold circlet and said: "Under the law, I claim the right to trial by combat."

The court stirred and Edward glanced to his left, where Cuthbert DeBoeuf stood, massive and impassive, a vast rock of a man with shaved head, overbearing brows and thighs that looked as if they could power a boulder across a river. The King's Champion was prepared for the challenge.

Marian and Philippa had been sure to get word to his handlers, assuring him that I was a weakling and a coward. Edward stood up from his throne. "So be it. The matter is in God's hands." And in my sword, I thought bitterly as my onetime friend the king swept out of the chamber.

The next day, an hour after dawn, the King's Champion and I met in the lists at Windsor. An area about 20 paces square was marked off with willow wands laid upon the ground, a bishop intoned a grace and an exhortation against sorcery – both Cuthbert and I had to swear we were neither bewitched nor had employed a sorcerer to aid us - and we stepped into the marked area, choosing opposite corners.

I carried Salvation, the beautiful, balanced sword Edward had gifted to me and fervently wished it would live up to its name. I wore a mail shirt but no other armour. Cuthbert glanced at it in contempt. He wore no armour at all, just trews and a sleeveless leather jerkin that displayed his huge arms and an assortment of illegible blue tattoos. It was a powerful statement of confidence, but it did not cow me. He swung a long, edged mace and I noted that he wore heavy, steel-tipped boots, and considered how to avoid the kicks I felt sure he would employ.

An hour before our combat, while I was still incarcerated, I had asked Master Leatham, my old archery tutor, to survey the fighting ground and he had reported it dry, absent of grass and fairly firm. He could not tell exactly what patch would be used – the judges chose it on arrival – but he felt it would give best traction to a ridge-soled, lighter shoe. And that was what I wore, tightly laced. The ground looked firm enough, sandy, with a scuffed patch of soil to the east.

The bishop, important in his buskins, wallowed in the moment and sonorously informed me that if I lost this combat I would be adjudged guilty and hanged here. He looked around to see if anyone had erected a gallows, but there was none and he seemed disappointed. He droned on about the rules and declared that if I could defeat Cuthbert or at least survive his onslaughts until sunset, I would be let free. He seemed confident I would not last beyond his second breakfast. He made no mention of what would happen to Cuthbert if I won, but I knew the champion would be liable for fines and the king's displeasure, which could mean a loss of his royal duties and even of his standing as a freeman. The big man yawned. He'd done this a score of times before, it was just another brief encounter and a smash-down victory.

"Save yourself, serf," he called. "Strip naked, leave your weapon with your clothes and crawl away out of the arena after you thank me for my mercy." I shook my head. "I think I'll take you down and feed your carcass to my pigs." I paused as if in thought, then added: "Of course, I'll have to knock out all your teeth first. They don't digest well, and I don't want you upsetting my pigs' stomachs. It's considerate of you that you shaved your lumpy head – they don't digest hair very well, either." Some foot soldier laughed, and I saw that Cuthbert was getting angrier by the minute. Good, it might impair his fighting skills.

A herald blew a few notes, and Edward rode up. He looked tired. "Get on with it," he snapped, and the bishop – I never did find out his name – scurried out of the arena. There was no ceremony, no declaration, just a sudden rush at me by the enraged Cuthbert. Master Leatham had warned me it was the big man's favoured tactic and I was ready. I screeched, looked panicked and as he swung his deadly mace at me, fell sideways to my left. His speed and bulk carried him past, I got in one swift jab with Salvation. It sliced through the leather jerkin and slashed his ribs for a minor wound, but it was still enough to keep his anger boiling.

Cuthbert bellowed more in rage than pain, but I was light-footed and on my toes already, flitting to the eastern edge of the square. The king's champion scraped those heavy boots in the sand, pawing the ground like an enraged bull, then came at me again, but more steadily this time. I crouched to one knee, ready to leap aside and try to sting him again. I had Salvation pointed at his crotch and he eyed the blade warily. My left hand rested, palm down, on the ground where the sandy soil was scuffed. Cuthbert twitched, I rose fast in a half crouch, sword still levelled and demanding all his attention and he boomed in, launching himself at me with impressive swiftness for such a big man.

I scooted left, raising Salvation to beat away his swinging mace and from my clenched left hand flung a handful of sand and soil into Cuthbert's eyes and bellowing mouth. His mace clanged against my blade, jarring my arm to the shoulder with its power, but it was only one swing. His empty hand was scrabbling at his eyes, he was spitting out sand from his mouth.

In a single heartbeat, I was around his right side and back-swinging Salvation in a vicious counter attack. The flat of my beautiful blade hammered hard against the unguarded back of Cuthbert's shaven head and he dropped forward onto his knees.

There was no mercy in my next motion: to drive two-handed the heavy pommel of my sword and crash it down on top of his head. It was a coup de grace that split his scalp and sent Cuthbert facedown into the sand. I walked to him, he was groaning, so I kicked his ribs but he did not stop. 'Finish him,' my mind urged, so I stamped my heel hard onto his head and he was silent. I put my foot under him to roll him onto his back, but he was too heavy to move. I shrugged my shoulders, stuck Salvation point-first into the arena and walked towards Edward to drop to my knees in front of him.

"Your grace?" I asked. He stared at me. "By God's beard, that was fast," he said. "I think you broke his skull. Poor Cuthbert, he's lost his post, now." The king paused and nodded. "And you have won your freedom, but I do not wish you near me. Just leave my country, Thomas, you have the status of a wild wolf and any man can kill you, under law. Your lands are forfeit, your title is withdrawn. You have until dusk tomorrow and after that, you can be taken and slain with impunity, wherever they find you."

Somewhere behind him, a raven croaked. It was a good omen if it came from the right, but I couldn't tell where the sound emanated. I sighed and scrambled up from my knees. Edward had cheated me. I snapped up Salvation. That was a weapon I would not surrender.

***

And so I sailed back to Flanders. Now I was penniless, but there was money to be made in tournaments or with the lawless *routiers* who practised brigandage. If I had to wear the wolf's head of an outlaw I would at least earn my outlawry. If all else failed, I could join the crusade to retake Granada from the Moors and acquire plunder that way. I had won my trial by combat but, I reflected bitterly, the king had cheated me. It may have seemed safer to flee England, but what I did not know was the terrifying silent danger that awaited me on the continent of Europe. Men called it the Great Mortality, or the Black Death, and that dark angel was to claim one person of every three across Europe. And it had come ashore there.

Chapter 20 - Plague

We sailed into the Baltic on a large cog-built vessel nearly 70 paces long, a Hanseatic trader that was flat-bottomed at midships, lapstraked in oak and caulked with tarred moss. Cogs were useful, sturdy ships, capable of operating close inshore as well as being able to cope with open sea voyages. Apart from being convenient for river navigation, their shallow draught was needed to get through the treacherous, sandbar-choked Limfjord, the western entrance to their home Baltic that avoided the dangerous trip around the peninsula of Jutland.

All this a grizzled German mariner told me as we made our way to Gdansk, in Poland with a consignment of English wool and precious black jet from Whitby. We docked by a handsome row of merchants' warehouses and were preparing to go ashore to celebrate our safe arrival when several revenue collectors boarded us and began to ask questions about our voyage. I gathered from the shaken heads that our captain was denying something, but there was an air of foreboding about the officials, and I soon discovered why. The Black Death was stalking Europe and had already surfaced in the south of Poland. Had we, they wanted to know, been in contact with any plagued person? Was everyone aboard in good health? Would we summon the crew and prepare for an inspection?

We had all heard of the plague, called the Great Malady or Great Mortality, that was already raging in the eastern Mediterranean. The wretches who contracted the disease died quickly, after breaking out in swollen boil-like buboes and seeing their skin decay and darken in the black patches which gave it its name. Coughing, body pain and fever accompanied the victim for the short time he lived – for some only a few hours, for others, three or four days.

The information was scary, but I must sail on, up the Vistula River to Warsaw, where I hoped to meet an English routier called Knolles and join his force of Welsh and Cheshire mounted archers. Being in the ducal city would also permit me to sound out the possibilities of going on crusade or of joining the tournament circuit to win a fortune that way.

We reached Warsaw after a nervous voyage in which our captain forbade anyone from going ashore and received supplies only from small boats which had to lay off our vessel to minimize contact with people. "Plague," he said briefly. "I've seen plague in the east. The safest thing is not to be near people." He practised his credo, too. When we arrived to dock in Warsaw, the captain did not leave his ship, and refused to tie it up at a wharf. We were ferried ashore in a small boat and we dutifully took the precautions the captain had advised.

For myself, I opted to wear a leather mask across my nose and mouth, the whole thing soaked in vinegar. It made a stink and it halfway pickled the flesh of my cheeks, but the moderate sting was something to endure and a small price to pay to avoid the disease we were warned was lurking.

People were flowing out of the city, passing through the brick walls of its fortifications in a silent river of refugees trundling carts, carrying bundles and dragging wailing children in a desperate attempt to escape. I learned that the routier I sought was at least three days' ride ahead of me, headed for Prague, so I found a stable, bought a fine chestnut stallion from a horse courser. I examined the beast closely, sure it must have been stolen, for the price he asked was small. It is easy to disguise a horse, especially if it is kept with many others. It can be given an enema so that its head will droop listlessly; it can be clipped and rubbed with oak gall to darken the coat, its mane and tail can be cut, braided or shaped differently; there are a score of means to disguise a stolen animal.

The trader watched me examine the beast, then said: "He's not stolen, lord. There are a lot of fine mounts for sale – people die, people flee. Beasts are plentiful now." I accepted the explanation, bought a good, solid saddle tree to distribute my weight on the stallion's back, filled my saddle bags with dried meat and hard-baked bread and set out west to catch the band of brigands I sought.

The journey was long, even though I travelled from dawn until almost dusk, and it was ominous. I passed by village after empty village, the silence broken only by the lowing of byre-trapped cattle lowing to be milked. I soon avoided riding through the villages themselves, preferring to pass by them in fields, for often shrouded, putrid bodies lay in village streets awaiting the death carts. Sometimes I would pass an open pit where lime-doused corpses lay in untidy confusion, evidence of how they had been unceremoniously tossed, often without a single soul to mourn them because the entire family had died.

Even the fields were not empty of death. I passed the foetid, stinking bodies of swine, rats, rabbits and pathetic wool bundles that had been sheep. Not even the carrion crows that were sometimes the only living creature in sight would touch these evidences of the terrible plague.

Some few times, outside the villages I came across the unburied corpse of a human, spot-blackened and bloody, with great boils oozing pestilence into the air. I would cautiously touch my vinegar-soaked mask and urge my steed on past, through the silence of untended orchards, fields and gardens where a few animals roamed among the abandoned crops. Several times, I came across nuns and priests who were among the few to care for the sick, but they, too, eventually would succumb to the infections that swept their convents and abbeys. In fact, most closed communities like prisons, barracks, ghettos or castles were soon swept clean of life by the swamping wave of pestilence.

Once in a while I would see other travellers, usually a small family group, but we skirted each other, as we did the hamlets where armed men waved us away with threats. Once, I saw a place where villagers had set up baskets and coins a few hundred yards away from the hamlet's limits, asking travelers to leave food. At the River Oder, which I crossed on Wroclaw's fine stone bridge, I was met by armed men and a plague doctor hired by a city guild who seemed eager to question me.

He protected himself against the pestilence by wearing a long cloak, a bird-like beaked mask with glassed eye openings and a wide-brimmed hat. The beak was stuffed with herbs to purify the air he breathed and he carried a longish stick to use in examinations of his patients so he could avoid contact and the chance of contracting the plague himself.

"The plague follows a certain pattern," he told me, his voice muffled through his bird's beak. "A fever comes, with vomiting of blood, sneezing, coughing and great sweating. The patient complains of weakness, of aches and chills. Often the tongue is coated white, great red and black boils the size of hen's eggs appear on the body, especially in armpits and groin and throat. The end is close then, and the patient pisses black urine and stinks foully.

"For some, death takes only hours, for others, four days of blistering torment is their lot, with a madman's writhing dance of death in pain at the finish." The good doctor, who probably would contract the plague himself in short order, warned of depraved people who, infected with the pestilence, would threaten to enter the houses and contaminate those who had locked themselves away unless they were bribed to leave with money or sex. "Be prepared to defend yourself against such sinners," he warned. "Do not be afraid to use your sword."

From him, I learned that the Church, in desperation, had authorized even laymen to hear another's confession so the faithful could die shriven. The doctor also laid out what his burgesses had ordained as measures against the pestilence: ordering the infected to stay indoors, to mark the doors of the houses of plague victims and to shut them up for at least five weeks. Their bedding and clothes should be burned and the dead buried only in the calmer air after nightfall and at a place designated just for victims of the Black Death.

The living, he told me, should burn juniper or rosemary, sage, bay or frankincense to cleanse the air in their houses and should heat stones of flint in the fire, then drop them into buckets of vinegar to give off purifying steam. Floors, tables and food preparation surfaces should be scrubbed with a solution of mint, pennyroyal and vinegar. Butter, the plague doctor told me, his voice muffled behind his guardian beak, was a good preventive against the pestilence. A brew called Plague Water strengthened the body's resistance, too.

It was composed of distilled wine and an assortment of roots, leaves and herbs including chamomile, linseed, rose leaves, angelica, wormwood, rue, peony and wheat. "Drink such draughts," he told me earnestly, "and you may be spared. There are no reports of the pestilence west of here, so you may well be safe in Prague. See a confessor, though, it is best to be prepared."

After our conversation, I rode on past the raised pikes of the bridge guards, across the Oder and into lovely countryside. It was a springtime-green landscape of blossoming fruit trees, white for the apple and pear, pink for the cherries and glossy dark purple for the plum trees' foliage. Banks of bright daffodils, purple and white and yellow crocus flowers, views of wind-ruffled meres and lakes stood before distant purple-hazed hills, it was a vision of natural beauty, still untouched by the grim shadow of the Black Death and I rode gladly into it.

And in Prague, I found Sir Giles Knolles and a tough-looking company of routiers who nodded their welcomes. I was again among friends. William Lawton, an archer in the company of Sir Ralph Mobberley, came to greet me and gave me news of my son Hugh, who was now a child of 12 or 13 years, I was unsure which, but he was no longer at court. "His mother wanted him to live closer to herself, but he is still in good standing and is a friend of Prince Edward."

Here too, in Prague was a band of old friends: Richard Mascy of Tatton, Roger Swetenham, the Jodrell brothers William and John and my old friend John Stretton, all of them Cheshire bowmen. Only one of the group, Graham Lawrence of Swinton, came from outside their small area but all were skilled bowmen and hardy campaigners. The two Jodrells had similar birthmarks: a black stain that almost covered their left thumbs. We teased them it was the devil's mark, and warned them not to be caught by the French, who promised to hack off three fingers of any captured archer's right hand. I simply assumed the Jodrells had inherited the birthmark, but both looked thoughtful and debated whether it was truly a mark of the devil. Evidently the thought had not occurred to them previously and it left them nervous.

William Lawton, who brought me news of my son, told me something else, too: that Joan Plantagenet, a kinswoman of the king whom he knew was my sweetheart, had married the Earl of Salisbury. I no longer carried Joan of Kent's silken scarf, and now it seemed I no longer had her. It was a dismaying time.

Chapter 21 - Routiers

For the next two and a half years, we routiers brought fire, sword and fear to the French and sometimes, if the pickings were ripe enough, to the Flemish, Brabanters and Germans, too. We employed the tactics the Scots had used against the English, employing companies of hundreds of mounted men to ravage the country, destroying undefended villages, stealing their goods and beasts and burning their homes and crops. All this caused floods of refugees to flee to their lords' castles. The raids undermined the population's fidelity to the king who was not protecting them, and ultimately, the activity would force the king to a battlefield where he could lose everything. This was merely a by-blow of our activity, our purpose for the looting and violence was simply to gather riches, but King Edward's intent to displace King Philip was well served, too.

Our warband captured four castles in that period, used them as bases to carry out our raids, then sold them back to the original owners when we had scraped bare the surrounding region. We took noblemen captive and ransomed them, and brought such terror that mothers used our reputation to discipline their children. Especially feared was a brutish misfit called Kelvert of Barnstaple, who took a trophy ear from anyone who resisted him and strung them as decorations on his horse's harness. "Makes them afraid, makes my job easier," he shrugged when I asked him about it. We used the principle to cow villages and even towns into surrender. We always gave the burghers a choice: surrender and pay tribute, or be destroyed when we did get in.

As most of our targets were unwalled villages with only a church or manor house built of stone, they were essentially defenceless. The villagers might choose to hide themselves in the local church, and some even dug defensive ditches around the graveyard and stocked the building with crossbows, but they could not hold out against hundreds of soldiers armed not just with arrows and swords, but also with fire.

"I've burned a few churches," Kelvert told me, "and sent to hell the wretches hiding inside. They should have just surrendered." To encourage neighbouring villages to comply, he made a practice of blinding and mutilating any who resisted, leaving usually just one man with a single eye, to lead a pitiful troop of maimed, blinded people to the next village to demonstrate what would happen to those who resisted. Even so, many villagers did put up some defence. They knew that although we would ransom the nobles or the wealthy, a poor peasant with nothing to make it worth a pillager's time to spare him, might as well fight for his life.

We fought for profit, not for faith or country; we were organized, even having administrators delegated to collect and distribute our booty. Some groups wore actual uniforms, ours wore a sprig of broom on cap or collar in an ironic salute to the *planta genista* that was symbol of King Edward's Angevin ancestors. And, because we were mostly foreigners in the lands we pillaged, we had little fellow-feeling for our victims.

It was not a time of which I am proud, but I was bitter. I had fairly won my innocence but my king had cheated me and called me outlaw. If I were to be outside the pale of the law, then I would act as an outcast, and I did. We brigands grew rich, some so wealthy they bought themselves lands and titles, lived large and grew infamous.

Also, all the while we routiers were raiding and looting the French, we were actually helping Edward. Not only were we depleting the French king's resources, but disaffected locals in northern France called aloud for him to protect them, a cry which Edward heard and readied to answer. He set about remodeling his army, began buying horses from Brabant for his cavalry and built his treasury for the expenses of a campaign.

This news I had through the king's cousin, Henry of Grosmont, Duke of Lancaster, who headed the horse-buying expedition. Henry was our Lancashire overlord and a longtime family friend of the de Hollands and had not approved of the king's action in exiling me and when he was in Flanders he and I met cordially. It was good to see his familiar narrow face with its long nose poking out from a bushy black beard. During our conversation, he mentioned that he had attended a great wedding. It was not news to me, but I still felt sickened. Joan of Kent, the king's cousin and my lover, had married the Earl of Salisbury.

"She's a beauty, you know," he told me, "and it's an unusual marriage, Salisbury's no great catch, but she's a Plantagenet. I think her mother had much to do with the match." I listened numbly while Henry obliviously went on to tell how Edward planned a great tournament at Windsor, where scores of masons were rebuilding the old Norman round tower as well as creating a vast pavilion to provide a home for a Round Table fellowship.

"Edward's a good fellow, but he's had this notion to practice chivalry ever since his grandfather held those Round Table festivals. Of course, such an order would be useful – it will bind the nobility to him at a time when he'll need its support if he's to become king of France. I think you should consider coming to the tourney to make your peace with the king. I'll do what I can to help."

With that, the gallant old knight was on his way back to Windsor and I was left again with a sore heart at losing my Joan. I supposed she knew of my outlawing and of my exile, and had despaired. Now, she was married to someone else. I would not again wear her silk scarf or the small silver ring. They were tokens now with no value. Sternly, I told myself to focus on other matters, like Edward's tournament.

The idea intrigued me. A tourney of Europe's best could be a glorious and rewarding affair, and I resolved to act. I had a new destrier, called Hammerhead, bought from my looted fortune and I now owned a fine harness of polished German armour acquired from a castle we'd taken. With a shield innocent of any insignia I could compete anonymously among the several hundred knights at the tournament and it would be a poor thing if I could not re-establish relations with the king when he was feeling magnanimous. After all, it had been several years since my trial…

It was a cold winter's day and the thorn bushes were white-rimed, and glorious, but my first sight of Windsor made me gasp. The rebuilt Round Tower looked magnificent, but the king had done more: he had constructed an elaborately-decorated stone building for the festival. It was about 200 paces long, shaped like a cloister some 30 feet high, under a wooden roof supported by stone pillars. Seating for about 350 knights took the form of stone benches lined along the walls, all overlooking a central area in which the jousting, feasting, dancing and theatrical re-enactments of Arthurian legends took place.

I grew a heavy beard for disguise, but opted not to take part in the individual jousting, as the winners had to raise their visors when they rode up to salute the king and queen, but I fought in the melees and was noted as 'the Welsh knight' but still did not reveal my identity, being careful to shuffle behind others in my fighting cadre when we saluted the judges. After the day's jousting ended, I was careful not to speak English at the feasts and entertainments although my heart was sore to see Joan of Kent sitting beside her husband, the Earl of Salisbury. In my eagerness to taste Joan's lips again, I made two reckless bids to secretly see her, but she dropped a note from her chamber window to say she was watched, and I dared not endanger her there, so resolved to try again when she was back in her husband's Welsh castle.

Edward's desire to recreate Arthur's palace meant we had a week of entertainments, but I usually slipped away before the evening's dancing, and pleaded my ignorance of the English language to avoid being roped into the enactments. And so the week went, until it came to the last day's climactic melee. I was put into the Black Prince's company and we faced a powerful mixed force of Scots, Brabanters, Genoese, Spanish and Italian knights. Something about him seemed odd as I viewed the young Black Prince, visor down, in his distinctive black harness, but I shrugged it away. What I did not then know was that he had exchanged armour with one of his conroi, so he could fight anonymously and, he said, 'Earn my victories on merit.'

Soon enough, the heralds blew their brassy command, the two opposing lines thundered at each other. The clash echoed inside the great pavilion, as did the yells and groans of the triumphant and the unhorsed. I fought from Hammerhead, who earned his name from his habit of smashing his neck and head into the side of his equine opponents, surprisingly often flooring them, and usually was a considerable help to me in unseating the riders.

The fighting went as it usually does, and I had just back-swung Redemption across a Brabanter helmet, knocking its occupant sideways when a swirl in the combat showed me a tall, slender knight bearing on his helm the red ribbon of our cadre desperately fighting off three attackers. I spurred forward just as he dropped his sword and was toppled from his saddle. I barged Hammerhead into the side of one opponent, throwing him off balance and stabbed at a second, causing him to rear his horse up and sideways. My cadre companion was on his feet, swaying, and would soon be clubbed down, vanquished and liable to forfeit his valuable harness. My reaction was instinctive. Using my formidable archer's arm and back strength, I grabbed the back of his sword belt and scooped him up.

By the good fortune of St George, the fellow's destrier was standing stock-still a couple of yards away and in the same scooping motion that I lifted and swung the dazed knight forward, I also flung him somehow across the saddle. Hammerhead responded to my knee pressure and wheeled quickly, blocking the third attacker as my comrade settled his seat and pulled a mace from its place by the pommel. He was horsed again, and armed. I wheeled away to find another contest, dimly aware that loud cheering was going on in the crowded gallery. I glanced, saw nothing amiss, mentally shrugged and went back to clanging steel on steel until the heralds called the contest over.

Weary and battered, I was riding out of the arena when Henry of Grosmont spurred alongside me. He slammed up his visor and grinned at me, teeth white through his black beard. "By God's breath, that was a fine save!" he said. Stupid with fatigue, I mumbled some query. He slapped me hard on the shoulder. "The youth you saved! Now's the time to meet the king!" I had no idea what he meant, so he gripped my arm and hissed fiercely: "Go and kneel to Edward, right now!" Over the next 50 or so paces as our mounts walked to the paddock, he told me what I had unknowingly done: saved the Black Prince in his anonymous harness from defeat and the humiliation of having to yield to an unknown foreigner, to whom he would have had to hand over his royal armour.

So it was that I knelt to a grateful Plantagenet king, received the kiss of peace and found myself appointed to serve the teenage prince in his military matters. Too, I had the de Holland lands restored. Edward had the fearsome Angevin temper, but he also had a sentimental streak and it benefited me. "I did find it hard to believe that you had acted like a coward," Edward whispered to me. A king cannot be seen to be wrong, I knew, and it was all the apology I would ever receive, but my time in disgrace was ended and my life changed again as I began my new duties, guarding and tutoring the teenage Black Prince.

Lord Edward had been invested as Duke of Cornwall, with a circlet, gold ring and silver rod of office at age six. He was appointed Guardian of England the next year and became Prince of Wales at 13. Like his father, he admired King Arthur, and like his father, too, he was extravagant, martial and sometimes brutally ruthless. He somehow knew of my secret relationship with his cousin Joan Plantagenet, but although he admired her, was generous enough to leave that field as open to me as possible, given that she was married to Salisbury. The shared secret was useful in binding us, tutor and royal pupil, and Edward and I became good friends, with yet another link to strengthen the bond – my natural son Hugh.

As an extra reward, King Edward had ordered Marian de Trafford, mother of our son Hugh, to bring the boy to court to continue his interrupted military training and education. He would be a squire to the Black Prince, and as a boy of exactly the prince's age – they shared their birthday – would be a companion for the young warrior.

When Hugh of Mobberley – Marian had determinedly defied her father and held that he was not a de Trafford - arrived at Windsor, I met the boy awkwardly. I had not seen a great deal of him during the past decade, but he was mannered, showed good skills in tiltyard and schoolroom and formed a firm friendship with Prince Edward, who was grieving the loss of his longtime ally William Montagu, fatally wounded in a tournament.

For the first time, I viewed my son, result of a passionate affair, with dispassionate eyes and I was proud of him. He then made me more so, for my first duty with the prince was to help him oversee the Commissioners of Array. These were experienced military serjeants and captains assigned to recruit trained and armed men for a campaign of pillage and destruction in France, and I chose to include Hugh in the planning to make Lord Edward feel less isolated among older men. It was a scheme which worked well. The two teenagers were enthusiastic and intelligent, scouring the rolls for suitable captains, administering matters, gathering and allocating reserves – we needed 150,000 sheaves of arrows, for example - making decisions and planning a campaign with the help of our noble earls.

Each commissioner was indentured to serve for a set time and to sign up a specific number of archers, men at arms and knights. Some would be infantry, others would be mounted. In all, we mustered 12,000 men. A fleet of 700 cogs was being assembled at Portsmouth to ferry this new army across the channel where they would join two small English expeditionary forces already operating on the continent. One was in Flanders, the other in Gascony, the latter commanded by my old friend Henry of Grosmont. He had urged the king to act soon: King Philip of France was with his army in Gascony chasing Grosmont, leaving the northern coast unguarded.

Edward saw his opportunity and accelerated his plans. He'd not take the obvious, short route across the Channel from Dover to Calais. Instead, while the French fleet lurked in the narrows of the strait in hopes of intercepting him, he'd cross much further west, land at the Norman peninsula and raid east to Paris, ransacking as he went. The English army would live off the land, the booty would pay for the campaign and the disruption and terror might force Philip and his House of Valois from the throne. Besides, he had a grudge against Philip for the humiliating terms of homage he had been obliged to make early in his reign. Dethroning the arrogant French king would be a pleasure.

During our war councils, Edward quietly gave me some specific instructions: when we landed in France, he wanted his 16 years old son to be treated as a mere soldier. His rank was not to exclude him from the risks of battle, he would fight alongside his comrades in arms and earn his spurs: the king also shared that he planned to knight the boy once we were in France. Most importantly, in battle the boy would lead the vanguard of the English army, our powerful force of archers.

Maybe I blanched a little, for Edward leaned forward and caught my arm: "He has to learn, Thomas. My father did not teach me, and I was humiliated in Scotland. I resolved then that I would forge and temper my own son for his responsibilities. One day he'll be king, so he needs to learn about warfare. I'll put Warwick and Northampton with you, they're experienced men with the status to command respect, but I want Edward involved in all decision-making and in much of the fighting." All I could do was to lower my head and murmur acquiescence. Silently, I prayed: 'May God, English longbows and our noble Earls of Warwick and Northampton save us.'

Chapter 22 - Caen

A few crossbow bolts clattered onto the deck as we sailed into Saint Vaast at the head of our fleet but Edward laughed at them, exhilarated, and threw an arm around his son in pretended fright. "God's breath! That's a terrifying thing!" he shouted, gesturing up at the small fort which guarded the snug harbor. The prince smiled at his father's enthusiasm. "A fine town," he said, taking in the sturdy stone buildings and the square-towered church. "I hope it is a rich one." Two of our larger cogs eased past us and scraped along the harbor wall to debark a body of archers and pikemen who ran off to secure the town. The king and his entourage made a more leisurely landing and waited outside a tavern, drinking wine in the sunshine while their horses were unloaded. My son Hugh and the prince looked about excitedly, remarking on the foreignness of everything, impatient to be mounted and away, but the king sent for them, we all processed to the small church and the king knighted his son and several other young bloods, in preparedness for war.

After the ceremony, the nobles gathered in the king's pavilion tent to drink wine and make merry. At some stage, after drink had been taken, the young Earl of Salisbury, William Montacute, who had been knighted that day, blundered into my back. I turned in surprise and saw who it was: the upstart who had bribed the mother of my Joan to coerce her daughter into marriage, then had locked her away in a Welsh castle. "You are clumsy, my lord," I sneered. "Have you had sufficient wine?" "You are a scoundrel archer," he rejoined. "Why are you here, in such company?"

Our words escalated, I knocked him down and put my knife to his throat. He made a thin squeal like a rabbit caught in the needle teeth of a stoat but the prince intervened and I moved back. In my anger I blurted: "This godless fellow has stolen my wife." Edward was close to his cousin Joan Plantagenet and knew of our romance, and he tried to hush me as his retainers pinioned my arms. I would not be stilled until two of Salisbury's men led him meekly from the pavilion, no blood shed. "Be grateful, Thomas, that my father was not in here," the prince hissed, "you have offended him once before with your hot temper."

I apologized, then carefully explained matters, and the prince listened. Joan's marriage to Salisbury was invalid because I had married her first. I told him we had witnesses to the ceremony and consummated our love before I had to go on crusade, but we had kept our spiritual marriage – made without benefit of clergy - secret from the world. While I was in Prussia, Salisbury had influenced Joan's mother Margaret and other relatives to coerce the girl into marrying him, then had confined her to Mold Castle, away from the royal court, and me.

"If that is the case, we should inform the Church and have Salisbury's marriage annulled," Edward ruled, evidently not registering that no clergy had been involved, but I did not correct him. Nor did he ask about my fictitious witnesses. "I'll speak with my father. Meanwhile, stay away from Salisbury. I'll tell him the same." With that, I had to be content, for there was much to do and a campaign to begin. Seething with anger and jealousy, I went to begin matters, and we commanders started with unloading the cogs.

The majority of our fleet was unable to find berths in Saint Vaast's small harbor, so landed their men and equipment on a sandy beach nearby. I was one of several beachmasters, organizing supplies, directing men here and there and readying our march inland. The next day, we began our crusade of fire and sword, looted and burned Valoges and the next village, Saint Mere Eglise. A few militia resisted us briefly, but were soon cut down by our cavalry under the newly-spurred knight, Prince Edward. We had the wealthy lands of Normandy before us, unguarded and at our mercy, of which we showed little. For two weeks, we looted and burned, and the fine towns of Carentan, Saint Lo and many other, smaller places were destroyed, as were about 100 ships we caught in harbors. Meanwhile, some of our fleet kept pace with us, sailing along the coast and we made regular transfers of loot to them until their holds were full, when they ferried our prizes back to

England.

After two weeks of our raiding *chevauchee,* we came to the prosperous regional capital, Caen. "Looks strong," the Black Prince said as we gazed at the walled Old Town's curtain walls and stone, round towers. "Nearly as big as London, maybe just as rich," I added. "There are those abbeys, too," said the prince. "Useful bastions." He was correct, the old city, on the north side of a river, had a formidable castle; the new town depended mostly on the river for its defences, but those were supplemented by several fortified bridges and two stone abbeys which also had been reinforced.

The king and a troop of knights rode up, Edward slid from his horse and waved us into his pavilion. "Good news. I've looked at the defences, and they're flawed," he said briefly. "I'd expected we would need a siege that we can't afford to get into this place, but we're told that the burghers ordered the garrison commander to concentrate on defending the new town where their homes and wealth are. They've actually abandoned the best defences – the old town and castle – to hide behind the river and some scratched-together ramparts of timber.

"We will take the bridges and the new town first, then assault the castle. There are parts of the walls that have crumbled and what repairs they've made look shaky." Edward shook his head. "Can you believe it? I think it won't need a siege. An assault and escalade could do the task once we get those bridges under control. I suppose we'll have to subdue the abbeys, too, can't leave manned bastions in our rear."

Close observation showed that the castle was held by just a few hundred men, but more than 1,000 were in the new town. The prince and his earls began to ready their men for an assault and Edward ordered a small force to blockade the castle and protect our rear while we took on the bridges and the abbeys.

The first surprise was that the abbeys had been abandoned, so we seized them. The prince, following his father's orders, was moving troops into position to attack the fortified bridges when a contingent of Welsh archers, flush with wine, booty and two weeks' easy victories, took matters into their own hands and rushed the defences, eager to be first to loot the town.

I was with Edward and the prince when we heard the shouting and saw the premature assault. "Get them back," Edward was bellowing. "Get Warwick onto it, they're his men! Get them back, now." The order came too late, the die was cast, and somehow it rolled a six.

Warwick, even with the help of his fellow earl Northampton, could not gain control of his half-drunken men. They swarmed the gatehouse and bar, and other soldiers including a force of mercenaries caught the fever for loot and they too joined in. Soon, several hundred Welshmen were battling furiously with the defenders and had won their way across two of the bridges to the far bank. The French commander then made the fatal error of committing much of the garrison and hundreds of armed citizens to fight outside their fortifications and a horde of English and Welsh archers waiting for their turn to cross the crowded bridges discovered that the river was running low and was easily fordable.

I was on the bank when they began slipping into the water and firing up at the crossbowmen on the ramparts and bridge while they waded across. I joined in. We were under a light hail of crossbow bolts which claimed a few archers, but the men on the fighting platforms above us faced a withering rain from our longbows. I stood waist-deep in the Odon, with the strap of my quiver in my teeth to hold it out of the river and keep the fletchings dry. I hammered shaft after shaft at anything that moved on the battlements above until a great shout went up. The first English had breached the hastily-made defences along the riverbank and our pikemen and archers were spilling through the break.

I cast aside my empty arrow bag, unsheathed Salvation and waded to the far bank to join in. In two short, vicious episodes, we scoured the French from the breach, took the bridge defenders in the rear and opened the great gates to allow our comrades into Caen.

A clattering of iron-shod hoofs on cobblestones made me turn in time to avoid being trampled by a dozen or so French knights who were hacking their way out of the fallen stronghold. I was out of arrows, but my sword accounted for two men at arms who tried to pass on foot and then a torrent of maddened English soldiers the French called the Black Boars was pouring into Caen seeking revenge, blood and loot.

I checked the purses of the two soldiers I had just killed and found coins, a fine gold ring embossed with an ox head that must have been looted from a nobleman and a heavy silver chain. I added it to the hacked-up church plate several of us had shared and hoped for more. Then I went to find wine in a tavern that had been smashed apart and whose floor was already littered with our passed-out soldiers. One of them had a knife with an enameled hilt, and I took it, too.

The carnage lasted for five days. Packs of drunken soldiers hunted down the townspeople who had resisted them; fire, rape, murder and pillage ruled as the city was sacked. Bodies lay on every corner, the air was thick with smoke and the screaming and weeping of hapless women was to be heard everywhere. I went nowhere without weapons and a mail coat, for even my compatriots were not to be trusted not to kill me if I seemed to have loot they wanted.

Men piled up the bulkier plunder in the streets, anything from cooking pots to tapestries. I saw several torturing an elderly Jew, hanging him head-down over a small fire in an attempt to learn the hiding place of his money. On Edward's orders, the English cavalry swept out of town and across the region, cutting down refugees who thought they could escape by slipping into the hinterland. "They resisted us, they must die. I'll make an example of them. If the next place wants to resist, they'll know what to expect," the king said grimly, although he rescinded the order later. On that second day, marshals began rounding up citizens to dig mass graves, for fully half of Caen's population had been killed. In all, said the monks who buried them, 5,000 died in that bloody July massacre.

Edward was unmoved. He called his court together to pay homage in St Stephen's Abbey at the grave of his ancestor, Duke William of Normandy. Then he showed us a royal order someone had found in Count Raoul's solar. It was from King Philip to the Normans: their raiding parties were to ravage the south coast of England. "This justifies our cause in God's eyes,"

Edward said solemnly. Privately, I thought the declaration hypocritical, and in direct opposition to the Arthurian principles the king claimed to espouse, but he was unscrupulously ambitious and coveted the plunder we were taking. The 'justification' was valid in his eyes and gave a spurious legitimacy to our great raid, so we pillaged on.

Towns with names like Lisieux, Brionne and Pont de l'Arche fell to us, along with a score of hamlets, dozens of farmhouses and a handful of monasteries which yielded good pickings, including a fine gilded chalice which I still possess. Each day we sent cartloads of loot under escort to the coast to rendezvous with our cogs, who ferried it all back to Portsmouth.

At the beginning of our great raid, we nightly feasted on local beasts and crops, as ordered drank only moderate amounts of wine under the threatening eyes of our constables and slept encamped around some looted village, while the king, the prince and their nobles occupied the buildings. Our scouts gave us reports of the approach of Philip's army and of his son Duke John of Normandy with a second force he was bringing from the south. "First, they'll have to catch us, Thomas," Prince Edward told me gleefully, "and then we'll flatten them!" For my part, I wasn't so sure. The size of the French force was six or seven times greater than ours and it seemed critical that we avoid conflict until we could find an advantage of some sort. Also, the terrain was bare of forage and supplies, stripped at King Philip's orders to deny us the ability to live off the land. Feeding our men and beasts was increasingly difficult.

We reached the great River Seine south of Rouen to find that all the bridges, even the one inside the city itself, had been destroyed The city was out of our reach, too: the walls were heavily defended since Philip had ordered every able-bodied man to assemble there under his personal command. Edward called a war council. "The French are not yet well-organised but they have plenty of men and it's just a question of time. We can't let ourselves be caught on the wrong side of this river, we must have a means of retreat into Flanders and to the safety of our allies if needed. We'll move south and east along the river towards Paris and seek a crossing. We have to move swiftly."

Saint George favoured us, and when we were only a short distance from Paris, at a place called Poissy, which we burned, we found an unguarded ford and our sappers created a pontoon bridge. The job was done with speed, and although scouts reported that there was a French force not far away, we got our army across unmolested and for the next week or more raced north with the French in pursuit. We were travelling on a vast plain between two impassable rivers, the Seine and the Somme. The English Channel was to our north, but the ports were defended. Two French armies were coming from the south and we were caught like a wolf in a trap. Worse, our supplies were exhausted and the land had been stripped of crops and forage, with all food stores carried away. Although we passed through a half dozen sizable towns there was nothing to pillage.

In desperation, we marched our tired and hungry troops through, set fires and destroyed as much as we quickly could and finally arrived at the racing, tidal Somme, the last major obstacle between ourselves and Flanders. It was impassable. Philip had ordered most of the bridges to be destroyed, and the few that were left intact were in heavily-guarded towns.

In a bid to capture a bridge, Prince Edward led our battalion in two fruitless attacks against walled settlements, but we had no siege engines and we could not settle in for prolonged assaults, as the French army was only a day or so behind us. Our furious escalades were rebuffed and we moved on each time until we came to Boismont, where a force of ill-disciplined levies opposed us. Prince Edward and a cavalry battle rode them down, and in frustration massacred all of them. Here, the young knight began to earn his name of Black Prince for his martial brutality.

It earned us little. The town's bridge had already been destroyed, its granaries emptied and its pastures burned. We incinerated the town, angered and now fearful of the noose tightening around our throats. "Thomas, we have to do something about supplies," the prince told me. "We are running short of everything, and the men and beasts are starving. The French have stoppered us up, we need an escape route and we need supplies."

I led out squads to scour a wide area for food, but Philip's orders to scrape the region bare had been efficiently carried out. The most any of our gleaners brought back were a few half-empty sacks of grain and some root crops. Worse, our foragers were often attacked by peasants and we had to abandon some of our heavier carts because the starving beasts were too weak to pull them. At least, the carts delayed Philip's forces while they looted them. Matters got worse. Scouts reported a large French force ahead of us, just six miles away at Abbeville, and a deserter from Duke John's army told us that forward elements of the royal cavalry were only an hour's ride behind us. Philip's grip was tightening. We had to find a way across the Somme.

As I prepared to ride out of camp to seek a ford, Grosmont came to me, and spoke quietly: "Thomas, regardless of cost, we must cross this river. "We cannot, simply cannot be caught here. It will mean the death of Edward and the prince. Philip cannot allow them to live, he will never ransom such rivals." Hearing the doughty old warrior express our unspoken fears was a shock. "Even if we succeed in the crossing, it will not be over, my lord," I said. "No, it will not," he agreed. "What we must do is get across the damned river and find a defensible position where we can hold Philip's forces while Edward escapes, maybe to Flanders, maybe to Calais, so he can return home."

I nodded. This might be the place where we English would die, but we would at least save our king. I joined the quest, scouring the banks of the Somme in hopes of finding a way across. The search was hopeless, but I rode along the river bank in the dying light before sunset and a miracle happened. One of my archers raced back to me. "Ahead, Lord Thomas," he sounded excited. "There are cart tracks to the river." I rode as fast as my tired horse would move to see for myself. There they were, a double track left by wagons, heading down a cut in the bank and right into the fast-moving tide. It was too dark to see the opposite bank, but there were flickers I knew must be camp fires, and plenty of them, too.

"Away, quietly," I told my squad, "and find me a few locals." It took an hour before we had a prisoner, and he was volubly indignant, but after I gave the peasant a gold piece and apologised, he became compliant. The place was called Blanchetaque he said, and yes it had a difficult ford across the Somme. It was where the river crossed a ridge of harder limestone that created a natural weir. It made the Somme just passable for a very short time, twice a day at low tide. "We are three leagues from the sea, lord," he told me. "this is the lowest crossing place before La Manche itself."

At my next question, he paced out ten strides. "It is narrow, only this wide, but it is marked with white stone under the water." I estimated that a dozen men could crowd abreast to use the crossing. The critical question was how deep it was at low tide. The peasant shrugged. "To the chin of a small man, perhaps, but the current is strong. At slack water of course for a short time there is no current, but then the river is much deeper." He did not know how long the stand of the tide lasted but volunteered that the white limestone of the submerged causeway was most visible after high tide. After further questions, it seemed we might crowd a few thousand men across at the lowest tide, even though it was still running swiftly. I took the man and the information to the king, who slapped his thigh in relief.

Shortly before midnight, Edward called a council of war. "We cannot afford to be trapped against this river but we are not strong enough to force a crossing against Philip's men at the bridge at Abbeville, either. Rouse the troops, abandon the heaviest, slowest carts and impedimenta. We will break camp as soon as possible, move fast and hope for low tide." In the middle of the night, our army of 12,000 slipped away while the French slept.

Chapter 23 - Blanchetaque

The march was short, about three miles to the Somme and my
hopes were high. The summer dawn came early, and the church
bells would have been chiming for Prime when we saw the
tracks that marked the ford. It was shortly after high tide, the
river was running full and fast and plainly it would not be
passable for some hours. What was worse was waiting on the
slope of the opposite bank: three ranks of French soldiers, about
3,000 men arrayed around the elite of their force, 500 men-at-
arms.

Grosmont and I conferred. "You can only move a few men
across at one time, Thomas," he said in a worried voice. It will
be a few score archers on the causeway at once, only them
against thousands of the damned Frogs. There is no hope, my
friend." I think I grinned. "Have faith in our yews," I said
lightly. I had a plan. The river ran across a ridge of limestone
which formed a natural weir. At the lowest tide as the water
ebbed, the ridge would be, I calculated, six or eight feet below
the surface – enough for us to flounder the short distance across
that deepest spot. We could survive that.

We had to wait for low water, so we rested, ate what meagre
supplies we had and sharpened our weapons. Four hours later,
as the tide was flowing, not quite low tide yet, Sir Hugh
Despenser and I called on a selected force of our tallest archers
and we waded into the Somme, shouting 'For God and Saint
George!' Dimly, we could see the white ridge that marked the
submerged causeway under the brown water, and we moved
forward steadily, a quiver of arrows and our longbows held high
to keep the bowstrings dry, most men with a second quiver of
36 arrows slung across their shoulders, hoping that wet feathers
would still fly true, but knowing that when firing into a mass of
men even a wobbling missile would still do terrible damage.

More to the point, I had arrayed about 600 of our fellow
bowmen on the western bank, on a large sandy spit on a bend in
the river that allowed them to close the range. They would not

follow at once. Instead, they were to launch their killing arrows high and long, sending them hundreds of yards and high, to crash down into the massed enemy. A hail of arrows like a snowstorm would fall from distance onto the French, hammering their middle and rearward ranks into panicked frenzy. And while this terrible hail fell, we few who could use the causeway at one time must advance. The water level fell a few more inches, but then I saw something disturbing: the effect of the natural weir at the critical time during the ebb was to create a churning whirlpool on the downstream side of the ridge.

Any man who lost his footing, any man struck by a French missile, any man whose grip on a comrade was broken would be torn away, dragged under, drowned and his body raced to the sea ten miles away. The ford was more dangerous at the tide's lowest ebb than at any other time. I shook my head in disbelief. This was our only hope of salvation. We had to take it. "Unstring your bows, keep the hemp dry somehow, and follow me!" I bellowed, and our ranks stirred.

We waded in, crushed together, a dozen abreast in each rank, men grasping comrades' belts, with more ranks following at short intervals so they could fire over our heads. The *arbalestiers* on the far bank opened up, their bolts thumping home or splashing around us, cutting down men unable to respond as we struggled against the swift, swirling tide. I was in the front rank, urging on my men, and archers were falling like wheat before the reapers but no bolt struck me. For all my height and strength, I was struggling against the pressure of the ebbing current and stumbled and recovered three, four, five times. Once, a bolt glanced off my sallet and made my head ring, but I was unhurt, bellowing at my men to move, faster, faster. We were linking arms, grasping at our fellows, fighting to stay upright and not to be swept away to drown. Man after man cried out and sank under the brown water, quarrel-struck and sinking, but as soon as gaps appeared in our column, others pushed forward to fill them. The tide continued to fall, and the pressure of the outflow increased.

In our first ranks, we archers struggled, went under, surfaced spluttering and pushed forward, hanging onto companions through the deepest parts of the river. We were making a human chain, holding our bowstaves with one hand or with them jammed through our belts until we reached shallower water. There, under intense crossbow fire, at last we could respond, although many men had already been struck and carried away by the churning, swift current.

Once we had fought to that blessed water that was no more than waist-deep, we re-strung our bows and began firing, holding our weapons as clear as we could of the current. Although we could not stick our points into the river bed, which slowed our reloading, we were still firing four or five arrows a minute, about four times faster than the crossbowmen's rate, and as our rear ranks waded closer, the hail of arrows, even those that dipped and dove like porpoises because of their wet feathers, thickened into an unendurable storm. They dropped from shallow arcs to strike the massed French in the face and chest. I drew, marked and loosed; nocked another shaft, marked, drew and loosed again, hardly aiming, just pouring shaft after shaft into the mass of men opposing us at such short distance. We could not miss. I saw man after man fall to my shafts, men in the front ranks taking our fire from the river, men behind them falling to the iron hail from behind us.

Nobody could withstand such an arrow storm. The crossbowmen flinched and turned away, trying to shield themselves from the thickets of shafts that battered down on them, then they broke. A force of mounted men tried to ride us down, but Earl William of Northampton was ready. He led a battle of knights to swim their horses through and around our files of longbowmen and a vicious mounted scrimmage broke out at the shallows and on the riverbank.

Now, I was up the sandy bank and fighting two-handed. I was swinging my sword, hacking and chopping, thrusting and punching with sword and dagger. And all the time, arrows from our bowmen on the sandy spit fell from the sky onto the French ranks, dropping like deadly hail behind the first few lines of enemy to pound those waiting to join the fray. Men were groaning and screaming, many blinded from face wounds as the battering missiles plunged out of the sky, for it is human nature to look at approaching danger, even up into killing arrows. Their mass wavered, then the enemy began to turn to flee.

Panicked Genoese crossbowmen and French men at arms struggling to retreat crowded the shore and entangled the advancing French horsemen; more English splashed up onto the bridgehead alongside us and a ferocious struggle got worse. While the battle raged a score or two of paces from them, the work parties I had detailed drove heavy stakes into the bank. Work parties on the opposite bank had used stout trees as stanchions on their side of the river and made long ropes from cordage and lengths of harness. These they had fastened to timbers and a couple of empty wine tuns to act as floats which our bridgehead troops caught in the current and secured to the new stakes. Now we had a rope walk bridging the river which we could use to help men cross in water deeper than they could wade.

The time of blessed slack water was fast approaching. Soon, more reinforcements crossed, more horsemen followed, swimming their beasts across while one or two infantry clung to each horse's bridle and tail and the battle for the bridgehead ended with a logjam of dead in the water and a French rout.

Our cavalry broke through, their doomed infantry ran. And were slaughtered. The English cavalry mercilessly chopped down the fleeing soldiers, offering no quarter since Philip had flown the *oriflamme* that signalled total war. Only a few French nobles were spared for later ransom. Now we could urgently bring the rest of our army across in the stand of the tide. The water was deep, but the guide ropes gave support, and the cavalry swam their horses back and forth, dragging more archers and foot soldiers with them at each crossing.

We even floated a small number of the lighter wagons over, before the tide made it impossible. Our way cleared, we tramped away from the Somme soaked, tired and hungry to find ourselves in a land fat with loot and food. Philip had not believed we could possibly cross the river and had failed to strip the land of its resources.

Some hapless last stragglers of our army were caught on the wrong side of the flooding Somme by French under blind King

John of Bohemia and Sir John of Hainault, who butchered them at the ford but not before we slashed the ropes that could have helped the French to cross. We also lost our heavy wagons and some loot, but we moved on, heading north and east. We sacked two towns, captured a small fleet of wine ships and replenished our forage and food. While the army rested, I joined Prince Edward, our king and a few other captains and we found a defensive hillside position near a small village. We ordered the men up to it and rested them as we waited in our battle-ready positions for Philip's army.

Chapter 24 - Crecy

The village on the east side of the River Somme was called Crecy-en-Ponthieu and the king of England found his vital advantage there, choosing some high ground outside the village above a slope up which the enemy must advance. Both of our flanks were protected by the terrain. On the English right, the approach narrowed abruptly, constricted by the village of Crecy and the River Maye which anchored our right flank, while a series of vineyard terraces near the centre of the chosen ground would compress the French and funnel them into a small gap.

At the other end of the line, our army had its left wing secured by the village of Wadicourt and its rear protected by a vast wood some ten miles long and four miles deep. The only way for the French to attack was head-on, up the slope where they would be squeezed by the river and the terraces of the vineyard into a narrow corridor. Only after pushing through that chokepoint could they fan out again, and Edward of England had a plan for that.

"It will be like Dupplin Moor all over again," Edward told his commanders. "The French want to fight at short range, and we can do that but we won't. We can kill them 200 paces before they reach us. Our longbows are so fearsome our enemies trampled their own men to death to escape our arrows. They did it before, they'll do it again."

"My son Prince Edward will hold the vanguard, and that will attract the French to attack his standard, but they'll have to come through that narrows. We'll put a stopper in the gap and the French will be so crushed together by their own advance they'll be unable to move. Our archers will kill them before they can get close enough for hand to hand combat."

The king ordered most of our men at arms to fight on foot, not mounted and deployed the army in three battles, with the central vanguard under the Black Prince forward of the king's ranks, to receive the first shock of the French attack. The Earls of Arundel and Northampton would hold the line to the prince's left, I commanded the division on the right flank, where my force was mostly archers.

The two front battles were to be arrayed with the longbowmen pushed forward in a staggered line, so infantry could step through their ranks if needed and with reserves of bowmen and pikemen at the rear in the third battle, commanded by the king. Our horses and baggage were emplaced behind the entire army, near the crest of a small hill on which a windmill stood. King Edward would use this vantage point to direct matters.

The king looked around the board at the grim-faced commanders. "Now, about defences. I want a chequerboard of pits dug before our lines, and I want them fitted with sharpened stakes…" and a buzz of conversation arose.

We dug trenches, we scattered caltrops between them to cripple enemy cavalry and we brought up tens of thousands of arrows to be stored in readiness behind our positions. Placed at intervals across our line were five 12-barrelled volley guns called *ribaults*. They were not siege guns, just light artillery and were mounted on carts, but they fired a dozen iron balls at a time and their noise, impact and smoke would be a useful addition in confusing the French.

As the enemy viewed us, they faced a grassy slope up from the Vallee des Clercs to attack our front line, which was formed like the teeth of a saw in three zigzags. Battalions of infantry alternated with divisions of longbowmen, with the archers pushed forward of their spearmen comrades. Cavalry detachments were readied behind each battle, to counter-attack as needed.

Behind this front line, which was anchored with a defended village at each end, King Edward's force formed a second, reserve line higher up the slope under his new banner of leopards and lilies. It too was arrayed sawtooth style with archers on each flank and foot soldiers holding the centre. Because of the added elevation of the slope those longbowmen could fire over the heads of their comrades and arc their missiles into the massed French army. Behind them in a small park, the king positioned the baggage wagons and our horses, for we would fight on foot.

When that Saturday passed noon, our lines were formed, pits and trenches dug, banners and pennants set, supplies of arrow and spare weapons put in place and all readied. Constables went among the men with cooks and carts of food, ensuring that all were fed and soon the king also went among the ranks. He went quietly riding a small palfrey, carrying just a white wand and accompanied only by two of his marshals. He rode slowly, spoke cheerfully with the men, many of whom clustered around to touch his armour, and asked them to fight well and defend his honour and that of England and St George. He also reminded them: "No prisoners, men, and do not leave your ranks. We fight as brothers, shoulder to shoulder, we will not be chasing some impoverished Frenchman for the ransom of his life savings of a few copper *deniers*."

That made the troops laugh, and as the king moved on, the men were encouraged to relax, lolling on the turf, their helmets and weapons in front of them. It was a display of calm and confidence as they rested and awaited the French, who were still in the distance, toiling towards the battleground.

My own place was on the right of the central battle with the Black Prince and a battalion of his knights. There, I counted the earls of Warwick and Oxford, my lords Cobham, Stafford, Delaware, Harcourt, Clifford, Chandos, Latimer and Neville among the prince's nobles, and a fine display of banners, shields and pennants they showed. I was pleased to see my son Hugh in Edward's conroi and he waved gaily to me, eager for the fray.

Prince Edward sent for me, smiling as he surveyed the great black war bow I had slung across my shoulders. "Good Thomas, I'd like you at my right hand, but I also need your archers today. You're a fine knight, but I have plenty of those. You're also a fine archer and you'll inspire your men. Take command of the Cheshire bowmen and cut down the French so we may idle the day away looking on, while you do the work." I laughed and said that would be our pleasure and strode away the hundred paces or so to the archers who were angled just ahead and to the right of the prince's battle.

It was later in the still, muggy afternoon, a full 24 hours after we arrived at Crecy before the French showed in their colourful mass of banners and armour, trumpets and horse. They were not in disciplined columns, they did not even have outriders to scout the battlefield, but four knights detached themselves and rode close to us. "They're just reconnoitering, hold fire," I shouted and the four turned away unharmed. An hour later, a single screen of crossbow men - Genoese mercenaries by the insignia on their jupons – headed the French horde and set up opposite our front ranks.

We archers were sitting on the grass, talking and eating, a few were praying. The sharpest-eyed among us remarked how fatigued the Genoese looked, and they did slump down as soon as they were ordered to their positions. "They're in full harness and carrying weapons, no wonder they're tired," said Graham Lawrence, the Swinton bowman. "They're not carrying pavises, either. That'll be interesting, not having shields when the arrows strike."

The sky darkened, a shower of rain fell, and I ordered the longbowmen to keep their bowstrings dry, unnecessary advice as they were already unstringing and putting the cords under their helmets or leather caps where most already kept several spares. We all covered up as best we could, for the rain grew into a torrent and thunderclaps rumbled overhead. Finally, the storm passed over and we watched astonished as a murder of crows appeared and flew squawking right over the French. "That's an omen, that is," said Lawrence, "and a bad one for the Frenchies." The storm clouds dissipated and a brilliant sun shone through behind us and directly into the eyes of the Genoese, who were ordered to their feet and to advance. "Bowstrings, lads," I shouted, eyeing the sky for possible new rainclouds.

There was a bustle and stir as men bent their great war bows and slipped the hempen strings in place, all before even giving a glance at the plodding Genoese. Behind them was a vast swirl in the French as the front part of their army came on a short way, then stopped. They were not in orderly ranks, but were a horde, and seemed leaderless. Those at the back seemed to want to be further forward and pushed and surged into those ahead. I saw constables racing about trying to halt the advance, but a huge crowd of armed citizens in search of loot had appeared on the road from Abbeville and they too were pushing and urging the soldiers forward as any pretence of order vanished.

Some citizens caught sight of our serried ranks and began shouting in fear, others fell back while a large body of French knights spurred forward. At that the Genoese, who I later learned were the only professional soldiers in Philip's force, advanced again. Our troops stood up without concern, put on their helmets and took up weapons, calmly assuming their positions. The Genoese continued to come at us in ragged semi-order and gave a great shout.

"Quiet, boys," I called out, and our division stood still and silent. The Genoese shouted again, again we stood mute. The third time, some of them raised their crossbows and fired, but they were 150 yards away, and well out of range. "Wet bowstrings, Thomas," John Westwood muttered. "They can't slip them off the crossbow so easily." I stepped up and shouted to my squadron, who were waiting, nocked: "Now, you war hounds!" They took a pace forward, drew, marked and loosed. The silence ended in a musical thrumming of 2,000 bowstrings, then the air was dark with flickering, hissing shafts. Our longbowmen were snatching up the arrows they had stuck point-first into the turf before them, were nocking, drawing, marking, loosing and snatching up another shaft. Before the first arrow struck, each archer had two, sometimes three, more in the air to follow it.

It took just a few hundred heartbeats before the Genoese, who had left their protective pavises back in the baggage train, broke. Our bodkin points were slamming through their mail, lancing through the lighter plate that guarded their limbs and smashing with deadly force into their uncovered faces. Those who were not struck down turned and began to plunge back through the milling horde of advancing French knights, impeding their way, slipping and sliding on the soaked, grass slope. The impatient horsemen cut at their retreating allies, rode around, through and even trampled over their own *arbalestiers* to try to reach us, but our blizzard of arrows was so thick and brutal and punished them so cruelly that only a few reached our line. The pikemen took the first brunt and then our cavalry was swooping in to flank the broken French and hack them down.

Now we settled to a steady rhythm, sending an arrow storm as thick as wind-driven snow to shoot down onrushing cavalry, to butcher those who fell into our pits and trenches, to step aside to let our infantry filter through the bowmen's ranks and turn back the horsemen. Then we would move forward again, slamming volley after volley of birch, beech and iron into the enemy. By now, squeezed into the narrows between the impassable terracing at the centre of the battlefield and the bastion of the defended village and river, the channeled tide of French horse was breaking against the infantry wall commanded by the Black Prince.

I was standing on the right of the English line, watching my men, calling out special targets, hurrying the boys who brought sheaves of fresh arrows and urging on the dreadful punishment the French were taking. From time to time I sent arrows of my own, killing men who seemed to be leading others, picking off those who were not edging away from us. Those at the head and exposed flank of their mob – there were no orderly ranks and files of fighting men – flinched visibly and the whole mass of crouching men curved away from our ferocious hail of missiles and shuffled towards the centre. There, the French were chokingly constricted, piled up against the men and horses already dead and dying on the blood-slick turf and in the killing pits in front of our lines. Many in the press of bodies were so crammed together they could not wield a weapon, very many suffocated or were trampled to death by their countrymen and their mounts. Even those dying from arrow strikes were often unable to fall, held up by the dense press of humanity around them.

Some horsemen were forcing their beasts forward, trampling over their living and dead countrymen to attack Prince Edward's war hedge and I saw the royal standard swaying and faltering as its bearer died with a lance through his chest. A pikeman leaped forward to save it; the distinctive black armour of the prince was prominent, hacking at the faces of warhorses to bring them down, dragging a comrade to his feet, rallying a knot of knights to hold against increasing pressure. I saw him beaten to the ground, then hauled upright by two Englishmen. They were battling four Savoyard and German knights who were trying to drag away the figure in black harness, battering at them with mace and sword while a man at arms half-carried the prince, visibly swaying, back into a knot of Englishmen among whom I thought I glimpsed the red and yellow jupon of my son Hugh.

Where we stood on the field, the battle had ebbed since our blistering hail had caused the advance to curve away. I had time to see a horseman from the prince's battle urging his mount up the slope towards the windmill where King Edward watched the conflict. Instinctively, I knew the rider was a messenger sending for help. My archers were still steadily loosing their shafts into the enemy, but we were not besieged. I followed my gut: this was a turning point in the flow of the battle and the prince was endangered. Near me were my Cheshire bowmen and some routiers. A dozen or so men would do the business. I named them: "Calvely, Lawton, Leatham, Mottram, Timmons, Mascy, Leigh, Swetenham, Barnstaple, Stretton, Broggers, Lawrence, Jodrell, both Jodrells! With me, bows and swords too. To the prince!"

We ran across the slope, a hundred blood-squelching paces, paused in a ragged line, drew and loosed a thumping volley. The onslaught of arrows took the French in flank from 40 paces' distance. At that range, our bodkin points would go through three inches of seasoned oak, and no Frenchman had that much protection. Our flights scythed through steel and flesh of both men and horses and the kicking, dying mounts and falling riders disrupted the grim line of French knights who were hacking wildly to get to the prince. Fully one-half of them fell or wheeled away on staggering horses. The moment was near-perfect. Just as the French rank broke vulnerably open, cavalry sent by the king thundered down the slope and crashed into the enemy, blindsiding them and driving them backwards. In an instant, the French horsemen were no longer entangled with our foot soldiers and our archers could be employed.

Our arrow storm descended in hissing carnage and the

nobility of France were falling, arrow-struck, dying in heaped huddles under the sleet of iron. Even King Philip of France was hit in the face by an English arrow. The oncoming enemy faltered and turned, and we ceased the storm of missiles so our Welsh and Cornish foot could race through the archers' lines with sword, axe and spear to finish the wounded.

Later, I would consider matters. The spearmen who slew our wounded victims were working in hot blood, but we archers were killing almost without passion. No enemies faced us within stink of their breath, we saw them at distance, drew and loosed and killed. We worked, that is all I can say. We forgot to hate, we simply destroyed. Slaughtering the king's enemies was a task, not something else, something personal, some blood-crazing effort. If they drew close enough to threaten us, we withdrew and allowed the infantry to filter through our ranks to fight them off. Then we reloaded, stepped forward and with volleys of feathered birch and iron, killed again.

Once, as I paused for breath, I saw a solitary French knight on a fine black charger being helped back onto his horse by a page. He was entirely on the wrong side of the conflict, as he was behind all three of our battles. He had charged right through our ranks but the horse had fallen, injuring him badly so he could not return. We did not break ranks to capture him. The order of the day was neither quarter nor ransom. We fought, we killed, and only occasionally did we get a drink of water from the pannikins the bearers brought around. I had no idea of time, the battle seemed to have been continuing for the whole of my life, but after a blurred nightmare of hours of killing, shouting and misery, the moon was out, and the great mass of the French had moved away. Small groups still attacked, and were being overwhelmed one by one, for we held our ranks past the sunset hour of Vespers and even under the moonlight, until at the king's order we rested our weapons and sank down without great noise or riot.

Sunday dawned in a dense white ground fog and we all tensed, wondering if an attack would come crashing out of the gloom, but when it cleared our scouts reported no sign that the French were gathering forces and although we had a few encounters with some levies that had not quit the field, the enemy were destroyed each time. Our battle was won, and the cream of the French nobility lay dead around us, victims to the blizzard of iron sent in tens of thousands of our arrows.

We spent a few days in the region, collecting booty that included more than 2,000 proud heraldic coats taken from the dead. Oddly, these tokens of the slaughter of the once-mighty were so moving that we were subdued, pensive and felt drained.

By the time we marched to besiege Calais, our spirits were lifting. We had convoys of loot, we had a rich city to capture and we felt we could take the whole of France. For myself, I had sent an iron chest of looted silver to the coast, for shipment to England. Lord Edward had guaranteed its safety and had also made me promises of land grants in France and in England. My prospects were bright. And then my world became dazzlingly brighter.

A messenger came to call me to King Edward's pavilion. I hastily sluiced my face of most of the accumulated dust I had acquired and smoothed my long hair and beard with bowstring-raw fingers before I stepped past a squad of guards and into the large striped tent that was carpeted and hung with looted tapestries. A great heap of captured French banners lay untidily at one side. Edward was sitting at a small table, fiddling with an ebony chessman, a black knight, I noticed. Henry de Grosmont was standing by the king, grinning at me. Surprisingly, there were no attendants inside the pavilion.

"Your grace, my lord," I was puzzled. The king waved a ruby-ringed hand at me. "My lord Lancaster claims I have mistreated you, Lord Thomas, and he is too fierce a man for me to defy." Edward gazed steadily at me, Henry's grin grew wider and I stammered something meaningless.

"Tell him, your grace," urged Henry, and the king grinned back at him like a schoolboy at mischief. I relaxed a little. "Henry told me that you did not turn your coat at Sluys and that I should compensate you for the time you spent wearing a wolf's head. So, I sent a bishop on a mission to Avignon," he said, and continued to gaze at me, to view my reaction. I had none, I was witless and mute.

"About my cousin, Joan Plantagenet, Thomas?" Light was dawning, my breath was painful. "Your grace?" My heart was hammering like horses' hoofs.

"Pope Clement has agreed to consider an annulment of her marriage to Salisbury because you both say you were already married to each other. As she is my dear cousin, and with our army rampaging through France, I suspect he'll be more than willing to please me by bringing back a decision I'd like. You may well soon be free to marry your Joan, Baron Holand. I just hope she'll take a dusty wretch like you."

Historical Notes:

Chapter 1 - Mikelgate

Mikelgate is the southern entrance into the Roman-walled city of York (*Eboracum*). It stands on the west bank of the River Ouse and is the portal through which at least six monarchs have entered the city. The name means 'Great Street' in Norse and the gatehouse, or 'bar,' was built in the 12th century and improved two centuries later. Notoriously, the heads of Richard Neville, Earl of Salisbury and of Richard Plantagenet, Duke of York and father of King Edward IV and King Richard III were displayed above it after the Battle of Wakefield. Plantagenet's head was mockingly adorned with a paper crown.

Traitors – and sometimes those who had simply displeased the king – died horribly, being half-strangled, castrated, eviscerated and then dragged behind horses to an execution site for decapitation. The more prominent offenders were butchered, their limbs, head and torso sent to be displayed on pikes over the gates of cities nationwide as a reminder of the king's wrath.

Churches: In 1327, York had at least 20 houses of worship, all but two of them inside the city walls. The oldest row of houses in the city, Lady Row was built in 1316, stands on the street called Goodramgate and almost completely hides Holy Trinity church, on whose burial ground it was built. The Lady Row houses themselves were small: 12 feet wide and 18 feet deep, and comprised two rooms, one on an upper storey, the other at ground level. Today, the row is one of small shops.

Chapter 2 - York

Wagons: Thomas must have woken early to hear the rumble of carters' wheels, for wagons were not allowed in York's notoriously narrow streets between dawn and dusk. Waggoneers were allowed to make deliveries only during the hours of darkness and some streets were designated as one way to prevent traffic tangles. At night, wagon drivers took their chances for the city was locked up and dark and few would venture out without an escort and torchbearer because the largely-unpoliced streets were the province of footpads, murderers and burglars.

Bakers: grain shortages meant that the poor usually supplemented what grain they could get with beans, peas and even acorns to make their bread. Cocket was a cheap white barley bread baked as a thin disc and imprinted with an official-looking seal not unlike that used by Scottish customs officers. Wastel was made with better quality flour, and cheat was whole wheat bread with the bran removed. Clapbread was made from barley and was slapped down onto the baking tray, flattened by hand and baked thin. The best quality bread was pandemain, which used thrice-sifted flour. It was generally reserved for the rich, who often used thick-cut brown bread as 'trenchers.' Hollowed, they were employed as plates and filled with broths ('brewets') or stews. Post-meal, the meat juice-soaked bread trenchers were given to the poor as edibles. The term 'trencherman' was used for those hungry enough to consume the meal, then to eat the bread container in which it came.

Pageant Wagons: designed as three-dimensional pieces of street furniture, these mobile theatres were owned by trades guilds and were employed on feast days. They were either pulled through the streets from station to station in a procession of *tableaux vivants* or parked in one place for the duration as a temporary stage. Some were viewed end-on, others opened the sides to their audiences but York's narrow streets suggest that the guilds there opted for end-on viewing. In Coventry, the Shearmen and Taylors and the Weavers' guilds put on 'Creation to Doomsday' pageants, a cycle also favoured by guilds in Chester. York's cycle included 'The Marriage Feast of Cana,'

'The Funeral of the Virgin,' 'The Purification,' 'Mary Magdalene Washing Christ's Feet' and 'Doubting Thomas,' this last put on by the Company of Scriveners.

Tiltyard Saracens were a training aid to teach dexterity in knightly combat. The horseman raced his mount down the 'list' or track to attempt to spear a wooden effigy of a Moor. This consisted of a horizontal bar mounted atop a pole so that the bar swung freely. One end of the bar held the target effigy, from the opposite end dangled a ball on a short chain.

If the rider accurately struck the effigy of the Saracen and rode at sufficient speed, he would escape a clout in the back from the suspended ball. If not, he paid the price of a blow which might unhorse him.

War harness: we'd call it a 'suit of armour' but that is a Victorian term. The medieval knight would refer to it as a 'body harness' and the plate version consisted of two dozen elements, from the strengthening 'comb' atop the helmet (the 'helm') to the sabatons which covered the fighting man's feet. Pauldrons protected the shoulders; breast and backplates covered the torso, a tasset guarded the upper thighs, cuisses did the same for the thigh down to the knee, and greaves protected the shins.

Hinged armour – poleyns for the knees, vambraces for the elbows and a gorget for the throat and neck more or less completed the harness, while armoured gauntlets acted as gloves. Some, like those of the Black Prince, had spiked knuckles to do further damage to a foe. The effigy on the prince's tomb at Canterbury shows them clearly. Under the whole carapace of metal some knights wore the cushioning of a padded gambeson, a tunic stuffed with horsehair or tow. Others favoured a leather jerkin well-soaked in greasy lanolin to allow the armour pieces to move freely.

The whole war harness was extremely expensive, so some fighting men opted for chain mail of linked rings worn over a heavy leather tunic; others used 'scale armour' of small overlapping plates sewn onto leather or 'splint armour' of metal plates rivetted to leather.

King Edward II had two notorious homosexual relationships during his long marriage to Isabella of France; the first with Piers Gaveston, the second with Hugh Despenser the Younger. In each, the king's favourite assumed unwarranted powers and riches and incurred the wrath of the establishment, and each suffered a similar fate. Gaveston was taken and killed by a group of magnates, Earl Thomas of Lancaster among them. Edward had his revenge after Lancaster was defeated at the Battle of Boroughbridge in 1322. He had the powerful magnate taken to the earl's own favourite castle, Pontefract, dressed to humiliate (*"bareheaded as a thief"*) and paraded on a scrawny mule to be abused, pelted with snowballs and tried for treason in his own hall. Although sentenced to be hanged and drawn before decapitation, two of those penalties were commuted on the grounds that Lancaster had royal blood, and he was beheaded *"with two or three strokes."*

Later, the captive Edward would die a suspiciously timely death, and both the Despensers would themselves be executed, Hugh the Younger wearing a derisory crown of nettles. The decapitated Thomas' brother, Henry of Lancaster did not participate in the baronial rebellions and in 1327 was granted the return of his lands and titles by Edward III.

Medieval cities were stinking places. Householders who routinely emptied their chamber pots of 'night soil' onto the street were repeatedly enjoined to sluice the area in front of their homes, but human and animal waste piled up before the residences of even the most scrupulous. By 1297 the burghers of London had enough of it. Householders were ordered to keep the fronts of their buildings clean and the street free of encumbrances. Failure to obey would result in a fine of a half-mark, (six shillings and eight pence, or one gold noble) which was enough to pay the annual rent of a cottage, or to purchase about 150 lbs of cheese.

On streets where traders did business, detritus from their products added to the usual fetid mud. Tanners, who used urine in their leather treatments, were noted for the eye-watering stench of their work areas, where apprentices cured hides by stretching them over a baulk of timber and scraping away hair and skin with a blunt, concave blade.

After removing flesh from the underside of the hide, it was softened by rubbing it with guano from chickens or pigeons or with warm dog stools, then soaked in fermenting bran to remove the resulting lime. Softening the hide for leather boots, for example, called for dipping it into a series of tannin baths then leaving it to soak for several weeks in a stinking pit of liquid, fermenting bran which removed lime deposits left by the dung.

Even the shoemakers who depended on the tanners' output were reluctant to work near them, but the butchers' shambles, where men killed animals right there on the street, and the fishmongers' quarter where the gutters were piled with stinking offal were also major offenders against the public gaze and nose. And, over all of the localised stenches often lay a pall of smoke from the bituminous sea coal used for smithing, heating and cooking.

Those fogs were so bad that in 1257 Queen Eleanor fled the royal chambers at Nottingham for Tutbury Castle because she was choking in the *"unendurable smoke."* The first English Parliament passed a law in 1273 prohibiting the burning of the soft coal, but it was so widely ignored that by 1307 a commission was appointed to hunt down wrongdoers. First offenders got a "great fine," or jail, repeat offenders also had their furnaces demolished.

Swine were also a target of official wrath. In 1281 a London regulation forbade allowing pigs to wander loose in the streets; 16 years later pigsties were also ordered removed from public thoroughfares. Offending pigs were to be slaughtered and their owners charged four pence per beast to retrieve the carcasses.

Marauding Scots: a perennial problem that had become worse since Edward's defeat at Bannockburn, border raids flared up as Robert the Bruce took advantage of Edward II's death to harry and plunder across the border. The English army, nominally headed by 14 years old King Edward but actually commanded by Sir Roger Mortimer could not trap their opponents to force battle, and eventually trailed back to face England's scorn. Soon after, in September 1327, the young king learned that his father Edward II had died at Berkeley Castle.

Edward II's death: Suspicion swirled around Roger Mortimer, whom many believed had ordered the former monarch strangled or suffocated. Wild rumours held that Edward had been sodomised with a red-hot spit, a cruel death if it happened, and a brutal reference to his homosexual liaisons with Gaveston and Despenser. Other rumours later circulated that he had not died at all but had been spirited to the Continent and ended his years in a hermitage. In fact, he was buried with pomp at Gloucester Cathedral, wearing his coronation shirt, gloves and coif.

Relics: medieval oaths were usually 'sworn on the relics,' and apprentices to guild craftsmen had to swear on some relic to uphold their contract of indenture. The wheelwrights' patron saint was St Catherine, who was broken on the wheel; the arrow-shot martyr St Sebastian was the patron of needle makers; St Mary Magdalen, who poured scented oil on the feet of Christ, was the guardian of perfumers, and St Clare, for clarity, was the saint who oversaw the wellbeing of mirror-makers.

Relics themselves fall into four different categories: first class, which is the body or body part of a saint, and second class, which is an item or partial item used or worn by the saint. These two classes of artifact are not generally entrusted to individuals. Third and fourth-class relics are objects that have been touched to a saint's first or second-class relic with the intent of conveying holiness, and these may be sold to the faithful.

The variety of relics was astonishing. Crusaders who looted Jerusalem returned with two 'heads of John the Baptist,' all 30 of Judas' pieces of silver, a dozen pieces of the True Cross including one *'as big as the leg of a man,'* and the Crown of Thorns, which found its way into King Louis' possession. He was undeterred by the other two Crowns already displayed in Paris and had a chapel built for it. In time it was transferred to the great cathedral of Notre Dame de Paris. In short order, and despite the crown being encased in rock crystal, the thorns vanished from the relic, stolen by the faithful, leaving only a circlet of ancient rushes.

Looters of Byzantium recovered one of Christ's baby teeth, fragments of the stone tablets on which God wrote the Ten Commandments and a number of 'authentic relics' of Christ's circumcision. The Emperor Constantine's mother Helena was an avid collector of relics and accumulated a number of iron nails claimed to be the ones used to crucify Christ.

To guarantee his safety, she had one inserted into her son's imperial diadem, another into the harness of his favourite horse. Other prizes in her possession included the tunic Christ wore during his Passion en route to Mount Calvary and the robe Our Lady wore at the foot of the cross.

Crusaders also liberated from the Persians the relics of the Holy Lance, the sponge that carried vinegar to slake his thirst, the right arm of John the Baptist, Christ's sandals, his iron collar shackle, the reed he held in his right hand and the winding sheets in which his body was wrapped after death.

A priest called Neotus acquired a piece of the True Cross *(Croes Naid)* during a pilgrimage to the Holy Land, and returned with it to Wales, where it remained until 1283, when Edward I acquired it on the death of Lywelyn the Last. Edward III had it installed at Windsor in the chapel there, but it vanished about 200 years later. Today, all that remains is a roof boss in the South Quire Aisle, which depicts Edward IV kneeling beside the relic.

Misericords: these 'mercy seats' were choir chairs which hinged up against the wall but had a small ledge on the underside which, when the seat was stowed, still allowed support for a standing chorister during long periods of prayer.

Chapter 3 - Edward

Bloodletting: excess blood was seen as the cause of many ailments, and removing the 'humours' of yellow bile, blood, black bile and phlegm could change a person's health. In humans, leeching allowed the 'bloodworm' (leech) to suck the illness out, while venesection meant a doctor would open a vein with his fleam knife and so drain the blood. Doctors attended both humans and animals and if they couldn't heal them, it was usual to invoke the name of a saint and hope for the best. Farriers took over as horse doctors and formed a guild in 1356 to enlarge and exchange knowledge. Iron fleams from the 12th century have been discovered at archeological digs in York and at Hornby Castle, Yorkshire.

Hildegard von Bingen includes much about **veterinary bloodletting** in her 1165 book 'Physica' and details ailments that affect animals, including colds that cause suffering in their lungs. She was specific, too, about rabies in dogs, and colic in horses.

Soldiers from Hainault: John of Hainault supplied about 1,500 mercenaries including *'fully five hundred superbly-mounted heavy cavalry'* (contemporary chronicler Jean le Bel) and provided Queen Isabella with ships to transport an invasion force. This alliance cost a price: a pledge to betroth her son Edward of Windsor (later, King Edward III) to 13 years old Philippa of Hainault. Those troops, mustered at York, came into conflict with English archers over a game of dice, and rioting spread through the soldier-packed city.

Campaign against the Scots: When Edward's cavalry raced for the Tyne in their unsuccessful bid to trap the invaders, they covered 28 miles in a day, on trackless moors and hills, then spent a miserable week starving under pounding rain before heading to the River Wear, where the Scots were encamped, but still failed to bring them to battle. Sir William Douglas led a night raid on the English, killing several hundred, and rode right to King Edward's tent, which he cut down just after the young king was spirited away.

The campaign fiasco made Edward resolve that when he had a son, he would thoroughly teach him the ways of war. This he did, and the Black Prince, aged only 16, was famously given command at the decisive Battle of Crecy in 1346.

Sir Roger Mortimer was rumoured to be treacherously double-dealing with the Scots, perhaps to plot Edward's death. More substantial rumours held that Mortimer, alarmed at tales of a plan by the Scot Donald of Mar to rescue Edward II from imprisonment at Berkeley Castle and restore him to the throne, ordered the former king to be suffocated. A Benedictine chronicler writing a decade later about Edward's death said, however, he *"was slain with a hot spit put through the privy place posterial"* as vengeful allusion to Edward's homosexual liaisons with Gaveston and Despenser. Murdered or not, Edward died six weeks after his son's abortive campaign against the Scots.

Hedger and ditcher: Edward II was mocked for his fondness for rowing – an unusual activity for a royal, and for his liking for the manual work of hedging and ditching, when he associated amicably with field workers and other commoners. He kept greyhounds but was not especially fond of falconry or hunting, nor did he take part in jousting although he was a good horseman.

He was generous to his friend Gaveston, and even asked his father to give the courtier Ponthieu county, at which the infuriated old king pulled out handfuls of the prince's hair. The prince and the courtier pledged a vow of constancy and sealed themselves to each other with a symbolic knot. The Bishop of Winchester
called Edward a sodomite, later explaining that he meant that it was not the late king but Edward's companion Despenser who was homosexual.

Chapter 4 - Archer

Isabella: Despite the supposed animosity between Edward II and his queen, they were married for 22 years and had five children, including Joan, Queen of Scots, and may have enjoyed a cordial relationship that only ended when Isabella let loose her persona as the She-Wolf of France. She wore widow's weeds after she escaped from Edward, saying she had enough of her husband's philandering with the hated Hugh Despenser and regarded their marriage ended. Once she decided to seize power, she went about matters forcefully.

She betrothed her son to gain the Hainault alliance, and began an affair with Roger Mortimer which would only end with his execution. For all that, Isabella must have retained an affection for her royal husband. The murdered Edward was buried by the high altar of Gloucester Cathedral, but his heart was taken in a silver casket to London. At her own death, Isabella chose to be buried in her wedding dress and had Edward's heart buried with her at Newgate Church.
Longbow: the term came into general use two centuries after

Thomas' time, and most in the 14th century would have used the term 'war bow' or 'English bow,' but 'longbow' was an understood contemporary term and it is used in this book for clarity, distinguishing it from lighter hunting bows.

Bodkin head arrows: in a skirmish in Wales, a war bow archer shooting at an oncoming cavalryman from about 50 paces sent a bodkin arrow through the iron cuirass that protected his thigh, continued through his leather skirt and saddle and went so deep into the horse that it killed the animal.

Archers were so valuable to the English army that the 'Assize of Arms' of 1252 decreed that all Englishmen aged between 15 and 60 years must be equipped with a bow and arrow. King Edward III took this further. In 1363 his Archery Law for able-bodied men made archery practice obligatory on Sundays and feast days, giving the king a ready pool of trained archers for his wars.

So many bowstaves and arrows were made that domestic supplies of suitable yew ran short and the wood had to be imported; the first documented delivery arriving in 1294. In the 18 years ending in 1359, the English crown is documented as obtaining 51,350 sheaves of arrows – 1.23 million missiles. At one stage, all ships entering English ports were required to bring at least four yew bowstaves for every ton of cargo. Another indication of the quantities used comes from the wreck of the Mary Rose, where 3,500 arrows and 137 complete longbows were retrieved.

Chapter 5 - Plotter

Tunnels: Nottingham is built on a soft sandstone ridge and for more than a thousand years men have dug caves and tunnels there as cellars, dwellings, workplaces and even a tannery. None are natural caverns, all 800 or so were excavated with simple hand tools. Edward and his soldiers used a semi-secret tunnel about 40 metres long which runs from a garden in Castle Grove to the current Castle Green, which in 1330 was the Middle Bailey. There are steps cut into the rock at the bailey end and an arched door at the top. The castle has long promoted an official 'Mortimer's Hole' next to Brewhouse Yard which was not secret: it was used to move goods up from the River Leen to the castle. Modern archeologists are confident that the Northwestern Passage was the actual entry point for Edward.

The solar was the ultimate retreat in a castle and was usually the abode of the lord. Its design was simple: a Norman hall built vertically on its end. In early motte-and-bailey castles (i.e. a wooden fortress atop a mound, surrounded by a palisade) the fortification was a simple wooden structure. The ground floor served as kitchens and stabling for animals; the first floor was reached up a defensible stairway and contained the great hall with central fireplace where the business of the castle was done. Benches and tables served for dining and were stowed away during the day. Alcoves along the walls served as bed spaces and although the lord and lady sometimes had a private chamber at one end of the great hall, the solar above it was their most defensible and private space.

Castles: When Duke William of Normandy conquered the English in 1066 CE he even brought a prefabricated castle with him, a wooden structure erected at Hastings. He also reinforced the Roman ruins at Pevensey and Dover. The Conquest completed, he began a massive 20-year building programme of motte and bailey fortresses to dominate and control the Saxon population, who were impressed to build the structures. Later, many of the 500 or so 'temporary' castles were converted to square stone keeps, and later still to concentric-walled castles that could house more troops.

Castle populations: Most of the servants and officials of medieval castles were men, thanks to the military role of a noble household, and the higher roles in what was essentially a small town were usually given to the lord's kin or to his favoured retainers. At the top of the hierarchy was the seneschal, major-domo or steward; then came the constable, who was responsible for pages, grooms and horses. The marshal oversaw discipline and arms, and all things related to knights, squires, men at arms and archers. The chamberlain oversaw the household, the wardrobe master attended to clothing and domestic matters.

The verderer administered forest law, the veneur supervised the chase, the falconer trained hunting birds, the huntsman kept the hounds (many lords employed dog boys who lived with the hounds in their kennels). Smiths and armourers worked metal and made weapons, other craftsmen included carpenters and masons, while the lord's lands needed farm workers, miners and a host of other labourers.

The castle kitchens employed scullions, cooks, confectioners, cellarers, poulterers, spicers, larderers, saucerers, and chandlers respectively taking care of cleaning, cooking, cake-making, provisions, chickens, (valuable) spices, meat and fish and the cool place where they were kept, sauce-making and candle-making. Many castles had a specialist scalding house to prepare meat and the ewery dealt with laundry, linen and napery. The pantlers were responsible for cheese, bread and napery (table linen) in the pantry and the butler with his buttery oversaw wine, ale and beer supplies.

The religious side of life was not ignored, as most lords had their own chapel and confessor. The almoner dispersed alms, the chancellor oversaw finances and accounts.

Chapter 6 - Trial

Leprosarium: a leper hospital operated by the Order of St Lazarus two miles south of Melton Mowbray was the national headquarters of the order and gave the village its current name of Burton Lazars.

The George Hotel, Stamford, Lincolnshire, was in 947 AD a property of the Abbots of Croyland and was bounded on each side by a religious house. One, the House of the Holy Sepulchre was a hospital of the Knights of St John of Jerusalem, also known as Knights Hospitallers. It hosted pilgrims on their way to the Holy Land and the knights who accompanied them as protection. King Richard ('Lionheart') gave the Abbey of Peterborough possession of the hospital, the house and the George Inn in December 1189. In later years, the inn became a famous hostelry with a distinguished and even royal guest list and is a thriving business today.

Richard of Wallingford did design a large astronomical clock, one of the most complicated in the world of that day, using technology he borrowed from the abbey mills. It told time and tides, monitored the orbits of the sun and moon and predicted lunar eclipses. Two decades after Wallingford's death in 1335 (soon after his bedroom was struck by lightning), the chiming clock with its dragon's tail cogs and wheel of fortune was completed by William of Walsham. The original clock was destroyed during the Reformation, but a recreation built in 1988 is displayed at St Albans Cathedral.

Abbey mills were such a major source of fee income that the monks discouraged their tenants from grinding their own corn. Soon after Edward's coup, Abbot Richard compelled the locals to surrender their hand mills and cemented the grinding stones into the abbey's parlour floor, where the monks walked on them daily as they went about their business, as a reminder of the power of the Church.

Mortimer: Sir Roger had been tried for treason after the failed Contrarian rebellion in 1322, as was his uncle Roger Mortimer of Chirk. The Mortimers were tried by the mayor of London, the chief baron of the Exchequer and three justices. Both men were imprisoned in the Tower. The younger Mortimer escaped by feeding drugged wine to his guards but was less successful in 1330 after his re-imprisonment, which ended for him on Tyburn Hill's common gallows.

Castle Rising: this stately seat of the d'Aubigny family is said to be haunted by the cackling ghost of Queen Isabella, who lapsed into dementia during the 28 years she lived after Mortimer's death. The hauntings are supposedly most frequent in the whitewashed upper chambers of the great castle.

Chapter 7 - Dupplin Moor

Under the terms of the **Treaty of Edinburgh-Northampton** of 1328 that followed a desultory Scots campaign by Isabella and Mortimer, the regents agreed to renounce England's claims to the Scottish throne occupied by Robert Bruce. The Scots handed over £100,000 for the peace and for the return of the Stone of Scone; Isabella promised six years old Joanna Plantagenet in marriage to four years old David Bruce and agreed to maintain the border as it was in the reign of King Alexander. The English nobility regarded the agreement as humiliating, and the treaty lasted only for five years.

It took 668 years before Scotland's Stone of Destiny was finally returned.

Edward Balliol, son of John Balliol, likely understood the fragility of his cause. He was coronated at Scone a few weeks after the battle but, mindful of his isolation among enemies, moved to his father's old demesnes in Galloway. However, within a matter of months he was chased half-dressed across the English border by a group of soldiers loyal to Bruce. He could only hold his throne with the support of the king of England and his flimsy grip gave out when Moray surprised and scattered the Disinheriteds' army at Annan.

The battle of Dupplin Moor in 1331 was the opening of a series of clashes between the clansmen and the English, but the

Scots did not at first understand that schiltrons of spearmen unsupported by archers or cavalry would be so vulnerable to the deadly English longbows. King Robert the Bruce had urged his chieftains that the smaller and less-equipped Scots forces not face the iron might of the English in open battle but should continue the guerilla tactics which had won the nation its independence. He was not heeded, and the butcher's bill for Dupplin was 2,000 Scots men at arms and an uncounted mass of common infantry dead, as well as the loss of 23 nobles. The English, who lost 33 knights and 200 infantry did not lose a single longbowman, and at day's end well understood the power of their archers when supported. They went on to make the formation a template for later, vital victories in France and elsewhere.

Arrow wounds, especially those from hard-to-extract broadheads, were usually treated as Thomas describes, by having the missile pushed all the way through – a very painful business. If, however, the arrow had struck in a place where bone prevented such an extraction, physicians used specialized tools to remove the missile. The future Henry V was arrow-struck in the face at the Battle of Shrewsbury (1403) and his doctor John Bradmore first widened the wound with linen-wrapped elder dowels then used a specialized pair of tongs which he inserted into the socket of the arrowhead and forced apart to grip its inside walls.

Once the arrowhead was extracted, he dressed the wound with barley and honey mixed with turpentine. Medieval doctors knew of honey's antiseptic properties and the prince recovered, infection-free within three weeks. It was effective and less painful than the usual method: cautery, which called for red hot irons to be applied to the wound to seal veins and tissue and prevent blood loss and infection.

The Arab physician Albucasis designed an 'arrow spoon' to extract a detached arrowhead. The spoon was inserted into the wound and twisted to attach itself around the arrowhead and allow it to be drawn from the wound without causing further damage as the barbs were ripped out.

Mantle Child: illegitimacy in the Middle Ages was not always a great social burden although it did have a bearing on inheritances. Many marriages were made witness-free and without benefit of clergy, meaning that people would not necessarily know if a couple had been blessed by the Church. In turn, it taught that a child conceived out of wedlock would be made legitimate if the couple later wed in a church. The child would be blessed under the wedding mantle and so would be shielded by religion.

In no-witness, church-free marriages privately agreed between a couple, women were the usual victims of false claims, when their 'husbands' denied ever agreeing to a marriage contract. The practice was so prevalent that the bishop of Salisbury laid down an edict warning men against weaving straw rings on young women's fingers so they could *'fornicate more freely with them.'*

Chapter 8 - Conroi

Crouchback: Edmund Crouchback, first Earl of Lancaster (1245 -96) was the second son of King Henry III and younger brother of King Edward I (Ironsides). His grandson Henry of Grosmont was Edward II's first cousin and Edward III's second cousin, as well as being England's wealthiest man and most powerful peer.

Of the king's conroi, Grosmont was the acknowledged leader, intelligent, literate (self-taught in later life) and valiant. He was also a sensual womaniser who reformed his ways and wrote a devotional book confessing his previous licentious life. In gratitude for his spiritual redemption he became an ascetic crusader, fighting for the Church in Germany and Spain.

Feast of St Hugh: April 1st.

Seals: to allow a person to authenticate a letter or document, a matrix was used. Pressed into soft wax, it would create an impression which showed a noble's coat of arms or other insignia over his title, name or inscription of some sort. The seal of a nobleman was round, churchmen's and noblewomen's seals were oval. If lost, a town crier would announce that any agreements made under that seal were invalid. At the owner's death, the seal would be smashed.

Organisations, not just individuals owned seals, too. An abbey as well as its abbot had a seal; guilds, companies, universities, priories and the like all had their own official matrices to demonstrate that their communications and agreements were genuine.

The Great Seal: while the highest officials employed the Great Seal to authenticate state documents, for his personal letters, the king had his secret seal, a signet ring with a reverse impression so that he could endorse a missive or document with his own guarantee of authenticity. In all, there were four royal seals in operation: two versions of the kingdom's Great Seal, one of which used red wax, the other green, for Chancery and Exchequer use respectively; a Privy Seal used by its keeper to authenticate the king's documents and the Secret Seal which only Edward himself employed.

Edward's reference to the soothsayer's prophecy of a **'Great Bear'** like Arthur has roots in an old Britonic word: 'Art' for 'Bear.' Arthur is believed to have lived in the fourth or fifth century CE, when bears were still extant in Britain and it was a term for a lord of war. The last bears were hunted out by the 11th century.

Chapter 9 - Escalade

Berwick was captured by the Scots in 1318 and was held by them for 15 years. It was long a thorn in the English side, forming as it did a base from which raiders could ravage the borders. Some Scots wanted it back in English hands and joined King Edward. After Bannockburn, certain clan nobles (the Disinherited) refused to declare allegiance to Robert the Bruce, were stripped of their lands and fled to join Edward Balliol in England, hoping that he, they and the English together would triumph over Bruce. Balliol and Beaumont defeated the Scots at Dupplin Moor, and Balliol was crowned king of Scotland, but was soon forced to flee back to England. His return to Berwick earned him the crown but it was a short-lived reign and in only a few years the English and Balliol would be expelled.

In 1356 **John Balliol** released his claim to the Scottish throne to Edward III, receiving in exchange an English pension. His grave is lost, somewhere beneath Doncaster Post Office.

Iron cannons were employed in the siege of Berwick where they and traditional wooden siege engines did great damage to the town. Their fire was directed by the Flamand soldier John Crabbe who was in command of the town's defences in 1316 but joined Edward's forces after being captured and persuaded to use his insights against the defenders.

The siege was the first known use of cannon to bombard an English town, and the cannoneers used gunpowder made at the Tower of London. An account in the royal rolls speaks in 1338 of a ship equipped with three iron cannons *('iii canons de fer')* of five chambers. The guns were constructed like a barrel, comprised of iron strips bound together with iron hoops that were heat-shrunk to provide more strength. The ball would be rolled into the barrel, the powder chamber loaded and attached behind it and a linstock applied to the touch hole. Once fired, the separate powder chamber ('tankard') would be removed and a fresh, powder-loaded one attached. Using a separate chamber for gunpowder allowed the weapon to be fired more rapidly.

The highly-unsuitable battlefield of Halidon Hill was forced on the Scots army because agreed indentures between Edward III and the garrison commander at Berwick, Patrick Dunbar, Earl of March, specified a surrender by a certain date. The Scots army was slow to arrive, the date was imminent and if the Scots had opted to seek another battleground and withdrawn, it would have meant surrendering Berwick.

Chapter 10 - Physician

Arab physicians were much respected for their skills, and many were educated in Montpellier or Paris, the only medical schools in northern Europe, although several Italian colleges had newly arrived on scene. The prospective doctor underwent three years' preliminary training, five more years of instruction and another year as apprentice to an experienced practitioner. He was at the top of his profession, ahead of barber-surgeons who could set a broken bone, amputate an infected limb or pull a tooth. Next down the list were the apothecaries who created remedies from herbs, fungi, roots and animal parts, and below them were the village wise women with a knowledge of roots and herbs to cure common ailments.

Handicaps to the advancement of medicine included the Church's ban on the dissection of corpses for scientific study and that doctors had only a basic idea of hygiene. They battled insanitary arrangements that caused the spread of contagion and infection, knew nothing of cleaning or sterilizing equipment, often wore the same blood-stiffened operating gowns and used the same unsterilized instruments on patient after patient. Additionally, the population itself was largely unhealthy. People rarely had sufficient fresh vegetables or fruit; skin diseases were common, thanks to infrequent bathing and wearing harsh wool next to the skin. Pneumonia, typhoid and heart disease were rampant.

Most surgical operations held great danger for the patient and were undertaken only in life or death situations. The unfortunates in need usually underwent them without narcosis, although inhalations of the steam of boiled mandrake or of a sponge soaked in opium could be helpful, but other palliatives were potentially lethal. One concoction called for lettuce juice, briony, opium, gall from a castrated boar, henbane, hemlock juice, opium and vinegar, all mixed with wine and given as a draught. If the mix was too strong, it could stop a patient's breathing.

The mentally ill mostly went untreated but those patients were usually unconfined. Some were tied to the altar screen so they could benefit from hearing Mass, some had the shape of the cross shaved onto their heads to attract divine intervention. It was about all a medieval physician could do.

Hospitals, which could be almshouses for the old, sick and poor or were simply accommodations for pilgrims were surprisingly common: more than 700 were founded in England in the several centuries after the Conquest. Some were established for sufferers of leprosy; most were operated by religious orders to maintain the link between Church and the people. Some offered refuge for orphans, most used serenity, healing prayer, medicinal plants, simple food and cleanliness as the chief weapons against disease and illness, and although treatment was limited, cures were surprisingly often attained.

Chapter 11 - Falcon

Three leopards: Edward knew the value of image, and later amended his royal standard and even his body harness and shield to show, quartered in equality, the leopards of England and the lilies of France, thereby bluntly making a point of his claim to be monarch of both nations.

Two pence a day: Edward III employed more than three dozen falconers, and their daily pay of two silver pence was about the same as he spent on food for each of the 60 raptors in his mews. He was a dedicated hawker and ruled that any trained hawk if lost must be delivered to the sheriff for return to its owner. Like some of his nobles, the king had silver chains made for his hunting birds and even kept a few favourite birds on perches around his palaces. The peregrine is noted as the fastest raptor and has been timed at 200 mph when stooping for prey.

Hawking was a favoured sport of gentlewomen and the clergy as no weapons were involved and women with their nimble fingers could better manage the jesses, thongs and rings that controlled the hawks. Hunting, however, was much more a man's sport. Edward III kept 60-plus hounds – about four times the size of an average lordly pack – and spent about £100 a year on them and the huntsmen. Favourite dogs were given silver collars and once, the king splurged on Persian green cotton to make hunting tunics for the dozen magnates and 15 squires in his party and also provided a quantity of dark red cloth to adorn six noble ladies accompanying them.

Thomas lists Edward's weapons, but does not mention one much favoured by knights – the **flanged mace**. This weapon, with its heavy head and angular metal flanges had much more swinging force than a sword and could cut through armour. Many knights carried a mace as a spare weapon at the saddle and would use it in close combat. Also favoured was the spiked skull mace, which could pierce a helmet.

Sporting young noblewomen dressed as men: chroniclers at tournaments were shocked at the 'wantonness' of high-spirited girls who assumed male clothing, even to the fashionably tight trews some wore. Ingenious women who so displayed the shape of their buttocks made some concession to modesty by sewing foxes' tails inside the garments.

Chapter 12 - Salvation

Johan von Endorf attacked the Grand Master of the Teutonic Order, Werner von Orsein, at Malbork Castle, Poland, in November 1330, inflicting stab wounds from which von Orsein later died. Von Endorf was reportedly mad and was also a confirmed criminal angered at not being reassigned within the order, but it is possible that the assassination was carried out at a Church command over contested Pomeranian lands for which the Order was preparing to go to war. Endorf was sentenced to life imprisonment but seems to have been swiftly released.

Saint Bartholomew's Day (also Bartlemas, Bartlemytide: August 24th) Tradition said the martyred saint was flayed with a knife, so the monks of his patronal Crowland Abbey gifted pilgrims with knives on his feast day. At Sandwich, Kent where the small chapel of the medieval hospital (1190) is dedicated to the saint, his feast day is marked with a children's run around the church, after which they are given currant buns. (Adults get a biscuit marked with the chapel seal).

Woodstock Palace was already a couple of centuries old when Edward was born there, for the rambling lodge had been a favourite haunt of kings since it was built by the first Henry. He kept a menagerie behind the park's high walls that included porcupines, King Frederick's leopards and other big cats, an elephant sent by King Louis and a giraffe, plus a fine stock of deer and pig for hunting.

Smithing: Medieval blacksmiths knew they must spend a lot of time heating and hammering. They knew only what was necessary to achieve quality iron, not understanding that the forge reduced oxygen and implanted more carbon into the steel. They could forge-weld small pieces of steel onto tools to provide hardened cutting edges and often re-used steel that way, meaning fewer artefacts survive today.

The medieval smith forge-welded items by heating them to yellow or white heat (nearly molten) then used silica sand or another flux agent between the two (cleaned and shaped) faces of the items to be joined. Because the faces were slightly rounded into shape, the weld centre joined first, then the smith hammered the join outward, pushing out the flux and any foreign matter that could weaken the weld.

Chapter 13 - Melee

Tournament of Peace: a tourney held at Windsor in 1278 which was designed to do no great harm to contestants. The swords were created from whalebone and silvered parchment, the shields were made from light wood and the helms were of boiled leather. The stricture about knights being helped to their feet was because jointed plate armour, designed to allow mobility, used about 90 lbs of metal. Mail weighed less but still burdened the knight with 50 lbs or more. A smallish man who'd been stunned by being unhorsed or by being beaten to the ground could have considerable difficulty standing without assistance.

Heralds did more than simply identify knights by their insignia, they knew who had the right to call himself who he did. By recording the genealogy of the great and good through generations, they established who held legitimate title to estates and castles, manors and farms. They alone determined who had the right to 'bear arms' – as in who was entitled to display armorial coats which illustrated their family history and connections, not just to carry weapons.

Spiked-knuckle gauntlets: The Black Prince's effigy in Canterbury Cathedral wears such gauntlets, along with his body harness with its decoration of the leopards of England and the fleurs de lis of France.

Chapter 14 - Feast

The etiquette of eating called for the lower ranked to aid the higher, and younger to help older, politely cutting meat, pulling a choice piece from the common pot or breaking bread for them. Most people shared drinking vessels, people brought their own knife to table or shared with another. Food was served on plates of wood or pewter or on hollowed-out loaves of bread – trenchers – and a **trencherman** not only ate the stew in his bread bowl but consumed the juice-soaked bowl itself.

Peasants rarely ate meat. Animals were too valuable for mere digestion and yielded milk, eggs and wool until old age made them candidates for the cookpot. After root crops like turnips, fish was most the most common food, and because no part of Britain is more than 70 miles from the coast, oysters, mussels, crab, lobster and other shellfish could be transported live. Eels and pike were kept in vats; many castles, monasteries and manorial estates had fish ponds if there was no river close by where weirs and fish traps could be employed. All that said, fish was not necessarily for the common peasant. He was not allowed to fish in ponds, rivers or lakes because the fish in them belonged to the local lord. Even if a sympathetic water bailiff let him keep a tench or two, its value was about two days' wages. Better to sell it and make do with eels, salt cod or pickled herring bought at market.

Chapter 15 - Calzand

King Philip's act in 1337 of moving his crusading fleet to the English Channel was the opening act of the 100 Years' War. Edward of England did not have the ships to counter the magnificent fleet paid for by the pope, he had only a dozen merchant cogs and the theoretical support of 57 ships of "The King's Pirates," a seasonal fleet from the Cinque Ports mustered under ancient duty. This he augmented with any wine ships, merchantmen, fishing boats or smugglers' vessels he could impress.

Cadzand is no longer an island, having been reclaimed as polder during the great Dutch engineering projects of the 17th century. An early seat of Mennonites, it is about 10km from inland Sluis (called Sluys in 1330) which then was a port.

An aside: Thomas never knew it, but his actions defending his friend meant it was he who fired the first arrows of what history would call the 100 Years' War.

Chapter 16 - War

Little is known about the **battle for Cadzand,** but it is not unreasonable to think that Grosmont and Mauny would employ similar defensive positions to those which had been so successful against the Scots at Dupplin Moor and Halidon Hill, namely a curving, enveloping battle line with archers at each end able to pour an arrow storm into the flanks of an approaching enemy. It is also reasonable that the English would have used the steep-sided dunes in their defences and would have employed pits and **caltrops** – horse-crippling spikes made by twisting together several nails so that however they were thrown to the ground, one spike was always upright. What is known about the battle is that only a few nobles were spared for ransom, and the common soldiers were slaughtered.

One aftermath of the battle was that King Philip VI wrongly thought that the Flamands had betrayed him and he set about exterminating the supposed traitors. The reign of terror he inspired alienated many of his supporters and was a great help to Edward of Windsor, who a decade later after making peace with France, apologised for the terror chevauchees he had ordered.

Thomas makes brief reference to **Joan of Kent,** a 12 years old heiress he likely seduced, but later claimed to have secretly married. Hers was a tangled life, and after her first marriage to Salisbury, she went on to marry Thomas. After his death, she married the Black Prince. Skeptics of her 'secret marriage' to

Thomas slyly called her 'The Virgin of Kent,' alluding to her more common label: 'Fair Maid of Kent.'

Chapter 17 - Sluys

King Edward's fleet was cobbled together from conscripted merchant vessels and from shipowners in the Cinq Ports who served an annual duty in return for trading privileges. Except for the royal flagship 'Thomas' and the 'Edward' which each carried several pieces of ordnance, the ships were small, carrying only 25 or so soldiers or archers and a small crew of sailors. The king's largest ship, the 'Christopher' had been captured by the French in a fierce battle in 1338.

The Chancellor of England in 1340 was John Stratford, Archbishop of Canterbury and he had news of Philip's fleet waiting in the estuary of the river Zwin to intercept Edward before he could reach Bruges and his allies. He was so convinced that the king's 130 cogs would go down to defeat against the larger French fleet that he threatened to resign his post unless Edward delayed matters so he could recruit more forces. The king used his best persuasive powers on the archbishop, who reluctantly withdrew his threat.

Edward attempted to hire war galleys from the Venetians, without success. Nor did his envoys to the pope at Avignon net him any vessels. The French by comparison mustered seven royal ships, 22 oared barges, 167 cogs and six galleys for Philip's "Army of the Sea." Reinforcements later brought the total to 213 vessels.

Edward wrote to his son the Black Prince after the sea battle to report that the English had captured 190 barges, ships and galleys and that only 24 had escaped, some of which were captured later. He estimated that more than 20,000 of his enemies had died, including their admiral, Hugues Quieret. The commander Nicolas Behuchet was captured and hanged from the mainmast of his own flagship.

Edward boasted to his young son that now he was "Sovereign of the Narrow Seas."

The news of the lost sea battle was so terrible no French courtier wanted to inform King Philip, so the task fell to a court jester. He told the king: "Our knights are much braver than the English ones." "How is that?" asked Philip. "Unlike our brave knights, the English do not dare to jump into the sea in full harness." In fact, some who did jump and made it to shore were clubbed to death by angry Flamands who resented the French seizures of their lands.

Observation: there were no fireships employed at Sluys. This is, after all, historical fiction.

Breaking Wheel: was also known as the Catherine Wheel, the instrument of torture for the martyr St Catherine of Alexandria. That legend may in fact be based on the death of Hypatia, a Greek astronomer slain by a Christian mob in 415 AD.

Bruges in the 14th century was one of the largest and most important cities in Europe thanks to the monopoly it held in English wool. Its river connection to the North Sea, 10 miles away was vital, but as the estuary silted up, the city went into decline as a centre of trade.

Chapter 18 - Trial

Trial by combat (aka Wager of Battle) succeeded trial by ordeal, which usually involved fire in the shape of the accused having to carry red-hot iron without being burned or to walk barefoot across nine or so feet of red-hot ploughshares. God evidently protected the innocent.

Hired champions were technically illegal but were sometimes employed. Some 'approvers' or rented champions came from prisons and could, after five victories for the crown, be freed. More usually, they were hanged.

Aside: the combatants usually had a squire to set up and attend the battle, to exchange gloves ('throwing down the gauntlet') with the opposing squire and sometimes to attend church and donate five silver pence, token of the five wounds of Christ.

Chapter 20 - Plague

Bubonic plague swept across Europe between 1340 and 1351 and took its name from the blackened skin and buboes – boils – that erupted in the groins and armpits of sufferers. The pandemic that took one-third of Europe's population in the 14th century was an iteration of the same pestilence that swept the Roman Empire around 542 AD and would return over and again in the 16th and 17th centuries. It has been called the world's greatest serial killer. The Great Pestilence ravaged England during 1348 and 1349 and about 1,000 villages were depopulated and vanished because of it.

In Germany where many Jews had moved after being expelled from England by Edward I, accusations during the Plague that Jews had poisoned water supplies resulted in organized massacres against their communities that destroyed more than 60 large Jewish towns.

Chapter 21 - Routiers

Thomas Holland was named by Froissart as a principal captain of the Black Prince and most of those he identifies as routiers appear in the Fine Rolls. Mascy was charged with rape and armed assault but was released to serve the king. Later, the fact that he was in the king's service earned him a pardon for abducting a girl. It was a not-uncommon Get Out of Jail card: the knight Sir Robert Marney was convicted of breaking into an earl's chase to poach deer and was locked up in the White Tower. After his release, he kidnapped another knight and forced him to sign over his inheritance. Under threat of outlawry, he joined the Black Prince's campaign and went to France, unpunished.

Others named by Thomas include the archer Roger Swetenham who was rewarded with gold and land for his service; the Jodrells received silver looted from blind King John of Bohemia and settled to prosperous lives in Gascony.

Windsor: Edward not only had the great Round Tower repaired and improved but began building an even bigger hall for the proposed Round Table fraternity in the courtyard of the castle's upper bailey. Hundreds of men worked on it for 40 weeks ending in November 1344, when winter halted the work. Edward did not have the funds to finish the hall and it was demolished, its final fate unrecorded.

The Black Prince did admire Joan of Kent, and after Thomas' death made her his wife.

Chapter 22 - Caen

Legend has it that when Edward came ashore on the sandy beach between St Vaast and La Hogue, he stumbled and fell face-forward into the sand. Shocked soldiers who witnessed this evil omen were reassured when the king jumped up and declared loudly: "The very land of France embraces me as its rightful ruler!" The story is apocryphal – it's also told that the exact same thing happened to Duke William of Normandy when he landed at Hastings.

The commander at Caen was Raoul II, count of Eu, Grand

Constable of France and the most senior member of the French military. When the city fell, he was taken for ransom, imprisoned in England for three years, then returned to France. There, the king promptly had him executed.

Sacked: the term comes from the habit of taking away loot in a sack.

Chapter 23 - Blanchetaque

The tidal ford at Blanchetaque, long gone since the Somme was canalized, was a limestone ridge that ran across the river, making a causeway in the river bed, hence the name 'white platform.'

Prime: the clergy's Offices of prayer were not evenly spaced but took account of shorter winter days so that the canonical bells that would sound for Matins at 6.40am in midwinter would chime at 2.30am in midsummer, and at 5.00 am at equinox. In August 1346, Prime, the second Office of the day, would have been marked around 4am, as daylight was dawning. The battle for the ford at Blanchetaque was fought about five hours later.

The chronicler Jean Froissart said the 16 years old Black Prince had '*made a right good beginning*' in the *chevauchee* that began on the Cotentin peninsula, and that he also distinguished himself in the battle at Blanchetaque against the forces of the seneschal Godemar du Fay.

Chapter 24 - Crecy (Saturday 26 August 1346)

The Genoese, King Philip's only professional soldiers, were indeed tired. Jean Froissart said they had marched six leagues (18 miles) that day, in full armour and carrying their heavy crossbows. "*They told the Constable they were not in a condition to do any great thing in battle,*" the chronicler wrote, but the Earl of Alencon dismissed them as 'scoundrels' when they retreated from the English arrows. King Philip's forces lacked strong leadership since the Constable of France, Raoul of Brienne had been captured at Caen

Caltrops: were four-pointed iron spikes so forged together that one spike must always stand upright. They were intended to cripple any horse or man who stepped on one, and at least had the effect to slowing an enemy cavalry charge. Also called: 'Crow's foot.'

At one point, German, Savoyard and French knights penetrated the Black Prince's battle and were engaged by infantry. Lord Edward was beaten to the ground and his standard bearer killed; the French took the banner, but the Sheriff of Cheshire, Sir Thomas Danyers of Tabley cut into the melee and retrieved it. The king sent a small group of reinforcements to Edward's aid; the rescued prince regained consciousness and fought on.

The Battle of Crecy took the lives of the elite of the French nobility, about 1,500 knights, and as many as 16,000 common soldiers, a considerable number of whom were crushed to death by their comrades' undisciplined advance. The English, who lost about 300 dead, withstood 15 or so French cavalry charges. King Philip himself was wounded in the face by an arrow strike, and the gallant, blind King John of Bohemia died when he was led into the melee with his horse tethered to that of two of his knights' mounts. His request was to be led into the engagement *"that I may strike one stroke with my sword."* His body was found in front of the Black Prince's line, the horses still tied together.

The chronicler Jean Froissart says that Lords Cobham and Stafford, with three heralds to interpret the arms and two secretaries to record the names, came across 80 banners on the battlefield and counted the bodies of 11 princes, 1,200 knights and about 30,000 common soldiers, a number he likely exaggerated.

Acknowledgements

No author writes alone, however much he protests that he does. Inspiration and direction came to me from Sharpe Books' Richard Foreman, who has midwifed more than a dozen of my historical fiction works to delivery. For all that he does, my grateful thanks.

Gratitude, too to my patient wife Jennie who suffers conversation about matters medieval for months on end, to my daughters Claire and Rachel, for their legal and publishing insights, to the admirable Kelvin Jones for his elegant cartography and to the King's College Fine Rolls Project team and chroniclers like Jean Froissart, who have so aided my research. Many of those medieval historians long ago became dust, but their contemporaneous look at events stays fresh today.

Author profile:

Englishman Paul Bannister spent his journalism career on national newspapers and the BBC in Britain and the USA and now makes his home in Oregon. He has two series of books published by Sharpe: the 'Lost Emperor' volumes which begin with 'Arthur Britannicus,' and the 'Crusader' series. All are available on Amazon, as is his autobiographical 'Tabloid Man & the Baffling Chair of Death.'

*

Printed in Great
Britain
by Amazon

32121012R00137